SEX ON THE BEACH

By

Sydney Somers
Beverly Rae
Betty Hanawa
Terese Ramin

Triskelion Publishing
www.triskelionpublishing.com
All about women. All about extraordinary.

Sydney Somers, By The Light Of The Moon
Her next to last day at work; her boss surprises her with tickets to Antigua for a final assignment. Presenting the job as if he is giving her a vacation at the same time, he then lets her know that the job is in a couples-only resort and that her least favourite brown-nosing co-worker is lined up to go with her nooo. What is a girl to do

Beverly Rae gives us Mr. Lonely
Miranda has finally finished the research she has worked on for years and now she has discovered his hideaway. Damian LeClare, recluse extraordinaire. And she has carefully worked out everything needed. Damian's life is going to get some spice and that will begin today.

Betty Hanawa sends us Love the Day
Artemis is very angry. Her handmaiden Lycida had broken her vows and had sex (horror of horrors) with a man. No longer virginal, she is also no longer a handmaiden. And not only that but she is now banished from Mount Olympus, the only home she has ever known, cursed by Artemis to forever give her body for pleasure to mortals.

Terese Ramin delivers HEX AND THE SINGLE (WEIRD) WERE-MONSTER (or How Janice Got That Way)
Causes Trouble had been blessed, shall we say, by the gods and goddesses right after her birth when under the guise of strength, courage and everything else expected, she was given additionally a bit of probably every hardship imaginable. She would be very gifted if only she and her life would reach some sort of compromise. Oh, the burdens of youth, even as a Shapeshifter!

Note: this last story is a prequel to Bewitched, Bothered and Revampyred These stories were all great! I enjoy anthologies, especially when I'm on the road and this selection of stories really appealed to me and all four authors well worth checking out. **5 Hearts! Glenda K. Bauerle, The Romance Studio**

Five Angels from Fallen Angel Reviews *By the Light of the Moon* by **Sydney Somers** – Hayley's scheming boss has a hunch that something fishy is going on at a couples resort in Antigua, and he wants her to go and investigate. The problem is, she needs a man to play her doting lover at the resort. Her buddy Cole is game to go with her, but can he keep his secret when he finds himself losing his heart to her?

Ms. Somers writes an amazing story, and one that is rife with series possibilities. Intriguing characters, a great setting, and a pack struggle make for an interesting plot. Simply   stunning!

Beverly Rae's *Mr. Lonely* – Miranda Raennia has come seeking
Damian LeClare, the one they call the Night Stalker. She is determined to have him, to make him see her for what she really is, and to be invited into his life. Will she be more than he bargained for? In *Love the Day* by **Betty Hanawa**, Lycida was one of Artemis' chaste handmaidens until a sexual romp ends her virginity, resulting in her banishment from Olympus and a the curse of a goddess. Every man she enters into a sexual relationship will die...and then she meets Benedict.

Ms. Hanawa's story of the power of love and the siren's call of the flesh is a wonderful addition to this anthology. There are underlying themes here, including the importance of seeing people for who they really are and being true to your word. Amazing imagery, mythology and knife-edged emotion combine to make a heartwarming, pulse pounding story.

Hex and the Single (Weird) Were-Monster or How Janice Got That Way by **Terese Ramin** – Let me just first say that this short story defies description and then I'll try to describe it. We've got Janice (AKA Precious Child and Causes Trouble), a woman on whom the Gods and the Goddesses bestowed gifts. We've got her mother, the Tribal Chief with an attitude and the determination to see her daughter mated and producing litters of grandchildren (or would they be called grandwerepups?). Lastly, we've got a host of werewolves, a superbly hung and unsuspecting lumberjack, and a waterfall used as a stimulating sexual experience. What else does one need?

Terese Ramin's unique writer's voice shines and entertains in her contribution to the *Sex on the Beach Anthology*. I laughed myself nearly to tears and then over the brink into semi-hysteria in the reading of this one. Run, don't walk, and don't stop until you have *Hex and the Single (Weird) Were-Monster or How Janice Got That Way* in your hot little hands.

Reviewed by: **Michelle, from Fallen Angel Reviews**

Triskelion Publishing
15327 W. Becker Lane
Surprise, AZ 85379 USA

Paranormal Romance / Anthology / Erotic Romance
Printing history:
First eBook release: November 2005
First mass market printing: July 2006

ISBN 1-933874-01-5

Ebook and cover design Triskelion Publishing.
Layout by Michelle Rouillard

BY THE LIGHT OF THE MOON

Sydney Somers

Dedication

To Jaycee…
For brainstorming, listening, inspiring, and talking
me down off the "I'm-stressing-and obsessing" ledge
on a daily basis.

Chapter One

"You want me to what?" Harley McKinnon dropped into the chair opposite her boss's desk, juggling the stack of files in her arms. She brushed impatiently at a loose strand of brown hair that worked its way from the clip at the back of her head. "It sounded like you were sending me on assignment."

Her boss pushed an envelope across the polish oak desk "You leave in two days."

Harley didn't so much as glance at the envelope. "Tomorrow was supposed to be my last day."

Mac leaned back in his leather chair, his Cuban cigar dangled out of his mouth. With his short, square, salt and pepper hairstyle and piranha personality, Harley always thought he reminded her of J. Jonah Jameson from *Spiderman* comics.

A pair of manipulative green eyes pinned her in place. "Harley, I took a chance on you three years ago."

She resisted the urge to roll her eyes. For three years, she'd heard this line and she groaned inwardly knowing what would follow it.

"Your dad and I are playing golf next week." He followed the reminder up with another pointed look. "You're not slated to start teaching your journalism class for another few weeks, and your mother told me you already sent the final revisions for your novel off to your editor."

This was why people didn't go to work for their parent's best friend. There was no separation from work and home life.

Harley managed to keep her sigh contained, mostly. "Fine." She was well aware if she didn't agree now he'd launch into wartime stories about how he saved her father's life and brought him back to her mom. One of these days the stories would stretch back as far as the Second World War knowing Mac.

Opening the envelope, Harley drew out plane tickets. "Antigua? As in the Caribbean?"

Mac winked. "See. It's not so bad. What else did you have planned for the next week anyway, wilderness camping and yoga? Aside from a little investigative work, you can even work on your tan under a tropical sun."

But she'd been looking forward to the camping and yoga. It had been forever since she took a little "me" time, and with being done at the magazine and shipping off the final revisions for her first suspense book, Harley needed the down time.

"There's nothing to this assignment, just a little poking around, asking a few question."

Harley skimmed the file for the rest of the information. "A couples only resort? I can't go alone?"

"Nope." Mac shoved away from the desk, set his Cuban in the crystal ashtray, and reached for the health shake his wife insisted he drink at least twice a day. Harley recognized the fruity aroma. Her mother began fostering it onto her dad at the same time. "I'm sending David along with you."

Harley bolted to her feet, almost losing the files to the floor. "No way." Harley couldn't get the refusal out fast enough. There was no way she'd share a plane, cab, or anything else with the brown nosing creep who routinely strolled into the women's bathroom, by mistake off course. *Sure.* His excuses were getting old seeing as how he'd worked for the magazine longer than she had. "I'll find someone."

Mac smiled at her and she realized he'd half expected a refusal. "Okay then. I'm sure you won't have a problem. Who would turn down an all expense paid trip to a five star resort?"

"Someone that may need more than two days notice, and already has a passport." Harley slid the envelope on top of the pile she carried.

He waved his hand towards the door. "Well David's on standby if you can't get anyone else."

A shudder snaked down her spine. She'd rather pay a male escort to go with her than even so much as share a conversation with David.

Mac drained his health drink then remembering his cigar, popped it back in his mouth. "Glad we have that settled. I have a good feeling about this one."

Harley pinched the bridge of her nose. The first stirrings of a migraine prickled behind her eye. "Tell me again what your source said."

"He told me there is something going on down at the resort he worked for."

What? Too much tanning and beach volley ball? Harley hitched her hip against the corner of the desk. "Such as?"

"He didn't get into it." Mac tapped a few keys, his eyes focused on the monitor on the corner of his desk. She waited for him to add something then realized he was reading his e-mail. Mac was, according to his very computer literate wife, an e-mail slut.

Setting the files aside, Harley leaned across the desk, her palms flat on the smooth wood. "Let me make sure I have this straight. You're sending me down there to investigate something, but you don't know what?"

He didn't take his eyes off the screen. "I've got a vibe."

Harley resisted the urge to snort. Mac's vibes paid off only fifty percent of the time. His last "vibe" landed her in jail for suspicion of scalping tickets at a basketball playoffs game. "So I'm supposed to go down there and pretend like I'm part of a couple and just poke around? Behind the pool bar maybe? Could be I'll find a clue by parasailing."

Mac stubbed out his cigar, his lips twitched, but he contained the smile. "The guy made all the reservations himself. It's harder than Fort Knox to get into, but you're all set."

"When did you make the reservations?"

He at least had the decency to look guilty. "Last week."

She could have hit him. "You knew I was going to be done this week."

"Don't get your panties in a bunch. You were wrapping up that whistleblower piece. I didn't want to divide your concentration."

Harley paced away from the desk. "No. You knew I'd tell you I wasn't going." She glanced over and saw Mac absently rubbing his shoulder. His old war wound, the bullet he took trying to drag her father out of an ambush.

Manipulative. Plain and simple.

Sighing, Harley returned to the chair. "So what else did this guy say?"

"Just that this story would put the magazine, and the journalist reporting it, on the map."

Harley didn't bother to remind him she didn't need to be made. With her first book done, and the journalism class this fall, she was perfectly happy with her life.

"If you're not sure," Mac continued, "I can send Val down instead."

"Val would spend ninety percent of the time smearing herself in sun block."

Mac stared at her expectantly. "So then…"

"I'll go." Harley crossed her arms. "But I want to talk to this source first."

The phone rang. Mac ignored it, punching the button to direct the caller to his voice mail. "You can't. He disappeared."

"Really?" She didn't bother to disguise the skepticism in her voice.

"We were supposed to have a meeting, face to face and he didn't show. What does that tell you?"

"That maybe he's just blowing hot air."

Mac scoffed. "Sometimes, Harley girl, I wonder how you're instincts ever pay off. Don't you smell the story here?"

What she smelled was bullshit, but she recognized the determined glint in Mac's eyes. She'd be on the flight to Antigua whether she really wanted to be or not. "So I leave in two days, huh?"

Mac smiled. "That's my girl."

*****

Harley set her bag down on the table near her front door, and kicked the door shut.

"Hey," an indignant protest came from behind her. "If you don't want me to stop by, you could just tell me." Harley smiled before turning around, her heart kicking up hearing the familiar sexy voice.

Cole leaned in the doorway, hands shoved in his jeans pockets, his blonde hair still wet from a shower, and those brown bedroom eyes that melted into her every time she held his gaze for more than a second. She turned away before he noticed her staring and headed into her kitchen. Cole strolled into the apartment behind her, flopped on the couch and stretched out like he did everyday when she got home from work. Cole was a freelance photographer and made his own hours, but she only saw him go on assignment once a month.

"So tell me beautiful, how was work?"

She'd got used to hearing him call her that, and even though she knew he talked that way to everyone, she still experienced that same warm tingle every time.

Harley slid the jug of milk into the fridge, fighting off the urge to walk over and jump him just to see what he'd do. "I'm going to Antigua in two days."

Cole sat up and draped an arm across the back of the sofa as he stared into the open kitchen area. "Really? You're finally taking a vacation?"

"Actually its work." She glanced back to the counter, focused on folding the paper bag into a square so she didn't have to look at him and pretend she wasn't really *looking*.

"One of Mac's vibes?"

Harley laughed, wondering when she'd gotten so edgy around him that she needed to keep her distance. "Yeah. Some tip about this couples only resort."

His eyes brightened before he jumped over the couch and walked into the kitchen. "Couples only, huh? You taking a mystery guy I don't know about. I thought you swore off men?"

"I did." And what had she been thinking with him just across the hall? Right... he wasn't interested in her. Well, that might not be entirely true. There were plenty of times she caught him watching her, noticed the brief flicker of heat in his eyes before he glanced away. One night after too much Tequila, she'd found her nerve and asked him why they hadn't hooked up. He gave her one of his sexiest smiles, said she was too good for him then brushed a kiss across her forehead, and said goodnight. That had been a month ago.

Cole stared at her, waiting.

Harley shook her head. "This is a business trip. I don't need to have a guy reading anything into it."

He cocked his head in that arrogant-and-I-know-it way of his. "So who are you taking?"

She shot him a sidelong glance. Harley swore she detected a hint of jealousy in his tone. Crazy. "I don't know yet. Mac wants me to take David. I told him I'd find someone else."

"I'll go."

"No." There was no way she'd be able to concentrate on work with him lounging around next to naked.

Cole's eyebrows crashed together. She ignored the hurt look she knew was just for her benefit. "Besides," she added, "You wouldn't be able to keep your eyes off all the other women. They'd know you weren't serious about me." She kept her tone light knowing he wasn't nearly as much of a playboy as he pretended to be. At her last count he only had three dates in the last six months.

"I'd behave," he promised. His gaze held hers for a moment longer than usual.

A slow heat stirred Harley's middle before she shifted her attention away from the six-foot temptation in front of her. "That's the point, you couldn't behave. We'd be pretending to be a couple. But, no." It was one thing to ask him on a date and get turned down, and another all together to go away, pretend to be into each other, only to return home and go back to the way things were.

"Come on, Harley. We've known each other for almost a year. Who else could you go there with and be perfectly comfortable? And I wouldn't be trying to take advantage of you."

That was the real problem. She wished he'd take advantage of her. Too often. She was almost at the point where she needed to read something dark and nightmarish before bed to fight off the dreams of Cole.

Harley shook her head. "No."

"You're not even going to consider taking me?"

Not unless she wanted to come back half-in love with him. She knew it would only take one thought, one "what if" and she'd be a goner. Ever since she kicked her ex out months ago, she'd managed to keep "what if" far from her mind her mind where Cole was concerned, unwilling to screw up their her friendship–aside from that last time with the Tequila– just because he still did funny things to her insides.

Cole grabbed her hand and warmth seeped into her skin. Tempting brown eyes tunneled into hers. "Please."

Lowering her eyes to their joined hands, she tugged it free. "Absolutely not."

*****

Cole paced his living room, trying to figure out what in the hell he'd been thinking. Go away with Harley. Pretend to be her lover. Get her into bed. Come home and go back to normal.

Jesus, he was an ass to think he could have his proverbial cake and eat it too. She sure as hell deserved better than a guy who just wanted to go away with her so he could get into her pants. Even liking Harley as much as he did, he'd been damn tempted to take her up on her offer of "hooking up" a month ago. Turning her down topped the list for stupid mistakes. But he knew then, just as he knew now, Harley wanted a guy who planned to stick around.

That pretty much put him out of the running.

And yet, there he'd been just a few minutes ago

trying to convince her to let him go along.

Cole flopped back on the couch, and rubbed his hands over his eyes. He needed a change of scenery and not just the temporary kind. He should go get a paper and look for a new apartment instead of picturing Harley in a skimpy two-piece swimsuit that left nothing to the imagination.

Living across the hall from her... it had been fine when she still lived with Greg. Watching her kick that bastard out–seeing, as he was just shy of doing it himself–made him realize Harley possessed more backbone than he imagined. Of course afterwards he got to know her, really know her, and it screwed up his plans of coercing her bed while she was on the rebound.

Cole stood up. Maybe if he promised to sleep on the couch, she'd let him go?

Cursing under his breath, he stalked around the room. This was stupid. Did he think they could go down there, drag her into bed, spend hours figuring out what made her scream the loudest, and then come back and pretend it didn't happen?

Maybe she'd go for it.

Jesus, he needed his head examined. No, what he needed was to get laid and take away some of tension that rose inside him every time he saw Harley. It would help if he didn't go over there every damn day, and it sure as hell didn't help that on top of her being sexier than hell, she was actually fun to be around. He'd even watched chick flicks with her.

The calendar caught his eye. Well that explained his enthusiasm to play her lover. The full moon was in two days. His desire for her was always the hardest to control at that time, which was why he usually made a point to take an assignment out of town then. His current employer changed the dates of his next job, leaving him across the hall from her at the worst possible time.

Which gave him the perfect excuse not to go anywhere with Harley. He'd never be able to keep his hands off her. With a full moon he could manage to control the shifting, but his desire would be a whole lot harder to tame if he and Harley were in some tropical paradise with a big bed, a hot tub and those patio loungers made for two.

He glanced at the door, knew it was Harley who stood on the other side even before she knocked. Crossing the room, Cole pulled it open just as she raised her hand.

Hand poised to knock, she frowned up at him. "How do you always do that?"

Cole propped a shoulder in the doorway, finding even the way her eyebrows scrunched together impossibly cute. "You couldn't find anyone else, huh?"

"Nope."

He tipped his head knowingly. "David called, didn't he?"

"Yup." Harley didn't roll her eyes, but he guessed she wanted to.

"What time do we leave?"

"Six-thirty am, day after next."

Cole grinned, tried and failed to remember all the reasons he should refuse. "Try not to look so happy about it, gorgeous."

Chapter Two

Harley fiddled with the ticket in her hand, trying not to look at Cole. The man should not have been allowed to leave the house looking like that, not when she remained determined to forget just how hot he was. Cole leaned back in the small airport chair, his long legs crossed and stretched out in front of him. His navy button up shirt revealed a tantalizing expanse of the smooth chest beneath, automatically calling to mind the one time she saw him in nothing but a towel. A pipe broke in his apartment and he asked to use her shower. Had she known how much she would enjoy the sinful sight of him, she would have messed with the pipes herself months before.

Beside her, sunglasses covered his Cole's eyes, making it impossible to see in what direction his gaze traveled. More than once she felt him watching her, but whenever she subtly glanced over, his face gave away nothing.

Had she imagined it? Wouldn't be the first time.

This was her last chance to get herself straightened out. In another few moments, they'd be boarding the small plane that would take them to the secluded resort. After that, she'd have to pull off an Oscar worthy performance–pretending not to be into Cole while she pretended to be into him.

Another migraine started to pound behind her eye. Harley closed her eyes, fighting off the approaching ache.

Cole's hand cupped the back of her neck, and she stiffened.

His warm breath caressed her ear. "Relax. If we catch it now, it won't get bad."

It wasn't the first time his fingers massaged the pressure points at the base of her skull, but each time he did it, his hands lingered longer and she found it increasingly difficult to move away. One night she had actually relaxed so much she leaned against him and drifted off. She woke a short time later to find he'd fallen asleep too. He woke seconds after her and all but jumped off the damn couch with an excuse about being late for a date. Cole's hand dropped away as he glanced around the small airport.

Harley tried to zero in on what captured his attention. "What? Hot chick at two o'clock?"

His lips twitched before he leaned back into the seat, but he didn't relax. He pushed his sunglasses down. Sleepy brown eyes took in every inch of her. "I only have eyes for you now, remember." Instead of the arrogant boast she expected, his voice washed over her, soft, sensual.

"I'll be back." Harley didn't look at him as she stood and headed towards the closest restroom. Once inside the small space, she studied her reflection. Loose strands of brown hair escaped from her clip and curled against her forehead from the humidity.

She couldn't do this. She couldn't. Cole was too… sexy, smart, sexy, fun, sexy, thoughtful, sexy— Damn it. Harley dug out her cell phone, relieved to see there was in fact a signal. She dialed her sister's cell number. With any luck she'd still be at work.

"How's it going so far?" Her sister's chipper voice came over the line and Harley relaxed.

Studying her amber colored eyes–nothing special about them–she groaned. "This was a mistake."

Kathy's indelicate snort made Harley smile. "It wouldn't be if you just told him how you felt."

"I tried that." *And just look how good that turned out.*

"So try again."

"Kath, we've been over this." Over and over and over. Why was she still so hung up on this guy anyway?

"Then why are you calling me?"

Harley leaned against the counter top, facing the stalls. "I have no idea."

"Because you want to tell him, you know you do."

"It might ruin our friendship." She'd rather have Cole as a friend then not in her life at all.

"And it might be the smartest thing you've ever done. Take a risk."

"Easy for you to say, your risk paid off." What did it really matter anyway? This was an assignment, not a pleasure trip. Even if she had the balls to come right out and say she had a thing for him, this wouldn't be an appropriate time or place to tell him. "I'll call you when I get back."

Kathy sighed. "You should tell him."

"I know." But they both knew she wouldn't say anything.

"Have fun," Kathy said before she hung up.

Harley tucked the phone in her bag, splashed some cold water on her face and left the restroom. She could do this. She could. If Cole could play the game, then so could she. She was a journalist and journalists did what they had to, to get the story.

Not paying attention, Harley collided with a solid chest, and nearly bounced off it. Two sturdy arms steadied her and she immediately stepped out of the way, barely acknowledging the dark haired man. He leaned towards her as she passed, and sniffed her?

Harley glared at him and headed back towards Cole. Some men were down right pigs.

*****

Where was Harley? The woman needed to explain a few things. He swung his head back towards the terminal door as another small group of passengers filed into the room. Not good.

None of the eyes passing over him could be considered hostile, but that made little difference to him.

The airport was full of werewolves.

Even in their human form, Cole had no trouble picking them out and every one of them that approached the small desk at their gate was definitely capable of shifting. It couldn't be coincidence Mac sent Harley to dig up a story at a resort that catered to werewolves if the crowd around him were any indication.

His gut tightened.

"What's wrong?" Harley appeared beside him, her golden eyes full of concern. Unfortunately, for him, she didn't miss much. Mac made a good call sending her, but it was damn shame they'd be getting back on the plane and going home.

"Where are we going?" Cole demanded. He

hadn't bothered with the specifics before. It made no difference to him what resort they were headed to in Antigua. Noticing the speculative glances aimed their way since Harley's pure human presence drew some attention, their final destination became damn important. "Where are we going?" he repeated in a lower voice knowing full well many could still overhear him.

"I already told you…"

She had? "When?"

"Last night when you stopped by while I was doing yoga."

Ah, well, that explained it. Some of those damn poses got him so hard he had difficulty concentrating. How could he not imagine sliding his hands over her pretty bare ass right when she slipped into another tempting pose? Even thinking about it now…

Cole snapped off the thought before it got him into trouble. "Who owns the resort?" He had a nagging feeling he already knew.

Harley tipped her head as though she considered how much to tell him.

He resisted the urge to strangle it out of her, his unease increasing by the minute. "Come on. I know you did your homework. Who owns the place, Harley?"

"A man by the name of Dash Windsor."

Cole dropped into the seat. Ah, hell. This was just what he needed. Why hadn't he asked her before this? He should definitely be in contention for moron of the year award.

The announcement to board the small plane

came over the speakers. Most of the gathered crowd headed for the gate.

Harley picked up her bag. Cole didn't move.

She started past him, and Cole grabbed her wrist. "We're not getting on the plane."

Confusion clouded her expression. "What?"

"We can't go to that resort." Knowing Dash owned the place only made the decision easier to make.

Harley perched on the edge of the seat beside him, and crossed her arms. "Why not?"

"Because…" He needed to come up with a damn good excuse. "Because I have a bad feeling about this." He tried not to wince at his *brilliant* attempt to convince her.

"Oh, well then, we better go back home," Harley teased before she stood up.

She took three steps before he caught up and sidestepped her. "I mean it."

The half smile fell away from her lips, and the corners of her eyes narrowed. "You wanted to come with me, so we're getting on the damn plane."

Cole shook his head. "No, we're not."

If a cartoonist sketched her now, smoke would steam out her ears. "Fine. I'll go without you."

"The place is for couples only," he reminded her.

If looks could kill. "Then I'll tell them I dumped my sad excuse for a lover on the plane and plan on leaving on the next flight. I shouldn't need more than a few hours to see if there is anything to Mac's vibe."

"Harley—"

"Look, if you don't want to go, and I frankly

can't figure out why you've just changed your mind on me like this, but I'm getting on that plane with or without you." She picked up her bag and spun around, striding for the gate.

Cole reached her side the same time her hand pushed on the door. "What did Mac say about this place?"

Harley sighed. "Only that a guy named Reginald called him and said there was a huge story here."

Dash wasn't going to be pleased. "But this guy, Reginald, didn't say what the story was?"

Shaking her head, Harley adjusted the strap of her bag. "He disappeared before Mac could get any more details out of him. Thankfully he already made the reservations for me and a guest."

Cole stared through the glass at the people–werewolves–boarding the plane.

She arched a brow, her lips tight at the corners of her mouth. "You change you're mind or what?"

He didn't bother to hide his annoyance. "Something like that."

Cole stayed close to her as they boarded. Harley seemed immune to the speculative glances the other passengers shot at her. He was thankful there were a few empty seats in both directions between them and the closest shifter.

Once Cole stowed their carry-on bags above their heads, he slid into the seat next to her.

Her eyes followed his every move. Cole knew his edgy behavior only drew more of her attention, but there was little he could do.

She gazed out the window. "I wonder what

Reginald was talking about."

Harley played with the hem of her skirt and his eyes were drawn to the shadow between her thighs. At any other time he would have imagined sliding his hand under the fabric. Right now his mind centered on how what would happen if Harley saw anything. A large group of wolves running around an island might be hard to miss.

Damn it, he didn't like this. Why was it that every time he looked forward to getting to know Harley on a more physical level, something like this happened? Then again, if he had to keep her from digging around, what better way to keep her occupied than make her beg him to fuck her again and again.

"What?" Cole asked, vaguely aware Harley said something to him.

"I wish I had got to talk to Mac's source, maybe then I'd know what I was doing here."

Knowing full well many ears could hear their conversation Cole did the only thing he could think of to make Harley stop talking.

Her eyes widened right before he leaned in and slanted his mouth across hers. For a moment, she didn't respond and he half expected her to shove him away or slap him. His body jolted with surprise when her hand gripped the front of his shirt. Warm lips opened under his and he swept inside, a burst of lust tangling in his gut at the first deep taste of her. A groan built in his throat as he inched closer, and slipping an arm around her waist, he drew her closer. Her breasts pressed against him as she tilted her head back, giving him better access to her mouth.

Harley shuddered in his arms, and the scent of her arousal hardened his cock. She draped one leg over his thighs, the provocative gesture an invitation he couldn't refuse. Cole nipped her bottom lip, tugged it between his as he slipped his hand under her skirt. Her thigh tensed, relaxed, then tensed again when he inched upward.

Not even in his most wicked fantasies, did he imagine she felt this good. Too good. And if he didn't stop now, he'd never want to.

Reluctantly, Cole pulled back. Swirling amber eyes stared up at him, questions burned in the heated depths. Questions he didn't even know he could answer.

Being the coward he was, Cole leaned back in his seat, closed his eyes and mumbled, "Wake me when we get there?"

*****

Harley stared at him. Wake him when they got there?

No. He didn't just say that, not after giving her the best kiss of her life. Hell, her muscles were still in meltdown and he was practically snoring.

Ass. Harley adjusted her seatbelt and tried not to recall how good it felt when his hand slid up and under her skirt moments ago. Her skin still hot to the touch, she would have happily spent the rest of the flight imagining what would have come next if the jerk hadn't decided on a nap.

By the time they landed, she was still annoyed. Harley tried not to let it show, and he didn't seem concerned about her response to him anyway. He was too busy watching everyone else to pay attention to her. Her white halter-top and yellow skirt covered more skin than some of the other women, so she couldn't begin to guess why so many of the other vacationers stared at her. She'd already checked to make sure there were no rips in the skirt or toilet paper stuck to the bottom of her sandal. Whatever their problem was, she didn't care. Just like she didn't care that Cole dragged her into one hell of a scorching kiss only to shut down on her seconds later.

After setting her bags down in the resort's open lobby, Harley took a seat at a small cocktail bar while the others in front of them checked in. Cole went in search of a rest room, leaving her to think up a hundred ways to pay him back for his stunt on the plane.

Raised voices caught her attention and she automatically tuned into the heated discussion.

"I'll take care of it." The man snapped.

"The way Dash took care of Reginald? We needed him." The feminine voice was low, accusing.

"Reginald is long gone."

Reginald? Mac's source, Reginald?

"Harley?"

She glanced up as Cole nodded towards the reception desk. Harley picked up her bag and walked the short distance towards the clerk. "Reservation for Harley McKinnon and guest." She shifted her attention towards the open door near the bar where the voices came from. A moment later a lanky blonde emerged followed by a giant black haired man on her heels.

Fingers tapping over keys brought her attention back to the desk clerk just as the young woman nodded politely. "One moment, please." She disappeared into an open door behind the glossy black counter.

"Problem?" Cole asked as he stepped up beside her. By the tone of his voice he didn't seem surprised.

Frowning, Harley leaned over to get a peek at the computer screen. "I don't know."

A moment later a striking man with blonde hair and eyes almost the same shade as Cole's emerged from the inner office. Dressed in casual island attire, his smile was polite, but tense as he approached them. Curious eyes passed over her with barely veiled appreciation then widened briefly noticing Cole beside her.

He returned his attention to Harley, held out a hand. "I'm Dash Windsor. I own the resort."

Harley noticed Cole tense as Mr. Windsor swallowed her hand with his. "Is there a problem with my reservation?" When the owner came out to talk to you that was never a good indication.

"Call me Dash. And yes, unfortunately there is a problem. It seems we've overbooked, Ms. McKinnon. I'm afraid I don't have a room to offer you."

Chapter Three

Cole studied the man on the opposite side of the counter, not missing the fact his eyes drifted a little too long over Harley.

"I'm sorry about the inconvenience, Ms. McKinnon. We'll gladly reimburse your flight costs."

Harley shot Cole a curious look, before she shifted and fixed her annoyed gaze on Dash. "I confirmed my reservation yesterday. You mean to tell me you gave my room to someone else since then?"

Dash nodded. "I apologize for the oversight. New computer systems. We're still working out the glitches."

Harley cocked her head and Cole knew she didn't buy it. She recognized a cover up when she saw one. And the more she thought there was a story here, the more she would dig her heels in. Harley might go home, but if Mac didn't send her back, he'd send someone else until he was satisfied.

Cole draped an arm around Harley's shoulders. He ignored the slight tensing of her shoulders and knew Dash hadn't missed it either. It didn't take a genius to realize she was pissed at him. "Maybe you should double check." Cole motioned to the computer. "Harley and I were really looking forward to this."

Dash's eyes shifted between them, his head tilting in silent consideration. "All right then. Let me see if another arrangement can be made."

Harley relaxed into him and for a moment Cole let himself get distracted by the warm weight of her body resting against his. The breeze blowing through the wide terrace doors to their left gently lifted her hair, and the apple scent of her shampoo drifted on the air. The memory of her hot mouth, soft and pliant beneath his, stormed through him. Cole edged closer, letting his arm slip from his shoulder to her waist. Her breath sucked in as he grazed the side of her breast in passing.

Cole caught Dash's arched brow and ignored the curious amusement that flashed in his eyes. "Well," Cole prompted.

"It seems I do have a couple of bungalows that may be suitable for you. I'll have Georgia show you the way."

Cole stepped away from Harley, forced his eyes not to linger on her mouth for more than a heat beat. "You go on ahead. I'm going to make sure everything is in order here."

She raised a brow, but didn't object as she followed a petite redhead out the terrace doors.

"My office then," Dash suggested, his lips twitching before he pressed them together.

Cole inclined his head, following Dash behind the counter and into the spacious office behind. Two entire walls were made up of windows that overlooked the resort. Beyond the palm trees and cabanas, sandy beach meant sparkling, turquoise water.

Cole didn't sit as Dash settled behind the glass desk and leaned back in his chair. "I have to say, you're the last person I ever expected to see here."

"It's a long story."

Dash idly tapped a pencil against the date book open in front of him. "She's not supposed to be here. Strict no human policy, you must know that."

"Yeah, well she thinks there is a story here, so if you make her leave she's only going to want to stay." The potential repercussions of Harley finding anything aside, he almost enjoyed telling Dash there was nothing he could do.

Dark eyes narrowed. "She's a journalist?"

Cole nodded, pretending to be engrossed in an impressionist painting of ocean from the view of the office.

"Well that's fucking perfect, another headache I could have done without." Dash scrubbed his hands over his face.

Seeing no point in remaining standing, Cole slid into the chair opposite the desk. "What are you doing here anyway? I didn't think you came down here all that often."

"There was a problem that needed my attention." He let out a breath. "So what kind of angle is she working?"

"That's the only upside. Harley doesn't know."

Leaning forward, Dash frowned. "Run that by me again."

"Her boss got a call from Reginald someone or other. He said there was a story here, but he didn't show for a meeting with Harley's boss. But he obviously said enough to catch the old man's interest."

Dash stood up, and stared out at the resort. "Well, Reginald is now unhappily abroad. So he shouldn't be a pain in the ass any longer."

"Is he why you came down here?" Cole relaxed into the chair, half wondering what Harley was doing at this moment. Maybe shimmying into a sexy little two-piece swimsuit.

"Seems he was getting a little too forceful with the staff. Rumor has it he planned on challenging me when I arrived."

With Dash being an Alpha, someone had to be incredibly confident or incredibly stupid to even think about challenging him. "Did he?"

Turing around, Dash smiled. "He'd already left by time I arrived. Some associates of mine caught up with him yesterday and I believe he's now roaming about Italy somewhere. He knows what will happen if he returns. Reginald's brother still works here, but I'm keeping an eye on him." He crossed his arms, his grin widening. "So how do you fit into all this?"

Cole opened his mouth.

"No, wait. You were so preoccupied with getting laid, you didn't bother to find out where you were actually going."

Cole let his glare answer speak for itself. He didn't need the obvious pointed out to him. This whole mess could have been avoided if he'd bothered to get more specific about the exact resort they were going to.

Dash shrugged, moved back to his chair. "Hey, you wouldn't be the first." He sat down, one golden eyebrow arching in curiosity. "You haven't claimed her, have you?"

Tensing, Cole leaned forward. "Don't get any

ideas."

"If she's available..." Dash's innocent look grated on his already aggravated nerves.

"She's damn well not available," Cole snapped.

"Oh, so you plan to claim her then?"

Not liking the direction the conversation headed in, Cole stood. "It's none of your damn business."

"She's very attractive—"

"And off limits."

Dash's grin faded. "She doesn't know about you, does she?"

Cole ignored the comment as strode for the door. "Let's not pretend either one of us gives a shit what the other is doing in their personal lives."

"What, a guy can't care about his little brother?"

Stopping, he glanced over his shoulder. "Half-brother. And no." Sure as hell not when Dash hadn't bothered with him after Cole's mother walked out on them.

"So why haven't you told her?" Dash leaned forward although he related sensitive information. "You care about her, it's rather obvious you know."

Annoyance gave way to anger. "Stay the fuck out of it, Dash."

"Fine." Dash stood up. "Keep her distracted and then get her away from here. I'll let the rest of the guests know. With their being a full moon tonight, you do realize I'm going to have to compensate everyone."

"I'll write you a check."

Dash nodded. "Good. Now about Harley..."

Cole spun on his heel and left the room. He

stopped by the desk to ask directions to their bungalow. He shoved all thoughts of his half-brother out of his head. If he didn't calm down, Harley would have something else to speculate about. The last thing he needed was her fixating on his and Dash's family connection.

The walk to the bungalow was short, and he found himself pleasantly surprised to find theirs built out over the water. He didn't see Harley in the main room as he scanned the cozy area, taking immediate notice of the king-sized poster bed. The wrought iron frame would be prefect for a little bondage play. Cole's insides quickened at the thought of wrapping Harley's pretty hands together, leaving him free to tease every inch of her until she screamed for him to fuck her.

Get a grip man.

Sliding open the terrace door, he found Harley leaning against the rail, her attention firmly on the turquoise water. Her short skirt hiked up her thighs as she leaned over the edge to look at something in the water.

He thought about walking up to her and simply slipping his arms around her waist. His cock twitched at the thought of pressing against her first class bottom. A quick stab of guilt prodded him in the chest. She'd be pissed to know he had no intentions to let her poke around, at least not without him.

Cole propped a shoulder against the doorjamb, and admired her legs a moment longer. "Nice view, huh?"

Harley tensed then turned around. The warm

breeze lifted her hair away from her face and Cole wished they weren't here because of the story.

She didn't comment on the view, but pinned him in place with a heated glance. "Why did you kiss me on the plane?"

Cole shrugged. He hadn't expected the question and with the memory of her warm mouth, the sweet brush of her tongue across his, his arousal increased ten fold. If she continued to look at him like that...

He changed the subject. "How do you know this Reginald guy wasn't just looking for his five minutes of fame when he contacted Mac?"

She waited a beat, long enough to make Cole think she wasn't finished talking about that kiss.

Harley leaned back against the rail. "I thought it was possible, likely even. Until I arrived. I overhead two people, a man and a woman saying Dash Windsor took care of him. What do you think that means?"

Cole could tell her the truth, about Dash sending him off the island, but then she'd only want to know where he learned that information. Seeing as how he wasn't ready to tell her or anyone, he and Dash shared the same father, he let it go. It was bad enough the questions were rolling through her mind about Reginald. Cole didn't need Harley asking him questions about his and Dash's nonexistent relationship. "Maybe they just meant fired him. Maybe he screwed up, Dash let him go and he decided to get back at them with a little negative press. That kind of stuff happens all the time."

"Maybe," Harley ventured, but Cole could tell by

the troubled light in her eye she wasn't convinced. And unfortunately for them, that meant he needed to keep her from digging too deep. She might be ready to put her journalist career behind her to focus on teaching and writing, but he knew when the story bug bit, and Harley was definitely infected.

"I think I'll take a look around."

He let her get as far as the middle of the room before he caught up with her.

*****

Cole's hand clamped around her wrist, drawing her back around. "Hold on a sec."

His brown eyes flicked over her face, pausing half a second longer than usual on her lips. Just long enough for her heart to pick up speed. Harley drew in a soft breath, all too aware Cole stood much closer than he made a normal habit of, but she couldn't make herself back up.

He leaned forward, blatant need reflected in his eyes.

"Nobody's watching," she blurted, then wanted to smack herself for interrupting him when he was only inches away from her mouth. But Harley couldn't just fall into some casual kiss and touch relationship. She knew it would be too easy to enjoy, too easy to get used to.

Too easy to be hurt when the game was over. Cole rocked back on his heels. "Right." His hand fell away as he stepped back.

Determined to find anything in the room to focus on besides the man still too close for any peace of mind, Harley started to unpack. "Maybe we should establish some ground rules."

"Ground rules," he echoed, following her to the bed where she'd left her suitcase.

Was that annoyance she detected in his voice?

"Yeah, I mean we don't want to get... awkward or anything." *Anything* meaning getting too attached to him.

His lips twitched. "So what did you have in mind?"

Space. Lots of it. Harley grabbed a stack of folded clothes and moved away from him. "Well, for starters I think we should save the affectionate displays for when we're around other people."

Cole stayed on her heels, closing the dresser drawer for after she slid her clothes inside. He planted a palm on the edge of the wood. "Like the kissing."

Harley's heart thumped, his sensually charged proximity disturbed her in every way. "Right," she managed.

He edged closer, his voice deepening as it lowered. "But don't you think we need to look... comfortable with each other?"

She swallowed past the sudden dryness in her throat. "Why wouldn't we look comfortable?"

"You froze up on the plane when I kissed you."

Her chin shot up. "I did not. Besides, you caught me off guard. I wasn't expecting it."

"But that's the thing, you have to be expecting it. Which is why a little practice might be in order." His arms encircled her, one hand resting against her lower back.

"Practice?" Did her voice just squeak?

He moved his other hand to her hip, and its warmth burned into her skin. "You can't be so jumpy around me."

"I'm not jumpy."

Cole leaned forward, blew a breath across her neck. Harley shuddered.

"See," Cole whispered against her hair. "Jumpy."

"That wasn't jumpy, that was…" She broke away as his mouth slid down her neck. Deliciously persuasive lips seared a path from her jaw to the top of her shoulder.

Catching her chin in his palm, he tipped her head back. "You were saying," he prompted.

She was? Right. She was about to say —

Cole's mouth melted against hers, and her world spun inward. Harley clung to him as his tongue slid past her lips. Sparks shot through her veins as she gripped his shoulders and hauled him closer. His arousal brushed her belly. Instinctively Harley rubbed against his cock, dragging a tortured groan from Cole in the process. His hands tightened around her waist before gliding upwards. At the edge of her halter-top, his fingers teased her exposed midsection then slid beneath the stretchy fabric. The pad of his thumb skimmed the underside of her breast.

His mouth caught the shaky moan that rose from her throat. Harley deepened the kiss as she stretched up on her toes and pressed herself against him. The soft ache between her thighs intensified at the tantalizing contact. Breathless, she pulled back and rested her head against his chest. "See, not jumpy."

Cole didn't move for a long moment, then he

abruptly stepped back. "Glad we've established that. It's hot, I'm gonna take a shower."

Harley stared after him as he disappeared into the bathroom. The click of the door shutting snapped her back to reality. How did he do it? How did he kiss her like that, hold her, make her feel things... and then just walk away as if it meant nothing to him.

Harley flopped on the bed. That was because it did mean nothing to him. He didn't have a thing for her. Although he obviously didn't find her completely unattractive or she doubted he would have agreed to come along, Cole played his part. Just like she was supposed to be doing. Only she failed miserably.

Refusing to mope, Harley waited until she heard the water turn on before she got up. There was no point in waiting here when she could at least take a look around. Outside their bungalow, she followed the short wharf to the beach, then a cobblestone pathway lined on both sides by towering palm trees. After passing the pool, where she glanced longingly at the small waterfall grotto, Harley turned away from the crowd, curiously aware of the pairs of eyes that followed her. She might have chalked the stares up to her more provocative clothes, but she knew it wasn't just men staring.

Disconcerted, Harley followed another path into a denser part of the surrounding jungle, unsure of where it took her. As long as nobody stared at her, she didn't care. A bird cawed overhead and Harley tipped her head back to watch the bright colored creature chatter down at her.

Her foot caught the edge of a stone and she shot

forwards. Stumbling, she managed to catch her balance. Harley glanced back over shoulder, frowning at the pair of shorts in the middle of walkway. Someone must have dropped them on their way to or from the pool.

Five steps further up, she spotted a shirt, and a... pair of boxers? Harley smiled. Maybe somebody had a few drinks and wanted to get a little closer to nature. Raised voices caught her attention, and she immediately recognized them from the resort's lobby.

Careful not to give herself away, she inched down the path, staying close to the thick foliage growing at the edge of the path between her and the couple in heated discussion. Sensing movement behind her, Harley whipped around. The pathway behind her was deserted. Frowning, she shifted her attention back to the couple.

Harley blinked, disbelieving the sight in front of her even as adrenaline pounded through her system.

A black and gray wolf blocked her path.

Chapter Four

Harley took a step back and froze as the wolf took a step towards her. Afraid to take her eyes off the large animal, Harley fought back the panic. Should she run? Scream? Curl into a ball and play dead? No, that was someone did with a bear, wasn't it?

The wolf's lips pulled back in a vicious snarl.

Heart thundering in her ears, Harley inched backwards.

"Easy," Cole whispered coming up behind her. "Don't move." Instead of being relieved to see him, her fear intensified at the thought him getting between her and the wolf.

He eased her behind him, his body tense, poised for attack. He could *not* be thinking of doing something stupid.

"Cole," she warned.

He didn't respond, his eyes never wavered from the wolf.

Harley's rapid heartbeat counted off the seconds in triple time.

Cole took a step towards the wolf, mumbling something Harley couldn't make out. Something about, *not her*?

Breath held, Harley waited.

The wolf stopped snarling, his bristled fur lowering before it turned and plunged into the foliage.

Neither of them moved for a long moment. Cole finally turned around, his tense expression relaxing. "He's gone."

Harley could only stare at the spot where the wolf disappeared. And just how in the hell did a wolf get to Antigua? They certainly couldn't be native to the environment, could they? "Where did it come from?"

Cole shrugged. "Maybe he got loose."

"You think he's somebody's pet?" Harley shivered at the thought of crossing paths with the animal again.

"Maybe. I'll walk you back to the room. You can change or shower if you want. I'll talk to the staff about it, then we can go to dinner."

Harley sidestepped him. "You don't find it a bit odd that there is a wolf running loose on the resort?"

"Not a whole lot surprises me anymore." Cole started back towards the pool. He glanced back over his shoulder. "You coming?"

"Yeah," Harley answered vaguely, wondering why he didn't seem the least bit concerned about the wolf. Left with little choice, she followed him back to their bungalow.

Picking up a lilac colored sundress, she slipped into the bathroom as Cole went to let the staff know about her run in with wolf. Washing off the sticky humidity made her feel better, but alone her thoughts drifted towards the kiss she and Cole shared not long ago. Next time, even if it meant begging him not to walk away, she would somehow convince him to do all the wicked things she dreamt about.

Harley just finished drying off when he returned.

"The owner's," Cole said from the other side of the door.

Opening the door, Harley frowned. "Dash Windsor has a big wolf for a pet?"

"Apparently. He's back in his pen now." Cole smiled. "You wearing that tonight?"

Harley realized she stepped into the room with nothing but the skimpy towel around her. His gaze slid over her, hot and hungry. Heat surged through her middle and pooled between her legs. "No."

He took a step towards her, the interest in his expression enough to put her on edge. Abruptly Cole changed directions and flopped down on the bed. "Hurry up then. I'm starved."

What the hell was a matter with him? He couldn't keep doing that. One minute look like he would devour her on the spot and the next act as if she wasn't even in the room. She let the bathroom door slam behind her as she finished getting ready. Some men were just so damn... The proper term escaped her, maybe because there were too many that fit, she couldn't settle on just one.

After she dressed and slipped her sandals on, Harley found Cole on the beach in front of their bungalow. He didn't even look at her as they walked in silence towards one of the resorts three restaurants. They were shown to a small table hidden from most of the dining area by wrought iron framework and green foliage that wrapped around the bars. A small dance floor stood off to their right where one couple swayed to a Latin beat.

Cole took the seat to her left, the table just large enough for her to avoid brushing against him.

He picked up the menu. "What do you feel like

having?"

Sex. "Not sure." Her eyes drawn to the dance floor once more, she watched as the couple maneuvered in an erotic tango. Harley felt Cole's attention shift to the dance floor as the couple's hands slid down each other, their caresses purposely sensual. The dark haired man brazenly cupped his partner's breast. Her back arched in response before he lowered her into an elegant dip. With her dress hiked up past her knees, the man's hand slid up her thigh, and catching her ass in his palm, he straightened them both upright.

One song melted into another as the couple swayed and groped each other in a seductive dance Harley felt helpless to look away from. With every turn and embrace, their hands explored and enjoyed, and Harley imagined Cole's hands doing similar things to her.

After the second song ended, the couple disappeared off the dance floor.

Ignoring the sweet pressure in her core, Harley shifted in place. The weight of Cole's eyes on her nearly pushed her to the floor. She swallowed, met his gaze and asked, "What?"

He said nothing. Harley set the menu aside. "Cole, you're staring at me."

He laughed and the smooth sound washed over her. "Thank you for pointing out the obvious." Cole lifted up her hand, brushed his lips across her wrist. His smile teased. "Better, not so jumpy." His thumb drifted back and forth across her skin. "Have to keep up pretenses," he reminded her.

"Right," she answered, her breath oozing out in a gentle whoosh.

A moment later their waiter appeared. Harley managed to get her order out, not missing the fact Cole's eyes didn't leave her once. When it was Cole's turn, she took a moment to study his handsome face, wondering how he so easily appeared to be in love with her. She needed to take a page out of his book.

Dinner was agonizing. Every other moment, Cole found an excuse to touch her. A gentle squeeze of her hand, the soft brush of his finger across her cheek as he tucked her hair back, and the soft whisper of his lips against hers when he noticed whipped cream at the corner of her mouth. By the time they finished, Harley's whole body hungered for him. One more heated look in her direction and she was liable to combust on the spot. Even knowing that once they were behind the four walls of their bungalow he'd drop the act, did nothing to slow the heat flickering under her skin.

Cole lead the way back to their room, guiding her along a torch lit path now that the sun had set. Music and laughter carried on the evening breeze, but they seemed to be moving away from it. She wished they could go down to the beach, have a bonfire and just…

But that was what real couples did. And she and Cole weren't a real couple.

Maybe once she reminded herself of that another thousand times she could be as slick about the whole thing as he seemed to be.

Cole stopped in front of her and she collided

with his back. "What—"

His arm slid around her, tugging her close. "Shhhh, listen."

Harley didn't hear anything beyond the breeze wrestling the leaves overhead and the very faint sound of music.

"I don't hear anything," she whispered.

"This way," Cole led her down another path and the surrounding jungle closed in on them. Harley couldn't help but think of the wolf from earlier. Soft moans filtered through the trees ahead of them.

That was what he heard? The passionate pleas were still so muffled she couldn't begin to guess how he'd heard them from where they stood moments before. As they approached, the moans grew louder. Cole tugged her off the trail and into the shadows as the path opened up in front of them leading to a gazebo. The same couple who danced back at the restaurant were now locked in each other's arms in the center of the wooden structure.

The blonde's head dropped back as the man's lips trailed down her neck. His hand moved under her skirt and, judging by the woman's groans, he caressed her in all the right places.

"We should go," Harley whispered, but didn't move, unable to peel her eyes off the couple in front of her.

Cole moved behind her. His arm came around her waist as he hauled her back against his chest. "No. He's going to touch her, fuck her and we're going to watch." His deep, raw command rumbled against her neck.

A delicious shiver curled up Harley's spine. "It's not right," she protested, only to find herself riveted to the erotic sight before her. The man pushed the straps of the woman's dress down, exposing two high breasts. His finger glided across her skin, covered one hard nipple. He pinched it lightly, then bending his head, flicked his tongue across the tip.

Harley tensed, warmth creeping through her system, all too aware of Cole at her back. Cole shifted closer and she felt the unmistakable nudge of his erection at her back. As she watched the couple on the gazebo she leaned more fully against Cole. He tensed and she waited for him to move away. The arm around her waist drifted higher the same moment the other man shoved his partner's dress up out of his way. His hands slowly slid up the woman's thighs.

She wasn't wearing any panties, Harley realized a moment before the man sank his fingers into her.

Between Harley's legs started to hum. She shifted in place both to ease the new ache and to contract her inner muscles around it.

Cole groaned behind her. His mouth grazed the side of her neck and her eyes drifted shut. A moment later he lifted her breast into his palm, his thumb making wide circles around her nipple.

In front of them the woman shoved the man away from him. She dropped to her knees in front of him, undid his pants, gripped the base of his cock and licked him from base to tip. The man's tortured groan rode on the air.

Cole tensed, rubbing himself against her bottom.

It felt too good to stop. Harley didn't care if it

was an act or not at this point. She wanted his hands on her too damn bad to worry about what would happen when they went home.

The woman's mouth shuttled up and down the thick cock in front of her, coaxing another loud groan from her partner.

Cole's hands slid under her dress. Through the thin cotton his fingers traced the folds hiding her clit. She shivered in wicked delight.

Growling, the man on the gazebo lifted the woman into his arms. She wrapped her legs around the man's waist as he leaned her back against the solid pillar. They both cried out as he drove into her, his hips thrusting in a savage rhythm that appeared to punish as much as it pleased.

Cole fingers slipped past the edge of her panties, and stroked her already damp slit. Harley bit her lip to trap the moan burning in the back of her throat. She squeezed her thighs together only to have Cole push them apart before he swirled his thumb across her clit.

Harley rocked back against him, her body strung tight by the desperate need swallowing her.

Cole nodded towards the couple still fucking in front of them. "Do you want me to do that to you, Harley?"

Hell, yeah. She managed a shaky nod, too caught up in the fire pulsing between her legs to speak.

"You want me slide my cock deep inside you?" He sank a finger into her, Harley jerked at the erotic invasion.

"Yes," she whispered.

The other couple's feverish groans ricocheted through the quiet night air as they found their release.

Cole pushed another finger inside her. "Tell me you want me to fuck you, Harley."

Fiery threads tightened and pulled in her body. "I want you, Cole."

His teeth scraped her neck. "You want me to what?" He pumped into her again, harder this time.

"I want you to fuck me." Harley squeezed her eyes tight, grasping for the sweet whispers of release.

Cole's satisfied groan rumbled against her shoulder. "How about we go up there right now?"

It took Harley a moment to realize the couple had vanished.

"Or we could do it right here." Another finger plunged inside her and this time Harley didn't hold back her moan. His thumb rolled back and forth across her clit.

"So," Cole prompted. "Here or there?"

Someone coughed directly behind them.

*****

Harley stiffened in his arms, the scent of her arousal fading as she shoved her dress back in place.

Cole didn't need to turn around to know who stood behind him.

The son of a bitch had some fucking timing.

Keeping Harley discreetly positioned behind him, Cole turned around. "Evening,"

Dash nodded politely. "Sorry to interrupt. I just wanted to reassure Ms. McKinnon that my friend was back in his pen."

Cole resisted the urge to knock him out, Alpha or

not. "I already informed her of that." And the bastard damn well knew it.

"Good."

The three stood in an awkward silence before Dash finally nodded again. "Well, good night. I hope you're enjoying your stay."

Harley didn't move until Dash left.

"Tired," he asked, taking in her flushed cheeks and sleepy eyes.

"A little."

Setting his hand at her lower back, he steered her back onto the path. "Let's go back to our bungalow."

She didn't say anything beside him. She didn't have to. Her desire, her arousal still lingered on the air and for the first time he realized just how much she might want him too. But it didn't matter. It would never work between them. How couldn't he do this to her? God, he wanted her, but would she be able to go back to the way things were when they got back to the city? And they'd have to. He wouldn't hurt her the way his jackass friend had. She deserved better than a man who had no intention of committing to any woman. Ever.

At the steps leading to the wharf, he paused. "You go in, I'll be right there."

He knew it was on the tip of her tongue to ask him why, but she only nodded and continued on.

Cole stared into the darkness. "Stalking me now? I don't think that's a very brotherly thing to do is it?"

Dash grinned as he stepped out into the light. "Nope. It's a full moon tonight."

Crossing his arms, Cole glared at him. "No

kidding. I think I missed the memo."

"I won't be able to keep most of them from shifting tonight. You know that."

"Harley won't be going for any midnight strolls if that's what you want to know."

Dash nodded. "Good." He turned away, then swiveled back around. "I have to know… are you serious about her? Because if you're not…"

"I already told you, she's not up for claiming."

"You must have some will power. Even I couldn't willfully resist someone I cared about tonight."

Cole said nothing, knowing exactly how close he'd come before Dash interrupted them.

"So you still have no plans to claim her then." Dash shoved his hands in pockets. "Why not?"

"I would never bite her without her being aware of what would happen."

"Well, she can hardly make the choice for herself if she doesn't know about you."

Cole started down the wharf.

"You should tell her."

He whipped around. "And you should fuck off."

"She won't leave."

Irritated now, Cole snapped, "Leave it."

Dash didn't seem concerned at the underlying growl in Cole's voice. "Just because your mother left when she learned the truth, doesn't mean all human women will."

Cole took a step towards him, stopped just short of knocking Dash on his ass. "Back the fuck off."

"That's what's stopping you, isn't it?" Dash

cocked his head as though he had a light bulb moment. "You care for her, you want her, but you won't claim her."

"What I do and don't do has never been your concern, nor is it now." Cole flexed his fist.

"Maybe. But if you aren't going to claim her, I just might have to."

He knew Dash intentionally pressed his buttons, but that didn't stop jealousy from rearing its ugly head. Cole grabbed Dash, yanked him towards him. He'd heard enough.

"Cole?"

Fuck. Cole turned around at the sight of Harley standing there, and released Dash.

She crossed her arms. "Is there a problem I should know about?"

Dash shook his head. "No problem. We were just having a bit of a disagreement about the loose wolf. I understand your boyfriend's concerns now." He nodded. "Good night again, Ms. McKinnon." Perhaps you'd like a full tour of the island in the morning. That is, if Cole doesn't mind. He'd be welcome to come along if he wished."

"She'll let you know," Cole growled, knowing it was another provocation.

Dash disappeared as stealthily as he'd approached. Cole waited until he was gone before he followed Harley down the wharf and inside their bungalow. She stopped in the middle of the room. Her eyes drifted around the room before settling on him.

"You can have the bed," Cole said before he

reached for her again. He couldn't cross that line. Not when he knew it would hurt her when he didn't stay. And he couldn't.

Disappointment flashed across her face before she nodded and turned away. She headed for the bathroom and he felt like an ass as he heard her get ready for bed.

Needing some air, he slid the terrace door open and walked out onto the deck over the water. The bright moon hung low in the sky and he felt the power of it pulsing under his skin. Maybe once Harley went to bed he go for a run, burn off the desire still clinging to him. The light went out behind him. He waited, listening for the sound of the bed covers being pulled back.

Silence.

The boards creaked behind him, but he didn't turn around. Harley stepped in front of him. Dressed in a pale yellow silk gown that came to mid-thigh, her long brown hair cascading down her back, she looked so amazing standing there in the moonlight, his chest ached.

She tilted her chin up, her voice a silken wave that wrapped around him. "I want you, Cole. I know you want me too, at least a little. Can't you give me just one night?"

Chapter Five

He didn't move, didn't breath as she leaned up and brushed her mouth across his. Her body molded to his before her hands tangled in the ends of his hair as she tugged him closer. "Please," she whispered, her breath whispering across his neck. Her teeth nipped his jaw. "One night."

Cole closed his eyes when her hands moved between them, down past his waist. How could he stop himself? She was giving him what he wanted. To touch her, make love to her with no strings, no expectations. Offering herself to him.

But could he control the animal inside him that craved to claim her, to make her his permanently? If it meant the difference between having her tonight, or walking away right now, he'd take his chances.

Catching her chin, Cole tilted her head back. "You're sure? Because I can't be the man you want me to be. I can give you tonight, but beyond that…"

"I know." Her quiet voice stirred his heart, tugging at him in places he didn't want to acknowledge.

He captured her mouth, tasting her over and over, until he would happily drown in the sensations coursing through him. In place of his blood, lava burned through his veins, thick and hot. His cock ached to find its way into her slick center, but there was time for that. If he only had one night, he'd make damn sure it felt like much longer. For both of them.

Harley's hands slid around his waist, and

cupping his ass she rubbed against his hard length. Sharp and exquisitely sweet sparks zipped from his balls to his cock. The back of his knees hit the wide lounge chair behind them, and Cole realized she'd walked them backwards.

"Sit," she commanded, her eyes bright with determination.

His lips tipped into a wide grin, before she gently shoved him backwards. Harley stood motionless in front of him. He clenched his hands tight with the need to rip the tantalizing spaghetti-strapped fabric off her. She didn't say anything, leaving only the soft rush of the water hitting the beach and faraway nightlife sounds of the jungle between them.

Harley pushed her hair off behind her shoulders, and Cole followed the natural movement as he had a hundred times. She complained about the long tresses and every time she mention getting it cut, he'd persuaded her not too. He wanted to run his hands through it, use it to hold her in place when she would finally take him in her mouth. His cock twitched, both at the erotic image and the incredible sight she made before him as she tugged first one and then the other strap past her shoulders.

Riveted, he watched her push the nightgown down. Two full breasts, their firm dark pink nipples, taunted him.

Harley shook her head before he reached for her. "Not yet." Her lips curved in a sinful smile that promised more than he dared to consider.

She pushed the gathered folds past her hips and

when the yellow silk pooled at it her feet, she stepped free. The only indication of Harley's nervousness was the short gasps of air sliding past her lips, and way her fingers curled and then lengthened.

Cole held her gaze. His heart thumped at the eagerness, desire and hopefulness swirling in the amber eyes. Eyes he'd been haunted by since she booted that jackass of an ex out. What had that moron been thinking, not wanting Harley in his life? She was a strong, smart and fun, sexy woman. And she made Cole ache for her in ways no woman before had.

"You're the most beautiful thing I've ever seen." He meant it. Every word felt scraped from his throat before it squeezed closed. How would he find it in him to walk away from her?

Harley took two steps towards him. Cole didn't move, couldn't take his eyes off her.

She closed her hand around his wrist, and guided it to her. "Touch me. Please." Harsh need echoed beneath her soft plea.

Her eyes drifted shut when he lifted her breast into his palm. Cole raked his thumb across one pointed nipple. Harley moaned, and the raw sound whipped his insides into action.

Looping an arm around her waist, he hauled her down to his lap. Cole smoothed her hair back from her face, stared into her anxious eyes then crushed her to him. Her mouth softened before he devoured her with a savage intensity. Seconds later Harley parted her lips and invited him deeper. The first teasing swipe of her tongue made his hips rock upwards. Only his cotton shorts stood between his cock and pure, hot, bliss.

Harley planted a palm against his chest. She glanced away, drew in a breath then brought her attention back to him. "I know that whatever happens is only for tonight, but you have to know... I need you to know that I've wanted this, wanted you so much..."

He kissed her again knowing he couldn't say anything to reassure her it would go beyond tonight, but for the first time in his life he wanted it to. She felt so right in his arms, he wondered how he'd ever be able to let her go.

Harley straightened, bringing his hand back to her breast. "Don't stop. Not until the sun comes up."

In the distance a wolf howled, but she didn't pay any attention to it, he made sure of that. Cole caught the greedy tip of one nipple with his fingers and tugged. He did the same with the other, holding Harley steady as she arched into him. Leaning forward, he trapped her nipple between his lips, raking it with his teeth before he sucked into his greedy mouth.

"Yes," Harley groaned, her head dropping back. "Your mouth... had I known—"

He curled his tongue around the other one.

She shuddered, her breath catching. "...I would have jumped you months ago."

"Oh, yeah?" Cole drew lazy figure eights across her nipples. "What stopped you?"

Harley smiled shyly. "I didn't think you wanted me."

Cole took her hand and brought it to his cock.

"As you can clearly tell, you were wrong."

Her fist closed around him. "Good to know." Harley teased the head of his cock through his shorts, her grin widening. "Maybe I should take a closer look."

Because he knew the minute she stroked her tongue down his shaft he'd want to come, Cole caught her hand. "Not yet."

Shifting Harley around, he faced her outwards so she looked at the ocean, her perfectly sculpted ass cuddling his cock. He started at her shoulder, skimmed his lips up the side of her neck, nipping her ear lobe. Harley turned her head, and he caught her luscious mouth with his. Cole cupped her breasts, both thumbs grazing the hard points as she bumped against him. He groaned at the bolt of lust that speared him in two.

He slid a hand down her belly, felt the muscles tighten under his palm. Circling her navel once, he moved lower, past her hip and down the inside of her thigh.

She squeezed her thighs together. "I think you missed the spot." Harley caught his hand and settled it between her legs. "Here. Right, here," she murmured.

Cole tunneled through the curls, parting the slick flesh. "Is this what you want?" He gently pinched her clit.

Harley jerked in his arms, her ass grinding against him in shameless response. "Oh, yeah." Her voice was low, smoky, as she shuddered. "That's it."

Up and down Cole glided his fingers along her

slit, circling the swollen knot with slow, sweeping strokes. "Good. But just so you know, we're just getting started."

*****

Harley dragged in a breath, clamped her legs together, desperate to keep his hand exactly where it was. Sliver shards of pleasure stampeded through her with every long swipe of his thumb across her clit. And just when she thought the tight ache building in her core would implode, another gentle flick spiraled the exquisite tension higher.

Cole pumped his fingers inside her, and Harley moaned long and loud, not caring who might hear. She spread her legs wider, and at the same time pushed back against his cock until Cole's breathing quickened.

Fingers bit into the inside of her thigh. "Don't make me embarrass myself," he pleaded, right before he sank his fingers into her heat again, over and over.

Lifting her hips, Harley rolled into each thrust.

"Why don't you help me out here?" Grabbing her hand from where she rested it on his thigh to steady herself, Cole brought it between her legs. "Let me see you touch yourself." He teased the pad of his thumb across her clit. "Please."

Heat stole across her cheeks at the thought of him watching her do something she only did alone, alone when thoughts of Cole drove her to find some kind of release.

His breath warmed her neck before his lips caressed. "For me." He slid another finger into her, and hot currents jetted through her. She'd give him whatever he wanted just as long as he didn't stop.

With one hand between her legs, his other guided her fingers along her damp folds, his palm burning into the top of her hand. The combined intensity sent her simmering body into a hot, rolling boil. His cock rubbed against her bottom and Harley dropped her head back against his shoulder.

"Come for me," he coaxed, strumming her clit between her own fingers before he plunged harder into her center. Her inner muscles clenched as he rubbed the aching spot within, shooting Harley into a star-spotted oblivion that swallowed her whole.

Cole swiveled her around, trapping her beneath him. He caught her mouth in a fiery kiss she felt echo through her entire blissfully sluggish body. He scraped his teeth across her nipple. "You don't want me to stop yet, do you?" Hungry brown eyes held her captive.

"Absolutely, not."

His devilish grin made her smile. A second later he sat up and stripped off his shirt. Propped on one elbow, Harley slid her palm up the smooth chest, knew it felt better now than in any of her fantasies.

Cole caught her hand and brought it to his cock. "Do you see what you do to me, how badly I want to fuck you... how badly I want to make you scream my name?" The shorts came next and she admired his athletic frame against the silhouette of the full moon.

Leaning forward, he hooked his arms under her knees and jerked her forward. On his knees, Cole bent his head to her thighs and stroked his tongue along the seam at her middle. Harley clawed at the lounge mattress beneath her, her hips arched as he swirled around her clit. She couldn't come again, not yet. It was too soon. But every slick lash of his tongue nudged her back towards the edge.

Harley tried to wiggle away only to find herself imprisoned when his hands cupped her ass. She bit her lip, trapping a moan as his teeth dragged across the tight knot, tugging it between his lips. Two fingers slid into her again and she screamed, a second orgasm tearing through her.

Cole hovered over her. "I've wanted to sink my cock into you for so long."

It was her turn to tease him. She shook her head. "Not yet." Harley gripped his hips, tugged him up her body until his impressive erection hovered above her face. Flicking her tongue across the engorged tip, she gently scooped his balls into her palm.

A deep groan rumbled up from Cole's throat. His eyes slid closed. "Fuck. Do it again." He nudged his cock at her slightly parted lips and she opened, taking him in her mouth.

Big, smooth and hard, just tasting him stoked the fire already burning anew between her legs.

Harley sucked and laved, sliding her filled palm up and down to match hungry rhythm of her mouth. Cole's groans became strained as he braced his hands above her and sank himself past her lips.

His hips rocked harder as he pumped his cock into her mouth. "That's… wait… I don't want to… not yet…"

Harley curled her tongue around his shaft, teasing and nipping before sucking him deep.

Cole jerked back, slid his hands under her ass and plunged into her in one powerful thrust.

"Cole." Harley yelled against his neck, lifting her hips to meet him. Hard and fast he slid into her, and she clenched her muscles around him each time to keep him there. Over and over, he drove into her, his breathing as harsh and ragged as her own. For leverage Harley dug her heels into the mattress, cradling him between her thighs every time he drove into her.

Cole's mouth slanted across hers and his tongue swept inside. Under the scorching assault, her body ignited, and every feverish thrust sizzled through her bloodstream.

"You're mine," Cole growled before he kissed her again. He adjusted his angle picking up speed.

His body thundered against hers, hard, hot and fast. Harley tilted her head back. Fierce brown eyes blazed down at her, a flicker of tenderness swirling amidst the desire. Her chest caught, her heart no longer thumping from just the charged currents that whipped through her. Now her insides tightened with the knowledge she was definitely falling for Cole. Hard.

Very hard.

Cole's mouth found Harley's at the same time lightning speared her core. Everything inside turned hot and twisted sharply as pleasure crashed through her. One last thrust, and Cole tensed, his muffled groan more of a tortured howl.

With her pulse hammering in her ears, Harley held tight to him. She didn't want the night to end.

Above her, Cole brushed a kiss across forehead. For a moment Harley could only hope that the tenderness reflected in his eyes meant that maybe… just maybe, there would be more than just tonight for them.

Afraid to believe, Harley didn't cling to the possibility, instead banished it from her mind as Cole rolled to his side and tucked her against his chest. She wasn't cold as the soft evening breeze caressed her skin. With his arm wrapped tight around her, she drifted off to sleep, wondering if the howl of wolves in the distance were real or all in her imagination.

*****

Harley stared down at him, smiling at the gentle snores that started a few minutes before. Sitting up, she poked his arm. "Wake up, sleepy head."

Cole growled, snagged her around the waist, and pulled her close. "It's not morning yet."

Her laugh bubbled out before he nuzzled her neck and her thoughts shifted to the very naked male tangled in the sheets beside her. "Its actually close to noon."

He cracked open an eye. "Really?"

Harley nodded, her chest tightening with the knowledge that when he got up, the incredible night she'd forever remember, would be over. Her body pleasantly ached from the four times they'd made love.

"I don't think there is any reason to get up, is there?" Cole's lips curved into a suggestive grin.

Not even the spark of desire in his eyes could stop her stomach from rumbling. "Food."

"Ah." He closed his eyes again.

Because she didn't want to be the one left in bed whenever he decided it was time to move on, Harley stood up first.

"Not with the sheet, sweetheart." He caught the corner of it and tugged.

Grinning, Harley let it go and smiled as he sat up. She dodged his groping hands. "I'll go, get us something to eat, and then you can have me for dessert." Harley waited, half expecting him to hold her to her one night only bargain.

Cole lips parted in a devastating smile. "Sounds great to me." He flopped back in the bed, put his hands behind his head. "Don't be long."

Slipping on her undergarments, she followed them with a pale blue sundress. "You don't have to worry about that."

Harley smiled as she left the bungalow. She wouldn't think about anything beyond the last few hours and whatever time she had left with him. No matter what came next, she wouldn't regret what happened between them.

Just outside the closest restaurant, Harley caught sight of the same woman she'd heard arguing in the resort's main lobby. Forgetting about breakfast, she followed the woman down a path that led past the pool. She called out, but the woman either didn't hear her, or ignored her.

By the time Harley rounded the next bend the woman had vanished.

Into the jungle?

No.

Maybe she'd scared the girl off. Hurrying her

pace, Harley jogged further down the trail, noting the cobblestones gave way to a dirt path. Around the next bend two piles of clothes were bunched at the side of the path.

From the same fool who lost his clothes yesterday no doubt.

Not knowing where she was going, Harley thought about turning around, but her curiosity got the better of her. More clothes were strewn across the path and she could only wonder if there wasn't some kind or orgy going on close by.

Hushed voices reached Harley's ears. She slowed her pace, creeping forward so as to not give away her presence. "We burn it to the ground," an angry voice snapped.

Someone snorted. "He'll hunt us down."

"So then we take care of him too," another voice chimed in, a woman's.

Take care of who?

Something smashed against a tree, a glass? "Dash shouldn't have kicked Reginald off the island. Maybe its time someone challenged the Alpha."

"Forget challenging him. We just take him out."

"Honor demands—"

Someone growled. "Fuck, honor. Dash Windsor didn't honor my brother when he barred him from the island."

They wanted to take out Dash Windsor? As in murder him?

"Maybe if Reginald hadn't gone to the press. He'd still be here," a calm voice reasoned.

The sound of a fist striking flesh froze Harley in

place and kicked her heartbeat into overdrive.

"My brother would never risk exposing us. The journalist would have been under control if Windsor let Reginald handle it instead of sending him to Europe. Instead we have her trooping under our feet as we speak."

Jesus, they were talking about her.

Harley took a step backwards and a twig snapped under her foot. She squeezed her eyes shut, her breath locked in her chest.

The voices continued. They hadn't heard her. Relief whispered through her. Turning around, she knew she had to find Cole. Together they could go to Dash, to warn him.

Harley stopped dead in her tracks.

Three wolves stood on the path, blocking her escape.

Chapter Six

As a group, they stalked towards her.

Fear iced down Harley's spine, but she didn't move.

One more circled around the others. She recognized the gray and black one in point position from before. How did he get loose again? And where had the others come from?

As she stared, the lead wolf curled his lips in a vicious snarl.

How far would she get if she ran? One she might have stood a chance of escaping, but four. The odds weren't good.

"Don't move, Harley."

Cole circled around in front of her. Where had he come from?

He squeezed her hand, but didn't look at her. "I need you to trust me, okay? Very, very slowly, I want you to edge farther up the trail."

The words no sooner left his mouth than another low growl sounded behind them.

Cole pulled her closer towards him as the wolves circled. "She has nothing to do with your feud."

Harley gawked at Cole. "I don't think they speak English."

Cole ignored her. "I suggest you back off. You know who I am. Think how difficult your lives will become if you fuck with me."

The snarling increased.

"Fuck," Cole growled. Keeping her close, he

tugged his shirt off.

"What in the hell are you doing?" Harley hissed. She could only stare as his shorts came off next. "Are you out of your mind?" Full-blown panic threaded her voice. "Cole." He was losing it.

He took her hand, but didn't take his eyes off the circling wolves. "I need you to trust me."

"I—"

The large gray and black wolf lunged at them. Cole shoved her to the ground, the impact knocking the air from her lungs. She rolled to her side at the same moment…

No… it wasn't possible… She didn't see… He couldn't have…

Harley blinked rapidly, unable to even drag in a breath as the man beside her only moments ago collided with the attacking wolf… only… he was no longer a man.

Werewolves?

The hysterical thought bubbled into her brain and she might have screamed at the insanity of it if one of the other large animals didn't pin her in place with laser precise eyes.

Scrambling backwards, Harley fought back the panic determined to immobilize her.

This wasn't happening.

The wolf circled, then charged towards her. Harley raised her arms to block the attack.

The bronze colored wolf… Cole…? skidded in front of her, the sound of vicious snarls and growls filled the air.

From behind him, the gray wolf struck, sinking

its teeth her protector's back.

Howling, he whipped around, shaking the gray wolf loose before launching at him. The other wolves stood motionless as though they cared who came out the victor.

Harley was too scared to move, couldn't take her eyes off the two wolves tearing at each other.

The gray and black wolf howled as he was forced to the ground. Teeth clamped over his jugular and Harley waited for blood. Instead, the dominant wolf held back.

Brown eyes flicked towards her.

Harley shook her head. No fucking way.

Howls filled the air and Harley's heart pounded faster.

More wolves appeared and surrounded the smaller group. One moved towards Cole. Harley didn't think, just moved, grabbing the branch and swinging it at the approaching wolf.

The silver wolf eyed the bat nervously, took a step back.

"Harley, it's fine."

Shifting her attention, she saw Cole on the ground, blood pouring from a deep wound on his shoulder. Behind him, where the small group of wolves cowered, three men and two women now stood. Completely naked.

What in the hell…

Only the recent arrivals remained as wolves.

Sensing no animosity, Harley ignored the silver one, and crouched beside Cole. She hesitated for a moment, then grabbed the shirt he'd stripped off earlier and pressed it to the still oozing wound.

Cole flinched, his face unreadable.

The last few moments sank in, replaying themselves in her mind.

Cole… And wolves?

Harley glanced over her shoulder at the silver one. His eyes were still fixed on the branch at her feet.

She couldn't have seen it. People couldn't turn into wolves. Not in real life. There had to be a rational, objective explanation. Right?

Pushing to her feet, Harley backed away. This was fucking insane.

"Harley." Cole tried to stand, but his knees buckled. "Wait."

She shook her head and spinning on her heel, she fled.

*****

Cole stared after her, the pain radiating down his back and chest stealing his breath. "Harley," he shouted.

Dash knelt beside him. "She'll be fine."

Cole dropped his head, wincing when his brother peeled back the shirt to examine the wound. "She wasn't supposed to find out like this…"

"Which is why you should have told her."

Cole snorted. "Aren't we a little old for I told you so?" Dash probed at his wound and he jerked away. "Do you mind? That fucking hurts."

"It needs to be stitched."

Cole shook his head. "I need to find Harley."

"Why, so you can bleed all over her? Go to the infirmary. I'll make sure she's fine, okay. I won't touch her," Dash promised at Cole's doubtful look.

Not liking it, but knowing he'd be good for nothing if he didn't get stitched up, Cole allowed Dash to help him to his feet. The ones who arrived with Dash led the others away. Cole felt some small measure of satisfaction seeing the wounds he inflicted on the small faction's leader. If he had so much as breathed on Harley...

"She's safe," Dash reminded him, damn near reading Cole's mind.

But she might not have been if Dash hadn't shown up. He grabbed his brother's arm. When Dash turned around, Cole offered his hand. "Thanks."

Dash gripped his hand, his grin widening. "Anytime."

*****

The resort's doctor just finished stitching him up when Dash strolled in.

"She's in your bungalow."

Cole didn't know whether to be relieved or not. "She is? I though she would have been half way to the airport by now."

Dash leaned back against the counter. "She's not your mother, Cole."

Thank God for that. Still that didn't mean Harley would be anymore accepting of his kind than his mother. "You saw the look on her face."

Dash shot him a *well, duh* look. "You shifted right in front of her."

"What choice did I have?"

"None, but she had no warning... nothing to make her think for a second you are what you are.

She just needs time to process it all."

Cole began to cross his arms, winced as the topical anesthetic was already wearing off. "And you think she's just hanging out in there thinking."

"Most likely. She's a journalist. She's probably trying to look at it from all the objective angles."

"Or she's packing." Chances were she already had.

Dash rolled his eyes. "You won't know if you don't go to her."

"So she can tell me how much of a freak I am?" That, he sure as hell couldn't handle.

"Fine have it your way. Sit here and throw her away. I know of someone who'd be more than happy to take her off your hands."

"If you wanted a mate, you'd have one already."

"Maybe I just haven't met a woman who would embrace the change." Some in Dash's casual shrug felt off.

Cole cocked his head. "Somehow I don't think that's it."

Dash stiffened, his eyes darkened enough to make Cole suspect he hit on a touchy subject. "We're not talking about me." Dash glanced at Cole. "But Harley would make a good, strong mate I think."

Cole growled and sidestepped Dash. "Don't go near her."

Dash shoved him back a step. "Then stop being a pussy and go talk to her."

He knew Dash was right as he brother strode away, yet it took him almost an hour to build up the nerve.

And it fizzled out on him the second he walked into the bungalow.

*****

Harley tensed as the terrace door slid open behind her. She wanted to turn around, see for herself that it was in fact Cole, but a fear she didn't understand kept her rooted in place. She wanted to believe she imagined that scene in the woods, but she knew she hadn't. It would have been easier to deal with if she had, could have chalked it up to stress or something.

But Harley didn't imagine it. The more she replayed the details in her mind, the more convinced she became. Yet... how was it possible?

"Is it a good sign you're not half way home already?"

Hearing his voice soothed her much more than she would have believed. He stepped up beside her, and instead of moving away from him, Harley inched closer. After a long moment she found enough to courage to look him in the eye.

Cautious brown eyes regarded her the way he might a timid child. "On a scale of one to ten, exactly how freaked out are you?"

Harley mulled it over. "Eleven."

"Very reassuring," he teased. Tight lines near his eyes showed his uncertainty.

"So," she prompted.

Cole nodded in understanding. "Where would you like me to start?"

"Somewhere between *A* and *Werewolf* would be good. And on the off chance the encyclopedia definition might be out of date, feel free to direct me to a website with the proper information."

"My father was a werewolf. My mother wasn't. She left when I was three after a full moon triggered my first shift."

"But there was a full moon last night. Did you..."

Cole shook his head. "Most times I'm able to control it."

"When can't you?"

"When I'm very pissed."

"Does that happen often?"

A pained frown crossed his face. "I'd never hurt you if that's what you think."

Harley reached for him. Not only to reassure him she could handle this, but because she needed to know, feel for herself, that Cole was still very much himself.

Strong arms held her tight as she closed her eyes and buried her face in his neck. "You could have told me before now."

Cole snorted. "If I had, you would have locked me out of your apartment."

Harley tipped her head up. "Not if you... did your shifting thing."

"Right," he mocked. "Then I would've had to catch you before you ran out of the apartment and ended up struck by a taxi because you didn't watch where you were going."

Given the fact that she ran just a short time ago, she couldn't argue his logic in remaining silent.

"So the ones who attacked us... They wanted to hurt Dash?"

Cole nodded. "The bigger one was Reginald's brother. Seems he was a little pissed Dash removed Reginald from the island for stirring up trouble."

"I guess Mac was right about his vibe this time." Cole stiffened, and Harley added. "I'm not writing a story about this place, or any of you."

He caught her chin in his palm. "Are you okay with this, okay with me being a..."

Harley smiled up at him. "It'll take some getting used to seeing as how I hadn't planned on falling on love with a werewolf—"

The second the words left her mouth, Harley tensed.

Cole lips parted in a satisfied grin right before his mouth swooped down to capture hers. The fierce possession behind it banished any remaining doubts about him... about them.

When they pulled back, Cole's smile burrowed into her heart. "I hadn't planned on falling in love with you either." He gently tucked her hair behind her ear. "I'm glad we came here."

Harley swallowed past the tightness in her throat. "Me too." Pressing a kiss to his jaw, she buried her face in his neck. Even in her wildest dreams, she hadn't imagined ending up with Cole in quite this way.

Curious, she glanced up at him. "So how does someone become a werewolf anyway?"

"Either by birth, or..." He angled his face away from her.

"Or," she prompted.

Hopeful brown eyes turned back to her. "By

choice."

"Oh." A hundred more questions trampled through her brain. Some that would no doubt require lengthy explanations, but those could wait for now. "So your dad's a werewolf too, right?"

"Yup."

She somehow couldn't picture Cole's bookish father trotting through the woods. "Huh. Any other secrets I should know about? Like a little woman tucked away somewhere having wolf cubs?"

Cole grinned. "Not quite. But I do have an older brother."

"I thought it was just you and your dad?"

"It was, for the last twenty years." He shrugged. "Turns out my brother might not be such as ass after all."

"Will I get to meet him?"

His lips curved in a secretive smile. "I think that can be arranged."

"Do you werewolf types, do anything else other than... turn into wolves?" If he told her he'd live forever, she'd be pissed.

One golden brow winged upward. "Not really. Why? What else would you have me to do? Fly?"

Harley shrugged then nodded pointedly inside at the bed. A naughty smile tugged at the corners of her mouth "So do I get to put a leash on you?"

His eyes flashed, and he leaned forward. "Only when the moon is full." He skimmed his lips across hers. "And only if I get to return the favor."

"There's still a full moon tonight, right?" Pressed from shoulder to thigh, Harley's body responded to

Cole, reaching out to catch his mouth as it passed. His fingers tunneled into her hair as he cupped the back of her neck, and deepened the kiss. With heated precision, Cole swept his mouth back and forth across hers, slowing the momentum until every cell hummed and burned for him.

Werewolf and all.

To learn more about Sydney Somers visit

http://www.sydneysomers.com

Arriving in print in August 2006,
Somers' contemporary romantic suspense

TRUST ME

And in 2007 watch for her fantastically popular
fantasy series

Watchtowers: AIR
Watchtowers: EARTH

MR. LONELY

Beverly Rae

Dedication
To Gail Northman, Executive Editor with Triskelion
Publishing, who gave me the idea for *Mr. Lonely*.
Keep the story ideas coming, Gail!
~Beverly Rae

Chapter One

"We're here, Miss Miranda."

Miranda Raennia rolled down the tinted windows of the limousine and studied the beach house. The two-story house, situated on a secluded beach along the Californian coastline, along with a dusting of other homes of similar size, shape and color, settled into the rolling hills near Pismo Beach. Weathered by years of assault from rain, sun and winds, the gray wood of the exterior blended into the night. Upon closer examination, however, this house held one vital difference from that of its neighbors. Black blinds covered every window as if a state of perpetual mourning enveloped the home and its occupants. A mist cloaked the house and its surroundings in a billowy cloud, but Miranda could still see brief glimpses of light escaping at the sides of the shades.

Miranda gave her driver, Charlie, a thumbs-up and he switched off the motor. She scooted to the edge of her seat like a child anxious to join her friends on the playground, and studied the house one more time. Without questioning her life-long caregiver, Jerome Pickering, for details, Miranda knew she'd found the right house. And, if her research was correct, the right man.

Gathering her thick, red hair behind her, she twisted a scrunchy around the mass of waves to keep her curls off her face. She opened the car door and swung her legs to the ground. Jerome, the only soul she would allow to second-guess her actions, questioned her, his British accent growing more precise with his distress.

"Are you quite certain, Miss Miranda? Do you consider this a wise idea? I can't help but wonder what your parents would think."

Sliding onto the rear seat again, Miranda sighed and offered him a comforting smile. The ancient face of her parents' former butler and family servant since before Miranda's birth, creased deeper with concern. How could she not love the old man? His undying loyalty to her parents shifted to her after her parents' deaths twenty-seven years earlier. Throughout the years, he'd become her best friend and confidant, as well as her surrogate parent.

"Jerome, relax, man. I'll be totally fine. I'm going to check things out first. Nothing more."

"But this man's reputation leaves me a bit unsettled, Miss Miranda. Don't forget the locals call him the Night Stalker because of his solitary and unsociable habits. Perhaps we'd best return home and seek other, more agreeable male companionship?"

His eyes twinkled a bit with his recommendation and she hated squashing the gentle man's hopes. "Since when do we worry what name locals give someone? Besides, you know how I like challenges. And Damian LeClare is definitely a challenge."

"Perhaps too much of a challenge?"

Stretching her long frame towards Jerome, she tweaked him on the nose before patting the leathery skin of his cheek. "You worry too much about me and I love you for it. You and Charlie hang tight. I won't be too long, I promise."

Without giving him another opportunity to object, Miranda slipped out of the car and began her trek to the beach. The well-worn path guided her behind the house and down to the ocean, leaving some distance between the deck overlooking the sea and the waves rolling onto the sand. A perfect location to do surveillance before contacting her target.

Five young women, most of them close to Miranda's own twenty-nine years, giggled around a small bonfire. Taking off her shoes, she settled on a piece of driftwood close enough to the group to eavesdrop on their conversation, yet far enough away not to draw attention to herself.

"Hey, Carly, someone better fill you in fast. Has anyone told you about the Night Stalker yet?"

A cute, curly-headed brunette shook her head. "I heard a little from my new landlord, but nothing much."

A voluptuous blonde danced around the fire using a wine bottle as a microphone to lip-synch with the music playing on their CD player. In between song lyrics and sips, she relayed the local legend for the girl's benefit. "Well, then you probably haven't heard the best parts. See, this guy came here a long time ago. My mom remembers him living here and she's really old. Anyway, he lives in that house, but he rarely leaves. And no one has ever seen him during the day."

The chubby girl seated nearest the fire couldn't help but add her two cents to the story. "Yeah, and no one knows for sure what he does for a living either."

The attractive blonde shot her a warning not to

interrupt her story. "Anyway…" she dragged out the word to emphasize her annoyance at her chubby friend, "people say he's some eccentric scientist working on a cure for Aids because he gets these deliveries of blood and other medical stuff every month."

Miranda stifled a chuckle, bending her head to act interested in a crab crossing the sand in front of her. How could intelligent people believe such dribble and miss the so-obvious truth?

"Tell Carly the best part, Katie." The anxious expression on the chubbette's features told Miranda she valued Katie's approval more than she should.

Katie accepted the ass-kiss with fervor and bestowed an imperial nod to the chubbette. "I'm getting to that, Brenda. Anyway, the best part is he's drop-dead, movie-star gorgeous. We're talking hot with a capital "H" here. And…" She paused to make certain all eyes were on her. "they say he has magnetic eyes that can make a woman do anything he wants."

Her audience gave a collective gasp and she puffed up under their attention. Tossing her hair in the confident manner of a beautiful twenty-something-year-old, Katie made the ultimate announcement. "They say he brings in prostitutes from other countries to satisfy his sexual urges. He's never taken a local woman to bed. Until tonight." Katie preened under their astonished stares like a princess basking in the adoration of her subjects. "I'm going seduce him tonight. If he comes outside, of course."

Miranda had to hand it to Katie. She knew how to play an audience. Silence followed her bold declaration until another young blonde woman spoke.

"No way, bitch. You're just talking."

Ah, a competitor. Miranda ran her eyes between Katie and her opponent for the group's attention. Within seconds, she realized the long-standing rivalry between the two.

Katie glared at her rival. "You watch me, Brit."

Brit laughed and pointed toward the house. "Well, here's your chance. Let's see you put your bod where your mouth is."

The bold gleam in Katie's eyes died for a moment before she could rally her bravado. To her credit, she raised her chin, combed through her hair, and pivoted to face the house. Miranda heard her sharp intake of air in the same instant she saw him.

The figure stood on the upper deck of the house, a black form nearly invisible against the dark gray exterior. The wind picked up his shoulder-length hair, drawing awareness to the broad expanse of his shoulders. He stood straight and tall, a stationary front against the wind and fog, with a bearing that shouted strength and resolve. Yet, even with her acute sight, Miranda couldn't make out any facial features.

He's the one. She glued her eyes to him, unwilling, unable to let go. The culmination of three year's research had lured her to this place, this man, yet now her body wouldn't respond to her mind's call. Her thoughts screamed, begging her feet to carry her to him, but her heart warned against such a foolish action.

"Go get him, Katie. What are you waiting for?"

Having forgotten the girls, Miranda jerked out of her trance. Katie bit her lower lip, glanced at her friends, and shook out her long tresses. Thrusting out her chest, she moved toward the Night Stalker.

Mesmerized and curious to see his reaction, Miranda settled on the driftwood again to watch. Katie lifted her sweatshirt over her head, exposing a bikini-clad body any mortal man would give their right testicle to claim. Skimming over to the house, she stopped near the lower floor's patio to scrutinize the figure on the deck above her. Her body shook for a moment and Miranda wandered what she'd heard or seen to make her shudder. Did Katie tremble in fear? Or shiver in excitement? She ached to know but held fast to where she sat.

The silence surrounding the group of girls splintered as one of them punched a button on the CD player and cranked up the volume. Startled, Katie twisted around to check out the noise.

"Come on, Katie. Seduce the Stalker. Show him what he can have for the night."

As her friends egged her on, Katie began swaying seductively to the pulsating rhythm. She ran her hands up and down her body, sliding her palms over her large breasts while gyrating her hips. When no response came, the girl gave a stripper-style show, fondling her private parts and bending to wiggle her butt at him. After several minutes of the suggestive dance, Katie paused, assumed a pose resembling a swimsuit model's stance, and waited for recognition. From her body language, Miranda knew she expected him to beg her to sleep with him.

The figure remained motionless, a statue carved into the night sky. But Katie wouldn't give up so easily. Starting to touch her breasts again, the buxomly blond reached behind her, unbuttoned her bra and slid the flimsy material from her breasts. Tempting him further, she shook her shoulders to the pounding bass, making her breasts bounce while she cupped them underneath.

"Oh, my God, I can't believe she did that."

"Shake 'em, Katie. Let him get an eyeful."

More catcalls came from the others and Katie revved up the show.

Miranda flitted her gaze between the man and Katie, unwilling to miss a single bit of the action…and his possible reaction. Still, he remained motionless.

Katie continued her strip tease for a few more minutes, pinching her tits and running her hand underneath her thong bikini. "Hey, baby, want to invite me in? I'd love to take a tour of your home. Especially the bedroom."

Miranda rolled her lips inward to keep from laughing. The poor girl didn't have a chance, but Miranda wouldn't be the one to tell her. In the end, she didn't have to.

Without a wave, without a sound, without acknowledging her presence at all, the man on the deck turned and entered the house. For one blinding second, light shot out from the interior, washing over the stunned, half-naked woman. *She ought to get the hint now.* Miranda waited for Katie to keep fighting or give up.

Snatching up her bikini top, Katie whipped on

the bra and shouted her frustration. "You lousy bastard. Who do you think you are? I wouldn't walk inside your house now if you flashed the biggest cock in the whole world. Weirdo! Freak!"

Slugging through the sand, she kept ranting while the others met her with comforting hugs. Their angry voices rang out letting the Stalker know their disgust and disappointment in his lack of manliness.

"I think now would be a good time to leave." Knowing the group was too busy to notice her, she ran up the beach to her waiting limousine.

*****

Damian poured another glass of blood-red wine and listened to the shouts the angry girls' hurled his way. Their curses didn't bother him. After all, he'd suffered similar attacks in the past and much worse. Although his body may have responded to the young girl's advances, mentally he'd felt more amused than aroused by her exhibition. On the rare occasions when he could no longer ignore his desire for sex, he would import expensive, skilled prostitutes. Beautiful, fully-grown women who satisfied his hunger without the need for anything more. He never trifled with the local women or the rare tourist who might stumble onto his beach.

Sitting on his imported leather couch, he waited for this night to pass just as he'd waited through so many nights before. Since Christiana's betrayal over a hundred years earlier, he'd learned patience. After the first tormented years of traveling the world, seeking solace in one-night flings, he'd discovered he'd never love another the way he'd loved her. Or hate anyone the way he hated her. Christiana Constantine's rejection had taken his heart while her betrayal had broken his spirit. With time, he'd grown weary of the travel and settled near the small coastal community, hoping to hide from humanity in a private world filled with misery and memories.

Downing the liquid, he rose and sought the view out the windows. How many times had he peered out into the darkness? Yet, unlike a thousand times before, on a thousand other nights, tonight carried an urgency. Tonight, an intangible force compelled him to search the night for an unknown mystery.

Pouring another glass, Damian shook his head, trying to shake the tightening in his neck. "You're merely restless, man. You'll shake it off." Yet even as he spoke the words, he heard the lie hidden behind them.

Sarah Loury, his houseguest, entered the adjoining kitchen area on noiseless feet. But Damian heard and smiled. "I thought you'd retired for the night." He kept his back to the young woman, something another would have found insulting. But not Sarah. She knew him as well as he knew himself.

"I couldn't sleep. Those little bitches outside are caterwauling too much. What did you do to piss them off?"

Ah, good, supportive Sarah. He'd found her years ago, a homeless waif of a teenager, scratching out a horrible existence on the streets of Los Angeles. She'd attached herself to him and he'd brought her home.

Damian laughed, an infrequent sound in his house, but one only Sarah could get him to make. "It's more of what I didn't do that pissed them off."

He heard her lift the carafe and pour herself a drink. What role did Sarah play in his life? Not his lover. Not his servant. More. She was an infrequent companion and friend who gave him the space and solitude he craved in exchange for a future of her own. And he loved her in his own way, sometimes in spite of her own way.

"So why not give them a little action, Stud? I mean, what sane man turns down free pussy? I sure wouldn't. And God knows you don't get enough as it is." She giggled and his smile grew wider.

"I prefer my women with no possible emotional connections."

A wet napkin hit him right between the shoulder blades. Whirling around, he spanned the yards between them in a second. His hand closed around her thin neck, shaking her head and making the frizzy blond hair she never seemed to comb, flap around her face. Long, treacherous fangs lengthened, he bent over her, his mouth an inch from the vein pumping in her throat. "Don't goad me, child. Your skinny body wouldn't yield much, but I could drain a few ounces from you."

The girl's eyelids lifted, exposing more white around her eyes. "Oh, please, my lord. Please spare my pitiful life. If you do, I promise…"

"You'll promise what?" Damian held his breath in anticipation. As usual, her answer would be entertaining.

"I promise to take you to the dentist."

Damian's laughter echoed through the house. He loosened his hold on her and she squirmed out of his reach.

"Damn, man, don't you ever brush? And your breath. Wow. How about I make a run to the store and pick up some mouthwash." Her freckles jumped along the bridge of her nose when she wrinkled her nose in disgust. "Hell, I almost want you to suck the life out of me. Anything's better than smelling your rank breath."

He snatched a sponge from the counter and tossed it at her. She ducked, giggling at his rare playfulness. Running his hands over his straight shoulder-length strands, he downed more of the wine.

"Seriously, though. Ever heard of flossing?" She grinned her grin of crooked teeth.

He shot her a bemused look, warning her not to take the joke too far. "Funny. Why don't you become a comedian instead of a doctor?"

"Because I love blood as much as you do."

Her quip lifted the corners of his mouth, something only Sarah could manage. "I seriously doubt that." Seeing the shift in her body as the wicked gleam left her eye, he cringed, ready for the conversation to get serious. Did she need money again?

"Ya know what, Damian?"

He paused, the crystal goblet poised at his lips, before he answered. "What now?"

"You should at least try to behave more like a real vampire." Hopping up on the counter, she peeled a banana and shoved half of it into her mouth.

"I *am* a real vampire." Damian's dark mood settled over him again. "Be careful unless you want me to prove it."

"Okay, okay. Don't get your batwings in a tizzy."

Sighing, Damian headed for the window and the empty night.

"Did you see her?"

"The blond doing the dance?" He knew she didn't mean the dancer, but wanted her to confirm his assumption.

"You know who I mean. The one sitting apart from the group. She watched, but didn't join in."

"I know who you mean."

"I don't know what struck me about her, but something…"

"What?" Could Sarah experience the same sense of necessity? He glanced at her in her black jeans and t-shirt and wondered, not for the first time, if she'd learned more from him than how to survive.

"I don't know. But she reminded me of someone. Maybe Christiana?"

Damian gritted his jaw in the struggle not to drain her for real this time. "I told you. Never mention her name to me."

Her voice trembled a bit, but she continued. "Now don't get mad, dude, but I figured if I got that impression of her, you might have, too."

The cold fury inside him reached his eyes and he knew she saw the madness just beneath the surface. "She's nothing like Christiana. No one will ever be like Christiana."

"Yeah, but maybe—"

The strength of his voice rocked her and she flung her body off the counter, away from him, fright etching her features. He stalked toward her, a battle raging inside him to control his vehemence.

"Never speak of that witch again." His hands clenched, trying to keep the power of his alternate being in check.

"She wasn't a witch, Damian, just a grade-A bitch." She gasped when she saw his reaction to her words. "I'm sorry, man. I didn't mean to make you mad."

"Sarah, go and leave me in peace. Never speak her name again. Do you understand?"

She reached out for him, trying to placate, but he wouldn't let her touch him. The pain, the humiliation struck his core, chipping away another piece of his dignity.

Her sad eyes called to him, but he ignored her and refocused his attention on the starry sky. Hearing heard her footsteps on the stairs as she headed to her room, he let his sight travel to the driftwood and scan the rest of the deserted beach. He searched for her, the one he'd sensed, and found nothing.

Chapter Two

A deafening sound pierced the air in the yacht's cabin, sending Jerome rushing to her side. Rushing, at least, as fast as a man almost a century old could rush. "Are you all right, Miss Miranda?" His anxious eyes darted around the large stateroom until landing on her.

Miranda jumped off the bed and held up the CD player. She cupped her hands together and shouted over the noise. "Isn't this great?" Whirling around, she bobbed to the music and made her way past Jerome. With one finger, she hooked the package he held out for her and kept going. As soon as she'd taken the sack from him, he clamped his hands over his ears.

She laughed and shut off the machine. Dumping the contents of the sack on top of her crimson bedspread, she grabbed the first CD and clapped. "Terrific! I love *Coldplay*." She reached down to snag two others. "Cool. *Shania Twain* for country and *JoJo* for more rock. Did you get the new rap artist I told you about? Yes! Here he is. You did good, Jerome. Real good."

"Grammatically speaking, you should say 'very well,' Miss Miranda."

She wrinkled her nose at him. "For bloody sake, Jerome, I'm all grown up now. Don't you think it's about time you gave up on the grammar lessons?"

She caught a quick vision of the reserved, proper gentleman in the midst of the music store. On purpose…*hey, a girl's got to have a little fun*…she'd sent him to the busiest, nosiest store in town. "Did you have fun at *Musical Maniacs*?"

The wise face arched an aristocratic eyebrow, leaving no doubt he knew she'd sent him there on purpose. "Oh, yes. I had an awesome time." Dropping the sarcastic tone, he added, "Of course not. The world's lost all sense of decency since my youth."

"Damn, Jerome. You haven't been a boy since the first Model Ts rolled onto the streets."

He sniffed, at once acknowledging the truth of her statement and tossing it aside. "Miss, are you sure you want to go through with this scheme of yours? Perhaps we should ascertain more information about this Mr. LeClare before you do anything rash."

Miranda threw off her jeans and t-shirt, opting instead for a tight-fitting sequined tube top and black leather pants. Jerome, still unused to her displays of nudity, cast his sight down. "All done. I don't get you, Jerome. You raised me and seen me butt-ass naked hundreds of time. Why do you have to be so shy?"

"Because, Miss Miranda, you aren't a little girl any more."

Miranda bent her head sideways and surveyed her outfit in the full-length mirror. "Damn right I'm not. Plus, I have a helluva good body, if I do say so myself."

Full hips led to a slender waist and straight up to firm, perky breasts of ample proportions. Her long, cherry-red hair accented her pale skin. High cheekbones, the envy of many models, accented her sparkling green eyes. But her best feature, she thought, was her full, kissable lips. She picked out the perfect red lipstick and ran the tip over her mouth.

She saw his frown and knew his thoughts before he could speak them. "Relax. You know how much prep I've done for tonight. In fact, I think I could write a biography about Damian. Not that anyone would believe his story." She chuckled, excitement bubbling to the surface.

"Nonetheless, perhaps you should take a bodyguard along with you."

"Oh, shit, Jerome, don't be a pain in the ass."

She rolled her eyes, saw the hurt flicker over his features before he calmed them, and wished she'd been more sensitive to him. He cared for her like a daughter even when she acted like a brat.

Slipping to his side, she squeezed him in a quick hug. "Don't worry. You know I can take care of myself. Besides, you'll be waiting in the limo just up the road." Not resisting the temptation to torment him a little, she winked and added, "And I plan on having you wait until right before daybreak."

Taking his arm in hers, she dragged him along to the speedboat bobbing in the dark waters. Handing her satchel over to one of her men, she slung herself over the side and made quick work of descending the ladder. Two more muscular men helped lower Jerome while she bit her nails. She wanted to make him hurry, but reminded herself of all the times he'd shown infinite patience with her as a toddler. Now she could repay the favor.

Once settled in the boat, she nodded to the crewman at the controls. With a curt nod, he started the engine and aimed the boat toward the twinkling lights on the coast.

Miranda raised her face, enjoying the spray of water against her skin. "Life is good, Jerome, and tonight's the start of the best chapter yet." Pulling Jerome to her, she gave him a quick squeeze before standing up to hold onto the rail and watch the approaching coastline.

The minutes passed with incredible sluggishness until the boat docked at a small private port seven miles south of Damian's home. Without pausing, Miranda hopped onto the shore and headed for her waiting limousine. "Please hurry, Jerome."

She heard his panted breath behind her and slowed her pace. Taking in the peaceful, moonlit scene, she inhaled slowly, letting the wind carry the smells of night to her. When she reached the limo, the chauffeur held the door open and she paused before getting inside. Rotating in a circle, she held out her arms and made a proclamation. "Damian LeClare, here I come."

Once the elderly gentleman settled into the rear seat beside her, she knocked on the partition separating the driver from the passengers. "Take off, Charlie. The night's not getting any younger."

The black limousine flew down the coastline, following the narrow road bordered by beach on the one side and houses on the other. Her heart pounded as they drew closer and she wandered if he could sense her arrival. The car swept to a stop on the incline above his home and she held her breath, wanting to examine the shrouded home once more before placing her plan into action.

"Jerome, you'll stick around, remember?"

"Yes, Miss Miranda. I don't approve, but I do remember."

"Good. I'll see you later." A wild titter escaped her. "Or not."

Before he could object, Miranda gathered her stuffed satchel and pushed open the door. "Hot damn. I'm gonna have some fun tonight." She whistled a jaunty tune and set off for the beach.

*****

Damian stretched full-length on his couch, listening to the blissful melody of Mozart. Soft strands of soothing notes flowed over him, easing the frustrations of the night before. He knew Sarah wanted him to be happy, but her reminders of Christiana rankled his nerves. What he wanted, all he wanted, was quiet, solitude, and time to forget. Not, in his opinion, too much for a man to ask for.

He lifted the goblet to his lips and sipped his favorite wine. Although not a significant investment, his purchase of a vineyard in the South of France gave him the chance to experiment with different grapes and combinations. If nothing else, the winery served as a distraction in an otherwise boring existence.

His hand waved in the air, keeping time to the symphony playing through the speakers hidden in the masculine design of his home. The gray, brown and black of the décor blended mechanical devices with the other furnishings, providing a comfortable, serene ambience.

Closing his eyes, he followed the music, listening to the intricate weavings of instruments. He sighed, finding a rare moment of tranquility. Yet, strangely, the familiar music held an additional element tonight. An out-of-rhythm bass thumped against the piece, as different from Mozart's creation as a child's finger painting would be to a Rembrandt. He frowned, perplexed and irritated, as the throbbing grew louder.

The pound of the drum expanded, adding a singer's voice...if he could call the screech a voice...to the mix.

"What the hell is that awful noise?" A drop of wine sloshed from his drink onto the rug when he swung up to a sitting position. Making a mental note to send the Persian rug out for cleaning, he marched to the window and drew up the blind.

The sight below him brought a sneer to his lips.

Her.

On his beach. Making that despicable racket.

The girl from the night before hopped about the sand, waving her arms around as if to frighten off invisible sea gulls. He watched, captivated and a bit stupefied, as she made the oddest movements he'd ever seen. The terrible music filled the night air, driving all other sounds from the area, but the girl...woman by the shape of her body...appeared to throw her limbs in all directions to the beat of the song.

"How can anyone enjoy such wretched music?"

"That's rap music, Damian. Very popular stuff."

Damian cranked his head around when Sarah came up behind him. Without touching him, she nodded in the direction of the woman.

"Yes, I recognized the genre." Again, his lips curled in a snarl, displeasure surging through him.

"Isn't she the same one as the night before?"

He'd swear he heard a chuckle in the tone of her voice. But she was smart enough to keep her mirth restrained.

"Yes. Yes, it is." His sight fell on the wild female, hypnotizing him. Something about her total immersion in the music broke through his defenses and opened a tiny door to his spirit. For a moment, he forgot the awful music invading his world. She stretched her arms wide, extending them as if to catch the wind around her and tear it from the sky. Her willowy limbs jerked side to side, up and down, lengthening her tall frame to higher proportions. Long, waving hair caressed her neck and shoulders, cascading down the hollow of her back, leading his eyes to her rounded, firm buttocks.

Sarah's giggle interrupted his thoughts. "You're scoping her out, you dog. Not that I blame you. I'd be tempted, too, but I'm getting the impression she flies the straight path and not the down-low."

"Don't be ridiculous. She is an irritant. Like you." He tried to put as much sincerity behind his words as he could muster, but even he heard the false edge to his tone.

"Yeah, right. How about inviting her inside?"

He heard her soft intake of air when he actually paused to consider the suggestion. Shaking his head, he countered her suggestion with one of his own. "How about you running her off?"

"Aw, come on, Damian. You know you want her. I can hear it in your voice. Hey, maybe we'll get lucky and she'll swing both ways."

The woman jumped around the beach, wiggling

her tight little ass in tempting ways. His heart flipped over once when she did a somersault and her generous globes fell part of the way out of her tight top. Catching himself running his tongue over his lips, he swiveled away from the appetizing sight.

"No, Sarah, you know my rules. Go down and tell her to leave."

Sarah smothered a grin. "And if she won't?"

"Tell her I'll call the authorities."

The grin broke loose along with the sarcastic laugh. "Uh, huh. Like that'll ever happen. Summoning the cops would call attention to you."

Anger flared inside him and he let a touch of the flame loose. "Go!"

Sarah cringed and hurried from the room. He heard the door slam behind her and soon saw her approaching the beautiful dancer.

His hands gripped the windowsill, but he resisted opening the window. He knew if he did, he'd hear the woman's voice and be more drawn to her. Instead, he watched as the two women greeted each other.

Sarah and the woman shook hands and Damian smiled. Sarah swore she could tell someone's sexual preference by touching them. He doubted it, but one could never be sure. If she was gay, would Sarah want her to stay? Could he stand to let Sarah have her?

His smile grew wider when the woman frowned at Sarah and gestured at the beach towel, picnic basket and other items strewn on the sand. After lowering the volume on the CD player, they conversed awhile longer and the frown left the

woman's face. Instead, she threw back her head and
laughed.

What could she find so amusing? His curiosity
spiked and he shoved open the window. He had to
hear them.

"He'll call the cops? Oh, come on, we both know
he won't do anything of the sort."

Her voice, a melody all its own, caught his breath
and held it suspended, as he listened for more.

"Miranda, this is a private beach and Damian
doesn't like your music."

Miranda. A beautiful name for a beautiful creature.
He steeled his heart against the unwanted thoughts.
To permit such ideas access could spell disaster.

Damian gawked at the women standing on his
beach and smiling at each other. He growled,
unhappy with Sarah and with his own reactions to
Miranda.

"Well, Damian needs to get out more. This is
golden stuff. Tell him to pry the stick out of his
uptight ass and open his mind to new things and new
people."

Sarah bounced with the music along with
Miranda. "I agree with you, but I'm not risking my
neck repeating your words. So…you're sure you
won't leave?"

Miranda hopped closer. "Nope. If Damian
LeClare wants me to leave, he can damn well ask me
in person. But thanks for delivering the message."

"Sure. No problem." Sarah grinned at Miranda
and took a few steps toward the house before
Miranda snagged her hand.

Taking Sarah by her arms, Miranda pulled Sarah to her and pressed her mouth on hers. After a momentary hesitation, Sarah tickled her tongue against Miranda's lips and started to wrap her arms around her. Pulling away, Miranda cocked her head to the side and winked.

"Too bad I'm not bi, 'cause if I were I'd be on you big time. I hope you didn't mind, but I figured as long as Damian's playing Peeping Tom, I'd give him something interesting to watch."

*****

Miranda cranked up the music louder than before. Did he think a scrawny girl like Sarah, barely past her teens, could run her off? Instead, Sarah had asked a few pointless questions and hadn't even tried to persuade her to leave. No, Sarah had come on a fishing expedition, nothing more. Miranda had sensed the girl sizing her up in those few minutes and felt the enormous fortitude within the frail body, yet concluded Sarah couldn't match her strength.

Miranda twirled, pleased with the plan so far. She'd sorted out Sarah's role in his game right from the start and knew the young girl's spirit. Trying to act nonchalant, Miranda waited for Sarah to deliver *her* message.

Head down as she twirled, she closed her eyes, and got ready to meet the great and mysterious Damian LeClare. He would be dangerous and dark. And cool. Deadly cool. Everything in the investigator's report told her so. But would the reality live up to the image?

The song ended in the middle of a lyric and she opened her eyes. Black eyes gripped her, stopping her in mid-swing and she reminded herself to take in the next breath.

Damn, he's amazing. Stronger, leaner, *hungrier* than she'd imagined. Blue-black hair hung to his broad shoulders, providing a stark canvas for his angular features. His square jaw set, ready for a confrontation. Calling her away from the obsidian glow of his eyes, the lips arrested her attention, forcing her hand to reach for them.

Her hand never reached his lips as his grip surrounded her wrist, breaking her out of her dream. A jolt of energy seared up her arm. She hissed, gaped at his large hand wrapped around her wrist, and fought the impulse to hit him. "Let me go. And leave my boom box alone."

He stared at his hand on her arm as if only now realizing he held her. She saw bewilderment flicker across his face and she waited for him to release her. Gazing into her eyes, holding her, connecting to her, his lips parted a bit before he spoke in a rich and velvety timbre.

"No."

No? Confused, she fought the hint of fear lurking in her churning stomach. Everything she'd learned about the man told her he didn't get violent. Unless provoked. Maybe she'd pushed him too far already?

An indecipherable gleam shone in the recesses of those black pools, and she wanted to ask his thoughts, but couldn't, wouldn't take the chance. She'd felt the attraction between them the instant he'd grabbed her and hoped he'd experienced the same. If he asked, she'd follow him anywhere.

"Damian, you're hurting me."

Her whisper of his first name startled him and she wondered why. He'd overheard her conversation with Sarah, she was sure of it. So why would mentioning his name cause such a reaction?

However, instead of letting go, he bent his head. Soft hair tickled her arm while his warm breath heated her skin. But nothing prepared her for the moist touch of his lips on her wrist.

The jolt she'd experienced before held little resemblance to the lightning bolt scorching up her arm and down her spine. Her heart stopped and her mind shut down, while every nerve in her sprang to life. The kiss lasted a mere second, but for Miranda, time froze.

I'm right. He's the one.

With an explosion, her breathing resumed. An image of him leaning over her, his head tilted toward her neck, raced through her brain and she shuddered. An ache ripped through her when his touch left her skin.

"I'm sorry. I never meant to harm you."

Blinking at him, she cleared her throat and answered. "Sure. I understand."

Without warning, an invisible wall encircled him, leaving her on the outside. This, at least, she'd expected.

"Miranda, you have to leave."

Recovering, she shot him a cocky grin. "So you were eavesdropping."

Could vampires blush? Apparently, they could.

"I sent Sarah out to deliver my message, which you've decided to ignore." He glanced at her possessions scattered around them and arched an eyebrow. "So, I'm personally asking you to leave. If you don't, you'll force me to call the authorities."

She laughed, startling him, and hit the "On" button. Music blared and she had to shout at him. "Stop blowing smoke, Damian. You're not calling anyone." Prancing off a few paces from him, she renewed her outrageous dance. She glanced at him when she whirled, hoping to catch him watching her. When she did, she laughed at his surprised expression.

"Why don't you go to another beach? Where there are others like you."

She spun faster, enjoying the rhythm and his obvious distaste for her music. Did he mean "others" as in lovers of rap music? Or as in mortals?

"Lighten up, Big D. Live your life. You only have the one, right?" *Or several.*

"That crap you're listening to is intruding on my peace and quiet."

She slammed her foot in the sand, stopping her spin, and flipped the hair away from her face. "Damn, man, you act like you're some old recluse hiding from civilization. Are you really that up in years?" *Yes!* "Or are you just ancient in your mind?"

She waited to see if he'd reveal anything about his true nature, but he stood his ground without any tell-tale signs of recognition. She'd have to press harder.

"Simply because I prefer the classics to garbage doesn't make me old. Much less ancient."

She sent him an "I-know-you're-fibbing" smirk.

"Really? How about sharing then?"

God, how she loved the looks he gave her. She couldn't tell if he was more surprised or irritated at her suggestion.

"Sharing?"

"Yeah. You share your beach with me...and I'll share a steak with you." His eyebrows lowered and she knew he didn't understand.

"No, thank you." He shook his head and started to walk off.

"Damian?" She wanted to keep him with her. All night. But at least for awhile longer.

He didn't answer, but paused and lifted his eyebrows at her. His wonderfully, elegant, expressive eyebrows.

"I'll bet you like your steaks rare, huh? Me, too. The bloodier, the better." *Nudge, nudge.* Her satisfaction with this cat and mouse game increased when she saw the flash in his eyes. But he gave no other indication he'd understood her remark.

Wheeling around, he headed toward the house. Miranda called to him again, desperate to keep him outside with her. "Damian!"

He whipped around, scowling at her. "What now?"

Because she couldn't think of anything else to say, she lifted the top of her tube top and pulled the material down from her breasts. "Are these better than the girl's last night?"

Her excitement made her chest heave, adding to the show. Why didn't he answer? The warmth started at her neck and spread up to cover her cheeks. Embarrassed by his silent perusal, she stuck out her chin, defying her emotions. Since when did she ever get embarrassed, anyway?

He scanned her body, running the full length of her, taking several minutes to do so before considering her breasts a moment longer. "Actually, no, they aren't."

"Are you crazy?" She studied her boobs, perfect in both size and shape, each topped with matching taut nipples. "These ladies are spectacular." When Damian continued to walk away and ignore her, she shouted, "And they're all natural, baby. Not some medically enhanced bazookas like the slut's last night."

He waved his hand in the air, but didn't stop his progress.

Muttering under her breath, she added, "Damian LeClare, this means war."

Miranda pulled up her tank top while she watched him enter the house. "You can't fool me. You'll watch me some more. I'd bet all my money you will and I never bet on anything except a sure deal."

She popped the rap CD out and slipped in one by a country/rock performer. Switching the knob as far to the right as possible, she sat down on the towel to think. She needed something radical to get Damian's attention. Something that would knock his fangs right out of his head. Or make him drool like a dog in heat.

As the night settled in around her, she ate some of the cheese, and crackers packed in the picnic basket. She knew he checked on her. The impression of watching eyes, coal-black eyes, tingled her nerve endings. But she wouldn't give in to the compulsion to scope out his windows.

The full moon rose above her and she stretched out on the towel, awed by the brilliance of the milky-white light on the ocean's surface. A sly smile curved the corners of her lips, and she wiggled her toes in delight as inspiration struck. Such good ideas should not be wasted.

Rising seductively, she stood and lifted her face so the moon's rays highlighted her features. Positioning her front away from the ocean and toward his home, she tugged the tight fabric away from her breasts and over her head. Pausing, she slid her hands over her tits, enjoying the sensation and the self-teasing.

"Damian, I know you're watching. I saw the heat in your eyes. I felt the flame in your body. Keep watching, Damian."

Hooking her thumbs in the top of her slacks, she slid them along the waistline from her bellybutton to her spine. She wanted him to realize what she intended to do. More, she wanted him to want her to do what she intended to do. Bending over, she slid the pants down, letting them drop to her ankles to kick them off.

"No underwear here, Mr. LeClare." She wiggled her ass at him, wishing she could see the desire she knew her creamy form created in him.

Tossing her hair, she started for the water in a slow, easy swing. She gasped as the water hit her, shortening her breath, yet her lips remained steadfast in a Mona Lisa smile. The waves rushed against her body, leaving her chilled to the bone. But a little cold wouldn't keep her from fulfilling her destiny.

She dove into the oncoming waves and burst to the surface. Splashing around, she sliced in and out of the crests, enjoying the thought of his playing voyeur to her mermaid. Imagining his burning eyes on her, she ran to the shoreline, holding her hair over her head, arms raised, breasts jiggling. Standing at the water's edge, she squeezed giant drops from her hair and pretended to be shipwrecked on a tropical island. "Now what would I do if I were stranded on a deserted island all alone with no one to satisfy my womanly urges?"

Deciding to fulfill her needs while sending the desires of her unseen spectator soaring, she scampered over to her towel and stretched out her lean body horizontally to the house. The water droplets clinging to her skin chilled her to the bone. Yet even when her teeth chattered together, she vowed to keep the show going and, hopefully, his shaft growing.

Inch by glorious inch, she ran her hands over her body in slow torture. Pinching the nipple on one breast, she cupped her other breast and fondled it. She lifted her head and pulled the peak into her mouth. Closing her eyes, she licked her bud and brought it into her mouth, shivering both from the cold and from the spark of desire flickering in her abdomen.

Miranda lowered her head and skimmed her fingers down her stomach, slowing as she approached her mound. Bending one knee, she ruffled the small patch of hair left from her bikini wax and pushed her middle finger between her folds. Her breathing hitched and she envisioned Damian's own breath doing the same.

"Are you waiting for me, honey?"

Chapter Three

The unfamiliar voice shook Miranda to full awareness and she grabbed at the towel beneath her to pull the cloth around her. "Who the hell are you?"

The word "skuzzy" popped into Miranda's mind. The man could be described using various adjectives including ill-kept, bedraggled, stinky, and dirty, but skuzzy fit the bill best. Standing, he towered over her prone position, but she could tell he was small in stature and reed-thin.

"Skuzzy's" filthy clothes hung from his boney frame, while a tangled mass of dirty hair highlighted his gaunt features. A matted and overgrown beard added to his dilapidated appearance and Miranda wondered if bits of food got caught in it when he ate. His beady eyes bulged, making her hope they bulged from genetics instead of her nakedness. Her stomach flopped over when he spread his lips wide, sending her the unmistakable signal of someone thinking evil thoughts and she grimaced. Unlike the bulging eyes, she couldn't mistake the reason for the grin.

"Name's Billy. How about you and me getting to know each other?" He started to kneel on the sand beside her, but Miranda hurried up, spilling the basket and player off the towel as she stumbled away from him.

"Sorry, Skuzzy. I don't want to get to know you. In fact, if I were you, I'd get out the hell outta here as fast as I could. If you're lucky, you'll live to regret seeing me."

A slow burn began under her ribcage like so many times before. Taking a large breath, she pushed the almost overwhelming urge down, wanting to keep her burgeoning instincts buried.

"Now that ain't no way to greet a fellow beach lover."

Maybe if she made small talk with him, he'd think of her as a person instead of a victim. Didn't all the rape experts advise women to do that? Besides, if Damian saw them, he might come and lend her some help.

"Yeah, I'm a beach lover. So do you live around here, uh, Billy?" The name Billy didn't fit him. She'd always think of him as Skuzzy. She scooted farther away from him, but he matched her moves with his own.

"Don't matter." He gestured to her, prompting her to come to him.

Miranda considered diving into the ocean. Somehow she didn't think Skuzzy would be much of a swimmer. And going for a swim seemed like a better idea than tearing out his throat. He started narrowing the distance between them and she tensed, ready to run to the sea.

"Come on, girlie. You know you're horny. I saw you taking care of yourself. But now you don't have to. I'll take care of your snatch for you."

She shifted, dug in her left foot and prepared to escape. Just as she started to go for it, a dark shape appeared behind Skuzzy.

"No thanks. I'd rather he take care of me." Miranda inclined her head and wiggled her eyebrows.

Skuzzy paused, fisting his hands on his hips. "Aw, honey, I'd of figured you to be too smart than to use that old trick. Guess not. But that's okay. I like my bitches dumb and spread-eagled."

Skuzzy shouted as he flew through the air and into the surf. Face down in the ocean, he lay lifeless for a moment. Miranda whipped her head between them, keeping an eye on both the vagrant and Damian.

Damian, a dark, forbidding statue in black trousers and shirt, stood legs apart, arms to his side, a picture of serenity. Only the fury in his expression told a different story.

"Leave." The calm tone of the one word belied the raw power emanating from him.

Skuzzy leapt to his feet and started toward Miranda. Damian raised one hand and edged closer, immense energy rippling the air around him. Skuzzy realized his mistake, twirled falling to one hand, and took off in the opposite direction. He ran several yards before stopping to hurl insults.

"Fuck you, man! Nobody messes with Billy Chambers. You're going to regret you ever heard my name, you asshole!"

Miranda saw Damian's body tense as he raised one arm in the sky and flick his hand. Skuzzy's upper torso doubled over, putting his head between his legs, and aligning his sight with his butt. He screamed, jerking his body in a vain effort to get out of the grotesque hold. Miranda gasped, flinching at the impossible position of the vagrant's body.

Damian chuckled, a low, mean growl. "No, Billy.

That's an asshole."

Billy's cries unnerved Miranda and she swept nearer to Damian, wanting to take his arm, yet afraid to do so. "Please, Damian."

He glanced her way, lifted his arm again, and flicked his fingers. Skuzzy fell over in the incoming tide. Groaning, he struggled to his feet, shook his fist at Damian, and staggered away.

"The imbecile simply won't learn, will he?"

Again, Damian raised his arm, but stopped when Miranda laid her palm on his shoulder. "Damian." She waited to see if he'd heard her whisper.

He turned to her, the anger easing from him in shaky waves. Pitch-black eyes raked over her, burning her with a flame hotter than any before. "Are you all right?"

"I'm fine."

The ire she'd thought passed erupted again. At her. "What do you think you're doing, parading around like some two-bit whore? You're lucky he didn't have friends with him."

"Now, wait a sec. I can take care of myself. I don't need your help handling little piss-offs like him." Why she wanted to chew him out, she couldn't understand. Hadn't she wanted his help a few minutes ago? Yet somehow, the urge mixed up with the cozy sentiment of having him come to her rescue. A vision of kicking his butt mixed up in her head with an image of her sitting on his head while he lapped up her juices. Which, of course, led to wetness between her legs.

The wind blew his hair away from his neck, giving her full view of the vein pulsing there. She jumped to the strong angle of his jaw line, over to the lips slightly parted and fastened to the black magnets beckoning to her.

A dusting of dark curls peeked over the "V" of his shirt and she wished with all she held holy to reach out and see how far down the curls ran. The silk of his shirt emphasized his muscular physique while hinting at more below the silk of his slacks.

Do I see lust in his eyes? Or is my imagination, my dream, conjuring up false images?

"You're a foolish woman, Miranda."

Now why did he have to open his mouth and ruin the moment?

"I ordered you to leave. This wouldn't have happened if you'd obeyed me."

Obeyed him? Oh, Damian, you have so much to learn about me.

Neither of them spoke for a minute, each gauging the other's level of frustration, anger…attraction? His heated glares intensified the throbbing in her crotch and she swallowed, trying to hold on to her irritation. Opening her mouth to speak, he held up his hand and she wondered if he would flick his fingers at her.

Without another sound, he spun on his heel and stalked up the beach. She ached to follow him, but stood her ground, shivering under the thin towel. "Okay, Damian. I'll go. For now."

She grinned at the shadow of Sarah standing at an upstairs window, waved and quipped in a Terminator-style voice, "I'll be back."

*****

"She's something else, huh?" Sarah flipped a pancake onto the counter next to the stove. Sliding the spatula underneath, she scooped it into the pan. "You know she did her show last night for your benefit, don't ya?"

Damian paced the floor of his living room. "Why are you cooking pancakes at night? And why are you here anyway? Whatever happened to our arrangement of you staying out of my way when I'm awake?" He scowled at her, hoping to put a dose of fear into her. This time, however, she kept her head down, avoiding his intimidation tactics.

"I'm curious, is all. I mean, here you are, the ultimate recluse…except for me, your trusty aide…and up pops this wild woman. But, unlike others before her, you can't get rid of her. Wonder why? Do you think you've met your match? Or are you not really trying?"

If he could sprout feathers, they would be ruffled big time. "Do you see her here tonight?" He stopped, hoping she'd take up his challenge.

"No."

"There. You see? I did get her to leave. Now maybe I can enjoy a life of peace and quiet again. That is, if you'll stop haranguing me with your constant chatter." When she didn't answer, he pivoted and paced the other direction.

"So you believe she's gone for good?"

"Yes. Most definitely."

"Then why are you pacing?"

He stopped, her question calling awareness to the nervousness inside him. But he'd damn well not let her know. "This has nothing to do with her. I, uh, have a financial situation to resolve. Absolutely nothing to do with her."

"You're repeating yourself."

He heard her giggle which annoyed him further. "Because you're irritating me. This has nothing to do with her."

"Oops, you did it again." She sang the words to the Britney Spears song and laughed out loud before she clamped one hand over her mouth.

Damian stalked toward her, raising his hand in a threatening manner and baring his fangs. Sarah grabbed the pan, a pitiful weapon against his power, and held it out with both hands. "Okay, okay. I'm kidding Damian. Keep the bloodlust in check, okay?"

The fangs withdrew as his aggravation subsided a bit. "Be careful, Sarah. Be very careful."

Her eyes crinkled, a sure sign her brain had zapped into high gear. "You been watching those late night horror movies again, Damian? Like maybe *The Fly*?" Shaking her head, she dismissed her own question.

Her lips rolled under in an attempt to stifle another laugh and she answered his command. "I'll be careful. But will you?" She pointed out the window and a lump formed in his throat as he shifted to see.

Miranda sat on her beach towel, one leg in front of her with the other stretched out above her head. With her boom box beside her, the first lyrics of an old classic filtered into the house.

Sarah dropped the pan to the stovetop and skirted to the other side of the room, giggling. "Oh, man, she's playing your song."

"What are you talking about now?"

"Don't you recognize the song?"

"It's vaguely familiar." *Very familiar. And not at all funny.*

"She's playing *Mr. Lonely*. She's playing the song for you, Damian."

Damian vanished, hearing Sarah's laughter ringing in his ears. He reappeared outside his home on the ground floor patio. The black shirt and slacks he wore hid him from her sight while he stood, struggling to rein in the emotions spiraling through him.

Controlled, he flew over the sand, eating up the yards between them. A force, amazing in both strength and surprise, sparked to life within him when he caught her cat eyes, and his blood rode a tumultuous ride through his veins.

She rose to greet him, the graceful ease of her ascent noted in his brain, and he placed his feet at the edge of her towel. They stood, faces inches apart, and stared into each other's eyes.

"Miranda." He spoke her name with firm conviction, yet lost his momentum to continue the speech he'd rehearsed.

"Damian." Her eyes twinkled in the moonlight, at once calling to him, teasing him. Her lips, painted a bright red, dragged his attention down, and he resisted the desire to touch them. "Why did you return?"

"I love doing yoga on the beach. Especially under the stars. The stars are lovely, don't you agree?" She glanced toward the heavens and he did the same.

What was it about this woman that irritated him so much? What was it about her that made his blood boil? He ached to reach out and slide his fingers, his teeth, along her slender neck. But he wanted more than a taste of her blood. He wanted to lick her sweat, smell the aroma of her skin, drink the juices of her womanhood

"Why are you playing that song?" He gritted his teeth, keeping the fangs withheld. He'd made a vow to himself. Never again would he crave a woman so much. Never again would he alter his life to fit the needs of a woman. He'd learned the painful, yet valuable lesson from Christiana and he never made the same mistake twice.

She smiled a slight, easy smile, yet alluring enough for him to hold his breath. "I don't get into classical music, but I thought you'd like the classics. And what's more classic than *Bobby Vinton's Mr. Lonely*?" She arched an eyebrow and queried, "Unless, of course, you'd prefer the version by *Akon*?"

"Who?"

She laughed a delightful, light sound, rushing his adrenalin in a race through his system. Perhaps he could bend his promise for one night? For one woman? A resounding "*No!*" shouted through his brain, bringing order to the chaos within.

"I figured you wouldn't know who Akon is." She skimmed a finger along his neck, ricocheting a shiver down his spine. "Never mind. Classics are better because they've stood the test of time."

Her intent perusal drew him to her, and for the

second time in his immortal life, he let another person inside his soul.

"Classics outlast all others. Living on through the decades. Don't you agree, Damian?"

He cleared his throat, trying to form words, but couldn't. Instead, he stood unmoving, waiting for her to speak. She didn't, yet what she did do catapulted his heart into flight. Sliding her hands around his neck, she inclined her head, and pulled his lips to her flesh.

He inhaled sharply at the touch of his lips on the curve of her neck. Fangs sprang forth and he opened his mouth, eager to taste, eager to take. She sighed, a small, satisfied sigh, and he pulled her to him.

Gathering all the strength he could, he fought his primal urge and placed his palms on the sides of her face. Changing position, his brought his lips to hers, and drove in with his tongue. The warmth inside drove him closer to the precipice, but he held on, staying away from certain doom.

She moaned, digging her claws into his shoulders. His fangs withdrew in the second before her tongue explored his mouth, and his shaft pressed against her bikini bottoms.

"Damian. Invite me in."

He wanted to. Wanted her inside his house, under the covers of his bed more than anything else. Yet another voice, growing more tenuous by the second, wouldn't allow him. This woman wouldn't be a fling, a one-night stand, a whore he could pay for a night's pleasure. No, this woman would be so much more. More than he could resist.

Thrusting her away from him, he gasped for air

as she wrestled to breathe, too. Wheeling around, he strode away, hoping his resolve would last until he made his way safely inside.

But Miranda wouldn't let him go without having the last word.

"Damian, I'll let you in if you'll let me in."

Even in his anguish, his lips curved up at the corners at her jest. Reaching the darkness of the lower patio, he snapped his fingers and disappeared.

*****

Damian stood at a window with the blinds pulled open, and cursed himself for being a besotted fool. Scanning the beach for the hundredth time that evening, he groaned, unable to stop the churning in his stomach. "Where is she?"

He glanced around the room, thankful Sarah was out for the night. Bringing the wine glass to his lips, he paused, staring at the ruby liquid. "Why am I attracted to her? She's arrogant, bull-headed, rude and has awful taste in music."

A frustrated growl escaped him as he twisted the rod to close the blind. Catching a movement out of the side of his eye, he froze, and squinted. A crouched form ran from one of the palm trees lining the side of his home and into the darkness of the lower floor.

"Oh, goody, I have a visitor. Not the one I'd hoped for, but maybe this one will serve as an entertaining distraction."

He listened for any unusual noises and soon heard the bumbling sounds of an intruder's presence. A door creaked open on the floor below him, a banging noise followed, and a man's voice uttered a low exclamation.

How far should he go? Rarely did he allow his true personality to show in the small community and surrounding towns. Better to go abroad whenever he needed to hunt. Yet if the intruder was the same man who'd bothered Miranda…and Damian could make that assumption…then he would love to teach the man another lesson.

The untamed tumble of sensations burst alive in him, searing his internal organs, readying them for total transformation. His fangs grew, sharpening as they lengthened, and he almost drooled at the prospect ahead.

The change drew him to the heat, every fiber of his being electrified, burning with the thrill of the hunt. Yet, somewhere deep inside his mind, he heard the warning and heeded it.

"All right, all right. If I can't drain him, I can at least have a bit of fun." Snapping his fingers, he disappeared.

Damian's reappearance almost cost him the element of surprise. He "landed" against a hallway wall, managing to pop into Sarah's vacant bedroom before Billy turned around and saw him.

Flattening his body behind the opened door, he waited. He heard Billy jump into the other room and curse under his breath.

So the coward's hoping to sneak up on me while I'm sleeping, huh? Too bad he doesn't know my sleeping habits more. He tensed, hearing Billy's approach.

Billy rounded the corner of the doorway and ran toward the bed. With a knife in his raised hand, he stood over the empty bed, ready to thrust the blade into any poor soul lying there. When he realized no one slept in this second bed, he muttered an expletive and tore off the comforter.

"Where the hell is he?"

"Are you looking for me, Billy?"

Damian grinned at the startled Billy. "Oops. Sorry to frighten you, Billy. Come for a visit?"

Billy gaped at Damian, the fear of a cornered prey springing into his eyes. "Uh, yeah. Uh, no." Billy snarled, gathering what crumb of courage existed inside him. "Let me pass or I'll slit your throat."

Damian feigned an expression of terror, holding his hands up to ward off any oncoming attack. "Oh, no. You wouldn't hurt me with that big, ugly knife, would you?"

Billy missed the sarcasm in Damian's voice and adopted a cocky attitude. "You bet." He ran his thumb along the edge of the blade, slicing open his skin and drawing blood. "Ow."

Damian chuckled. "Want me to kiss it and make it better?"

Again, Billy snarled, and quit sucking on his finger. "Shut up. I'm here to pay you back for the other night."

Damian let the fake fright fall from his face. "Oh, my. Well, to be fair. If you use your knife on me, then I'll be obliged to use these on you." Curling his lips up, he bared his dagger-like teeth at Billy.

The knife dropped from Billy's hand, sticking into the floor. Uttering a small cry, the vagrant backpedaled away from Damian and ran into the bedroom wall. "Jesus and Mary, Mother of God, please help me."

Damian took a few steps toward him, his fangs dripping with saliva, his forehead creased as he opened his emotions to the force growing inside. Shaking his head at Billy's frantic actions, he slid his mouth wider and grinned. "What's the matter, Billy? Isn't a confrontation what you wanted? Or do you prefer attacking helpless women alone on the beach?" Glancing at the bed, he paused and raised his eyebrows at Billy. "Or do you prefer sneaking into bedrooms to kill people while they sleep?"

Billy scrambled over the bed, toward the window. He grabbed at the blind, tearing it off, and fumbled with the latch. "Please, God help me."

"Billy, I'm sorry you aren't enjoying my hospitality. Here let me help you." Reaching past the cowering Billy, Damian flipped the latch and opened the window. "There you go, little man."

Billy's huge eyes snapped between Damian and the window. Squatting below the window, he inched his way up, and tried hurling himself out onto the patio.

Damian gripped the collar of his shirt and tugged him back inside. "Darn, Billy, where ya going? We're just starting to have a good time."

Damian chuckled at Billy's strangled cry as he sent him flying across the room. Billy landed with a "*thud*" against the opposite wall and fell to a lump on the floor. Moaning, he rolled into a ball and hid his head under his arms.

"What? You don't like flying?" Damian vanished, reappearing next to Billy and, using one hand, picked up the terrified man. Billy's feet dangled in the air as Damian held him high. "No problem. I aim to please all my guests." He snarled, sending a shudder through Billy's body. "Well, if you don't like flying, how do you feel about dying?"

Spit dribbled down Billy's chin as he struggled to get free. Lowering Billy's feet to the floor, Damian clutched Billy's scraggly hair and yanked his head to the side, exposing his grimy neck. "I usually prefer my snacks washed, but one has to make sacrifices for guests, you know."

Damian widened his mouth, exposing the fangs to Billy's terrified scrutiny and bent over his neck. The tips of his teeth pressed against the rank-smelling skin and he punctured deep enough to draw a drop of blood from two holes. As predicted, Billy executed a heart-stopping scream and struggled for his life. Damian's grip lessened on his hair and Billy wrenched free, scurrying into the hallway.

With his fangs extended to their full growth, he shook his head, sending saliva flying, and roared a primal cry. Mortals frightened so easily. But sometimes the results could be amusing. He walked out of the bedroom, following Billy's path to the front door.

Damian wondered at the path, surprised he'd chosen the front door instead of the door leading to the beach, but continued to follow anyway. The entry door stood wide open, a sign of Billy's rapid departure, and Damian went to close it. As he did, he overheard talking from the street above.

Sliding into the darkness, he bounded up the steps to the roadside running in front of his house.

Narrowing his eyes, his sight fell on Billy standing beside Miranda. Terror still oozed from Billy's every pore, but Miranda seemed controlled and in charge.

They exchanged a few more words, mostly Miranda's, and she waved him off, like a queen dismissing her servant. Billy didn't hesitate, but dashed down the street without a backwards glance. Damian frowned and ducked as she seemed to sense his presence. He could see the frown causing creases in her forehead, but the lack of another emotion caught his attention. *She's not afraid of Billy.* An image of her face as Billy threatened her flashed through his mind. *She'd never been afraid of Billy.*

Chapter Four

Withdrawn to her quarters below the deck of her yacht, Miranda dispensed instructions through Jerome to the rest of the crew. They'd have everything ready by nightfall.

Her plan with Damian needed a significant push. After all, she'd lost one precious night because of the actions of that low-life, Billy. When she'd arrived in front of Damian's last night, she'd gotten out of the limo and skipped down the steps to his house, ready to somehow, some way get invited inside.

Halfway to the front door, however, she'd stopped when a gut-ripping howl spilled out into the air. At first, she thought Damian might be in danger and she'd run around the side of the home hoping to assess the situation before she barged in. Skidding to a stop, she'd seen Damian in vampire mode throwing the worthless Billy around a bedroom.

Oh, how glorious! Even without releasing his full power, he'd been magnificent. She closed her eyes and relived the sight. His eyes blazed like a dragon's torch while his facial features morphed into perfect ridges and crowns. And his teeth. She'd never seen such wondrous fangs. Long, sharp, glistening white against his alabaster skin and dark hair. She'd lost her breath along with her soul, completely and utterly in awe. No wonder Billy's pants were wet when she'd stopped him. Damian had scared the piss out of him.

She giggled and hugged herself. Damian LeClare, strongest, most amazing vampire in all the world would soon be hers. She called for Jerome again.

"Yes, Miss Miranda?" His tired expression struck a chord within her. Once she and Damian were together, she'd have to speak with Jerome about retiring. Perhaps to her private island?

"Is everything ready? Is the sun down yet? Have the townspeople been invited? Have you arranged for the bars and refreshments? Do you think they'll come?"

Jerome shook his head, but gave an affirmative answer. "Against my better judgment. Yes, the crew carried out your orders to your exact specifications. And yes, the people are already showing up at Mr. LeClare's house."

She hopped off her bed and past Jerome faster than a runner sprinting to the finish line. "Well, come on, Jerome. We've got a party to attend."

She ran all the way from the yacht to the waiting limo. Fidgeting while Jerome hobbled to the car, she ordered the driver to go as soon as the old man's feet lifted off the pavement. To her order, Charlie hit the gas and they sped down the highway.

"This is it, Jerome. I can almost drink the magic in the air. Tonight's the night I become Damian's lover."

"Please, Miss Miranda. You know I can't tolerate talk of sex. Especially from you. Especially about you."

The car screeched to a halt in front of Damian's home. A caravan of cars and a couple of catering vans lined the street. Several people waved as they headed toward the beach.

She hugged Jerome to her. "Oh, you old sweetheart. Don't worry. I'll always be your little girl." From her hug, she leaned in front of him, and pointed at the scene on the beach. "All right! The party's in full swing."

Four giant speakers stood on poles forming an invisible square around a temporary wooden dance area. The music blaring from the speakers deafened her and she grinned thinking about Damian's reaction to the loud noise. A throng of people grabbed free drinks from the three bars set strategically around the perimeter and swimsuit-clad bartenders hurried to fill requests. Lanterns sparkled in the night sky, moving gently with the sea breeze.

Miranda danced into the crowd, delighted at the smiles and happy voices around her. Trying her best to pretend the house and the man inside didn't exist, she ordered a Long Island Tea from a sexy bartender and drifted among the other partiers. Men, boys, and even women asked her dance, but she declined, wanting to wait for the right moment, the right partner.

She sensed his intensity long before he placed his hand on her shoulder. Taking a deep breath, she bought enough time to settle her jumping stomach. Inching around, she took in a face of rage.

"Damian, how are you?" Sighing, she was thankful her voice hadn't deserted her.

As he pointed an accusing finger at her, he fell forward, catching Miranda off-guard and bumping into her. Her drink splashed over the front of his silk shirt in the same instant an intoxicated young man and his clingy girlfriend slammed into him again, sloshing beer onto Damian's Italian loafers.

"Aw, gee, dude. Sorry. No harm done, right?" Sticking out his hand, the drunk peered at Damian with bleary eyes and put his nose an inch from the vampire's. "I'm Jimmy."

Damian reeled as the drunken man's foul odor struck him. Uttering an oath, he stepped out of the drunk's reach, and picked the sticky shirt away from his chest.

Jimmy's girlfriend stared at Damian and shrieked a gleeful cry. "Oh, crap, Jimmy. You just spilled beer on the Night Stalker!"

The crowd milling around them froze and every eye latched onto Damian. Most people held their breath in awe of seeing their elusive citizen, but a few of them gestured and mumbled comments without having the courage to direct them to Damian.

"Cool, man. The Night Stalker walks among us!"

"He doesn't look like a mad scientist."

"Where's his Frankenstein? Locked in the house?"

"Hey, maybe we should go free the monster!"

"Free the monster! Free the monster!"

Other voices joined in the chant and the mass of people surged toward the house.

Damian's voice, authoritative and confidant, rang out over the crowd's mantra. "Stop! Listen to me!"

Everyone turned at his command. Damian, standing straight and regal, scanned the crowd. His eyes flashed with a ferocity hiding just below the surface while his nostrils flared with unconfined emotion. Without raising his voice, he instructed the throng of partygoers, his eyes darkening as he spoke.

"This is my house and my land. Enter at your own risk."

An uneasy quiet followed, and Damian stood between his home and the crowd with Miranda by his side. At long last, Miranda broke the spell Damian held on the crowd.

"Hey, who came here to par-tee?" She struck her arm into the air and was relieved when several people began chanting after her, "Par-tee! Par-tee! Par-tee!" The tension relieved, people returned to their night of fun and games.

With the mob dispersed, Damian seized her wrist and dragged her to the secluded area of the ground patio. She'd allowed him to lead her, but wouldn't put up with his brutal manner any longer. "Hey! Knock it off." Twisting her arm out of his grasp, she sidestepped, putting distance between them.

Did he grow larger? Hitching her head up higher than she remembered having to do before, she stood her ground. They'd be on equal terms in their relationship because she wouldn't tolerate anything less.

"Who do you think you are? Sarah told me about your invitations posted around town."

Could there be a darker color than black? If so, his eyes were that color. Hell, he'd made the word "invitations" sound ugly. Sweat popped out between her shoulders making her glad for the black halter-top she wore.

"So? What's the harm? I figured you could use a party to get the knot out of your panties. Don't you like parties, Damian?"

He seemed surprised by her lack of fear. But, of course, he couldn't know the whole truth. That would come later.

"No, I don't. And especially not on my property, without my permission." He threw out his arm, indicating the mob on his beach.

She decided on a different approach. Maybe she could throw him off guard. "Really? I'm shocked. I took you for a real party animal. You seem like such a night person to me."

His low, masculine growl set off alarms in her head and a flood between her legs. Pushing her farther into the dark, he cornered her against the wall of the house. She jumped when he slammed his hands against the wall on either side of her head.

"Take it easy, man."

His tone, edgy and malicious, sent tiny shockwaves of lust roaring through her. "First, you hire scum to invade my beach and my home. Then you bring unwanted people to act like idiots on my beach. This will not go on. Do you understand?"

Her desire mixed with anger, shooting her blood pressure into orbit. "What are you talking about? What scum? You mean, Billy?" Her mind reeled with his crazy accusation. "Oh, shit. You think I hired Billy to break into your house last night?"

A twinkle glimmered in his eyes, and she knew she'd said too much. "So you admit you know about last night?"

She lowered her eyes, upset at her mistake.

"Yeah, so?"

"Then why not admit you paid him to accost you on the beach the other night."

Her eyes locked onto his, indignant and proud. "And why the hell would I do that?"

His smirk widened and she thought she glimpsed the tip of a fang peeking between his lips. "So I'd come to your rescue."

She started to object, but he stuck a hand over her mouth. "And when I didn't invite you inside for your much-wanted sex, you decided to get a measure of revenge by having Billy break into my home."

She thrust her head to the side to free her mouth. "You're nuts. I wouldn't want Billy to harm you. And I never hired him to do anything. I don't need anyone's help in attracting a man.

He cocked his head to the side, mulling over her answers. "Okay, I believe you didn't mean for Billy to harm me. But as for the rest, well…"

The smug expression on his face cracked her last nerve. "Why you conceited son-of-a-bitch. Believe me, if I wanted to have you, you'd be down on your knees begging to touch me right now."

His eyebrows rose and he laughed.

He's laughing? At me?

Furious, she placed her hands on his face and yanked him to her. Their mouths met, hard against each other and, for a moment, she almost pulled away. But found she couldn't.

Tracking his hands through her hair, he kept her to him and drove his tongue into her mouth. She moaned and he echoed her moan, sending his breath down her throat. Her hands reached behind her to guide his to the hook of her halter-top.

With a single snap, the straps fell down, exposing her breasts to the night air and his ravenous eyes. She placed her hands on his shoulders and urged him to take a nipple into his mouth. Again, he groaned, a man yearning for more, and sucked her tit.

A cloud passed in front of the moon, making their hideaway darker still. Exerting pressure on his shoulders, she urged him lower.

He obeyed her request as he slid to his knees, tugging the flap of her wraparound skirt to the side. A delighted chuckle tickled the hair of her mound when he found bare flesh beneath her skirt. She smiled, knowing she'd planned well.

Yet when his tongue entered her folds, all thoughts of plans flew from her mind and her legs buckled underneath her. She flattened her hands against the wall, keeping her body erect and pushed her pelvis forward.

He drank from her riches, pausing every so often to sigh against her skin. Molding her buttocks to his hands, he sucked and licked until her release came, quick and hard. She growled, trying to be quiet as the crowd around them continued to play.

Rising, he caught her mouth again and she tasted her own sweet nectar. She sucked, pulling on his lower lip, nibbling at his flesh. As his tongue slid over her lips, probing her, her mind flew to his other probe. Pushing him away, she bent to her knees, leaving him to unzip his slacks. Once undone, she tugged them to his ankles.

She'd prepared for this night, reading everything

she could about him, knowing he'd earned a reputation for great sexual prowess. Yet all her preparation couldn't help her stifle a cry when his shaft sprang free. Thick and firm, his rod shouted virility. Eagerly, she wrapped one hand around his cock while the other cupped his balls. Her mouth sank onto his length, plunging him to the back of her throat.

Rocking her head, she licked and pulled, urging him to full pleasure. His hand gathered her long hair together as he guided her in and out, in and out. Soft groans accompanied her own for several minutes until, at long last, he pushed her from him and covered himself for his release.

Spent, they leaned against each other, trying to dress. The moon came out from hiding and Miranda stood so she could study his reactions. A shadow, not borne of any heavenly reflection, fell over his face.

"This shouldn't have happened."

Stunned, Miranda shook her head and tried to argue. "Damian…"

Without another word, he threw up his arms, palms out to silence her, and stalked into the house, slamming the door behind him.

*****

"Quite the rave last night, huh?"

Damian took in Sarah's messy hair and baggy clothes as she shuffled into the kitchen and started brewing yet another pot of coffee. "I can see you enjoyed yourself. Still recuperating?"

She ignored the dig at her appearance and doubled the amount of coffee she usually put in the coffee maker. "Right up until the neighbors called the cops."

Damian's neck tightened remembering how the policemen cornered him at the front door and ordered him to quiet his "guests." Not that he'd minded getting rid of all the people, but when the officer found two people having sex in his bathroom, he'd been mortified as well as furious. The couple were lucky the police had found them. If he'd walked in on them…

"At least they put an end to the disturbance."

Sarah giggled but kept her head down. "Shit, Damian, you're the only person I know who can throw a bash and not want guests to show up."

Damian grumbled, preferring to study the pink hue surrounding the moon. "I don't give parties and I didn't give that one."

Another giggle. Why did Sarah giggle so much? Or had the frequency increased since Miranda's intrusion into his life?

"You gotta give her credit. She's got balls. If you want my opinion, I think she's pretty cool. You could do worse, you know. A whole lot worse."

"I don't care to 'do' anyone." He sipped his wine and put the distance and the shadows of the room between them.

"Is that so? I think I saw you 'doing' someone last night."

He sputtered the drink at his lips and coughed. He didn't have to see her to know she'd added finger quotes around the word "doing." Instead of trying to deny her accusation, he didn't respond and hoped she'd take the hint. When she remained quiet, he puckered his lips and let out a small puff of pent-up anxiety.

Sarah, however, gave him another surprise. "Did you see the note she slid under the front door?"

Damian whirled on her, taking in the colored paper she held in the air. "What note? What did she say?"

"Well, I didn't think you'd want me to know, but…" As Sarah ran her nails under the envelope's flap, Damian sped over to her and snatched the note.

"My, my. Someone's excited. Got a thing for Ms. Balls, do you?"

Damian took in her leer, glowered at her, and snapped his fingers to disappear. He popped into his office located in a locked room off the bottom story of the house. This was his sanctuary within his sanctuary. His complete refuge. Even Sarah didn't enter here.

Mahogany wood covered the walls and ceiling while rich, dark leathers enveloped the eight-foot couch and its comfortable matching chairs nestled in one half of the room. An enormous black desk topped with a top-of-the-line computer system took up the other side.

Damian ripped the note from the envelope and sat down to read. Her message detailed her purpose, concise and to the point.

I'm coming tonight. Be ready to talk.

Damian examined both sides of the paper. "She thinks she can give me orders." He bristled at the attitude in her message, but a thrill, a quickening of his heartbeat, told of his desire to see her. "Fine,

Miranda. I'll be waiting. But our talk won't go as you hope."

How could he make her understand without hurting her? She couldn't know the impossibility of such a union. Yet would she accept anything less? Could she be content with a brief fling? Could he?

For a few minutes, he gave permission to let his mind wander, to envision the unattainable life with Miranda. But he lived in the night and only one way existed to make a joining between a mortal and vampire survive. He'd have to convert her. Yet he tried that once with horrendous results and he wouldn't try again.

"No!" He hurled his body off the couch and crisscrossed the small room. "I can't. I won't. I tried changing Christiana, but she couldn't take living in my world."

He paused long enough to pick up a crystal paperweight and hurl it across the room. The glass shattered against the wall, sending splinters everywhere. "Damn you, Miranda. Why did you come into my life?"

Running his long fingers through his hair, he dragged a hand over the nape of his neck. He'd never forgotten Christiana, recalling the pain of her betrayal, the heartache of her leaving. Remembering, he swore to harden himself against Miranda's charms.

"Damian?"

He snapped out of his thoughts, turning to the sound. Miranda stood in the doorway, her curvaceous form silhouetted against the light of the hallway.

"Damian." A statement this time. A declarative. A call to him.

"Sarah let me in the house. She said I could come on down. Will you invite me in?"

He heard her clear her throat. Did fear cloud her voice? Or something more?

Damian moved to his desk, seeking the fortress behind its granite top. *Who's afraid now? And of what?*

He watched the gentle swing of her hips as she skimmed over the carpet to him. A shot of yearning ripped through his groin as he remembered the taste of her lips, her skin, her clit.

"Miranda, I'm glad you came. Come in." He told the truth in more than one way.

"You are?" The hope in her voice lit a spark of hope in his soul. Violently, he doused the spark with a flood of reality.

"Is this your inner sanctuary?"
Strange she should know.

She took a few steps more, bringing her to the edge of his desk. He could see her features clearer now, the flaming hair swirling around her round, alabaster face. The slope of her neck, her luscious neck, leading down to her enticing chest. The mix of emotions locked in those glowing green eyes.

She's beautiful. More beautiful than yesterday.

He braced his hands on top of his desk and adopted his fiercest expression. "You have to understand this once and for all. We cannot be together. You will leave tonight, Miranda, and never return."

She smiled, a powerful weapon against the fortress he'd built around his heart. "You're wrong. We can. I want you tonight, Damian. All of you."

He shook his head, at once stunned and delighted by the strength behind her words. "No."

She paused, tilted her head and whispered, "Yes."

That one whispered word rammed through all his defenses, leaving his resolve broken into a thousand pieces. Rushing around the desk, he pulled her to him, pushing her on top of the desk.

She yelped, but made no effort to stop him. Instead, her hands fastened on his shoulders, bringing him to her neck.

*****

Miranda's pulse jumped as Damian's mouth raked along her neck and stopped directly over her jugular vein. Her fingers tunneled through his long hair and she closed her eyes, reveling in the flow of silk against her hands.

He tore her flimsy top off her, ripping her skirt from her in one swift motion. Naked, she gasped as his teeth bore down on her throbbing lifeline and paused. A muffled cry, filled with anguish rumbled against her throat and he pulled away. Desperate, tortured eyes raked her body, taking in all her curves and valleys.

"You, Damian." Tugging at the buttons on his shirt, she ran her tongue over her lips and watched him drop his slacks. Now she could feast on his body and she did so, pleased at what she saw.

"Miranda, I can't."

Raising her eyebrows, she gestured at his fully erect shaft. "Oh, yes you can." When his cock jumped up in response, she added, "If you can't, then no one can."

Pulling him to her again, she met his mouth with hers and imprisoned his tongue in her mouth. Their tongues rolled around each other, playing a sexual game of tag, while his hand molded to her breast.

The urgency inside her heightened all her senses as the whirlwind gained speed. The pumping of his heart answered hers, matching his rhythm to hers. A need, stronger than she'd ever known, burned in her, and she knew his need equaled her own.

His mouth broke free from hers and latched onto a tit. She arched, wanting him to take more of her into his mouth. Running her fingernails along the tight muscles of his upper arms, she dug in, marking him as hers.

"Oh, Damian."

He shoved his hand between her legs and rubbed her clit until she swelled, ready to spill open in pleasure. She shuddered through a small climax and he spread her legs more, placing them on either side of him. She obeyed his silent request by wrapping them around his waist and forcing him to her. His manhood pressed up against her throbbing pussy, rubbing her wetness onto his shaft.

Panting, she watched as his tongue enveloped the other heaving breast. She closed her eyes again, wanting to experience the full sensation of his coarse tongue on her smooth skin.

She'd known he'd be good, but she'd never dreamed he'd be phenomenal. Another wave of orgasm burst from her and she bit down on her lower lip to keep from crying out.

As if knowing her thoughts, he raised his head

and gave her permission. "I want you to scream. I'll make you scream, Miranda."

Grasping her under her arms, he lifted her and she clung to him. He carried her to the couch and sat down with her nestled on top of his lap. Thrusting into her, she shouted at the thickness, the length of him.

Another release broke free, drenching him, and she cried out again in ecstasy. He pumped her now, making her ride him and beads of sweat broke out along the back of her neck. Her pleasure soared to a new height, but came crashing down at the words he spoke between his panted breaths.

"Only-for-tonight."

A searing ache knifed through her chest even as his fingers dug into her bottom to keep her in place. Her nails jabbed into his shoulders, a result of both the sex and the pain he gave her.

"We-can-never-be-together."

She frowned at him, driving all her frustration, hurt and anger into pounding against him. Reaching the pinnacle, she yanked his head to her breast and he sucked her tit into his mouth, pulling harder as she screamed her release.

He came seconds later, digging into her buttocks, and groaning his satisfaction against her chest. She collapsed on him and they sat, still joined, while their breaths slowed and the air dried the perspiration from their bodies.

"You're wrong."

He froze and she wondered if she'd spoken the statement out loud. Pushing for a response, she repeated her simple statement. "You're wrong."

What would he do? Nothing? Would he simply ignore her? She lifted off him, breaking the physical bond between them in order to save the emotional one.

Damian kept his head bowed, his eyes averted from hers. Shivering, she pulled the afghan resting on top of the couch over her. Did she shiver from the cool night air hitting her sweat? Or from the panic rising in her throat?

He sat on the couch next to her, so aloof and unmoving. She swallowed, tried to think of an alternate plan and couldn't. Instead, she waited. Waited for him to decide the rest of her life.

She flinched when he leaned over and embraced her.

A hug? She'd expected so much more. Denials, accusations, demands. But she'd never expected a hug.

Rising from the couch, he gathered his clothes and hers. He passed her clothes to her without a word and pulled on his slacks. She dressed, unable to sort through the confusion in her mind, and waited for him to say something. Anything.

Several minutes passed and they finished dressing, a cold, lonely silence pervading the room. She watched him, unable to speak, until he walked to the door and started to leave. Her brain snapped out of the fog and into action.

"Don't you dare walk out on me, Damian LeClare!"

His hand hit the doorframe as he stopped. Slowly, he bent around, his features a mask she couldn't interpret. "Get out of my house, Miranda, or I'll throw you out."

The pain in her chest cut her in half. But she refused to let her dream die. Not yet. "Try it, Damian. You just try and throw me out."

The challenge ignited the fire in his eyes and she gulped against the awesome figure he made as he pivoted and stalked over to her. She forced her eyes to meet his and stood her ground, while a part of her wanted nothing more than to run.

His hand closed around her neck, not hard enough to hurt, but enough to hold. She could smell his hot heavy breath as he drew her face to his. "You don't want to make me angry, Miranda. You wouldn't like me when I'm angry."

Damian's words caused a stalemate and they blinked, he waiting for her response, she going over his last remarks. His eyes darkened when he saw the tips of her mouth quiver. Still holding her to him, her lips grew wider, and she let out a loud, whooping cackle.

He dropped his hand in surprise and backed away. "Are you crazy, woman?"

Miranda fell to the couch, clutching her stomach in a boisterous belly laugh. "Oh, Damian, you are so funny."

"Funny?" He frowned at her, perplexed at her strange reaction.

"Who do you think you are, the *Incredible Hulk*?"

Realization dawned on him, and he couldn't hide a smile. "Oh." Running a hand over his mouth, he added, "You mean like the movie monster?"

"Yeah, but remember? He was a nice guy

beneath all the green." She grinned up at him.

Recovered enough to regain some of his earlier momentum, he tried once again. "Never mind. If you won't leave, I will. Forever." Again, spinning on his heel, he stalked to the door, but her words caught and held him prisoner.

"I know your secret." She paused and held her breath.

He stayed averted from her, yet his tone carried his thoughts to her. "What are you talking about?"

"I know you're a vampire."

He whirled to face her, his features a mixture of surprise, anger and something more. He didn't move, however, so she came to him.

"I know you're a vampire, Damian. And it's not a problem."

He searched her, trying to understand. "You know?"

She smiled, getting ready to break the real news to him. "Yep."

"Then you understand why we can't be together."

She shook her head as she raised one palm to caress his cheek. "Yes, we can."

Damian yanked his head away from her touch. "Damn you're a stubborn woman. You don't understand. I've tried to have a future with another and it didn't work."

"I'm different."

He growled, shooting renewed lust through her body. "Okay, I give. So tell me. What makes you think we can have a future together?"

Trying not to be hurt at his caustic tone, she walked to the desk and leaned her back against it. "You know the rule about vampires, don't you?'

The glower he shot her lessened as he tried to understand. "What rule?"

Miranda stood tall, shook out her fire-engine mane and opened her mouth wide. Gleaming a pristine white, her fangs captured his full attention. "Once you invite a vampire inside, you have to let her stay."

Damian's joyful roar mixed with Miranda's, echoing into the night.

To learn more about Beverly Rae visit

http://www.beverlyrae.com

And read her delightful contribution to the

Still Sexy Ladies Guide to Dating Immortals

DANCIN' IN THE MOONLIGHT

Available in print now!

LOVE THE DAY

Betty Hanawa

Forward

Padre Island is a barrier island that stretches down the coast from Corpus Christi to the bottom tip of Texas. It's a wonderful place for families to enjoy the waves and sand, take a boat to see dolphins swimming or bird watching, go parasailing, go fishing, and just hang out. MTV discover it a few years ago. During the month of March, the South Padre Island, Texas fills with college kids on Spring Break. Despite the tourist boom, parts of Padre Island National Seashore are protected from development by the U.S. Fish and Wildlife Service and are as beautifully desolate as when the Island was first given to Padre Balli as part of a Spanish land grant.

When I was asked to participate in an anthology of island stories, I knew I wanted my story to take place on Padre Island. I've been lucky enough to live near it my entire life. The waves, sand, and sea air are such a part of my being, I have to go walk on the beach at least once a month to be part of it again.

The people, Benedict's bar, and the incidents in the story are fictitious, a product of my imagination. Any resemblance to real life people or places is coincidental. The parasailing, the water park, the miniature golf course are part of the attractions of South Padre Island, Texas. The wrecked shrimp boat Benedict and Lycida spend time at also exists and is being rapidly covered by the sand. And, yes, fishermen and others who traveled the shoreline northward from the county park do go past the beach area that technically and legally doesn't exist but does have a large sign with the red, hand painted letters that proclaim it "NUDE."

My thanks to Trisk-Heart for inspiration and companionship, to my husband (always), Laura and Tawny. This story is for Hope.

Betty Hanawa

Prologue

"You took a vow to remain a maiden." Artemis' anger, cold and clear as the light from her silver chariot, did nothing to detract from her beauty.

Lycida tried to tell herself not to panic. What was the worst that might happen? Ever since she allowed Damian to spread her knees and thrust his hard member inside her, she knew the act sacrificed her right to be a handmaiden to Artemis.

She had been curious about sex. That was all. It wasn't as though she wanted to marry Damian. The way he kissed her, the way his hands stroked her body made her ache. He told her he had the power to make the ache disappear, to make her more joyous than she ever had been in her life. Artemis insisted her handmaiden remain virgins. Lycida wished she hadn't listened to Damian.

"You chose to pleasure a man with your body, not remain loyal to your vows to me."

True, true. Unfortunately, she got no joy out of it. It hurt.

"From this day until Eternity ends," Artemis intoned, "you, Lycida, are banished from Mount Olympus and shall wander the earth with mortals. You shall pleasure men with your body. And the man who finds pleasure in your body shall find no other pleasure in his life."

The pain of loss cut through Lycida as sharp as Artemis' arrows. Leave Mount Olympus? She didn't want to leave the only home she knew. Temporary worship of her body by a mortals who eventually died, no matter how many there might be for Eternity, was temporary. Mount Olympus was forever.

Artemis raised her hand, her bow and quiver hung over one shoulder.

"I have spoken. Lycida is banished."

With a crackle, light shot from Artemis' fingers.

The silver light obliterated Lycida's last sight of Mount Olympus.

Chapter One

Her laugh went straight to his groin and sent him into hard-on overdrive.

Why her? Benedict Jones asked himself for the hundredth time in as many days.

Her name was Lucy Moon.

When she first started coming to *The Sinking Ship*, Benedict callously labeled her. Fat girl used by the pretty girls to make themselves look better. Part of the Spring Break college crowd slumming in the locals' bar. Using Daddy's money to buy her friends by buying their drinks.

But she had that laugh. Her laugh was unselfconscious, uninhibited, full of joyous notes that made everyone in the bar stop what they were doing to smile at her.

People gravitated to her table. Not just because the pretty girls hung around her. They *wanted* to talk with her, tell her jokes, maybe become the lucky one to trigger her laughter.

She drank strawberry margaritas with gusto and ate the bar food as though it was prepared by a Master Chef. His cook, retired from thirty years in the Navy, most of it in the galleys, heated up the pre-made hot wings, flipped pre-formed hamburgers, and fairly strutted in the cramped bar kitchen when the waiters popped in with "Lucy's compliments to the chef."

The Spring Break crowds ebbed and flowed through the bar throughout March. They left behind money and lurid stories, trashing the Island like the flotsam and jettison littering the northern part of the beach not manicured and sanitized for the tourist traffic.

During the third week of college kids, Benedict realized Lucy still came to *The Sinking Ship* three or four days a week with a different bevy of girls and boys in tow. He also noticed the majority of the boys had the strong, lean muscles of the surfer crowd and began to spot some to of the local surfers in the midst of out-of-towners.

Semana Santa, the Holy Week between Palm Sunday and Easter, caused barely a blip in bar's primarily locals customer base. The upper class Mexicans from Monterrey and Mexico City had no use for a small bar with indifferent food.

But Lucy still came. Sometimes she came with surfers, sometimes by herself. She never stayed alone at her table for long. Very soon after she wrapped her lips around the sugar-rimmed glass of her first strawberry margarita, people started drifting to her table, inviting her to play pool, join their domino game.

After Easter, the locals breathed a sigh of relief when they walked in, knowing they had a small break before the summer crowds ramped up the action again. By then, Lucy *was* a local.

Now she played dominoes with locals at the corner table. Benedict easily identified her companions: a maid from one of the hotels, a tattoo artist, and a masseuse. Benedict wasn't able to see the table from his spot behind the bar, but the way Lucy and the hotel maid were laughing, he figured the other two women were getting ready to lose big. Lucy held a domino above her head flaunting her last one.

She slammed the domino to the table. Her laughter rang out again. She jumped up and danced around the table. Her dark brown hair undulated in soft waves doing its own dance across her shoulders.

Lucy's jeans stretched so tight around her ass, Benedict found himself amazed they didn't split with her butt wiggling enthusiasm. Under her tight pink tee shirt, love handles snuggled above her beltline. Not that she needed a belt because there was no way in hell those jeans were going to come off without some serious tugging.

He had a sudden image of himself snuggling up to her body, then tugging those jeans off while Lucy encouraged him with her hands and laughter. He pulsed against his zipper.

Benedict tried to tell himself her body looked ridiculous, the way she danced around the table. But his mouth dried and his dick hardened until he hurt. His dick didn't know it was the twenty-first century and Rubenesque bodies were passé. It went primeval.

His eyes and brain tried to remind him the bar was filled with svelte, nubile, beautiful bodies. His hormones ignored all the other women in the room. His testosterone told him he saw the ultimate of the fertility goddess, the fertile soil in which to cast his seed. This overweight, laughing woman set his body jumping with unbearable hunger to celebrate life in the most primitive fashion.

But he had no reason to celebrate life. Nothing

was left in his life.

Damn it.

Benedict jerked his eyes from the domino table where Lucy's laughter still rang out. His shift was ending. He wanted to find a svelte, nubile, willing female for a few hours of no-strings-attached sex.

He refused get involved with someone like Lucy. He knew those kinds of girls. Overweight, no close friends, but everybody's pal. And needy, hungry. No, not hungry, but starving for love.

There was no such thing as just-for-fun sex with those girls. They latched on and hung on, thinking sex was the ultimate commitment. But all they got were their hearts broken.

He had no time for commitment. He just wanted hot sex. Quick, fun, over and done, then move on to the next female.

He definitely didn't want to leave a broken heart behind him. His family was already crushed and mourning. He didn't need any more attachments to grieve.

Resolutely, Benedict turned away from the attraction of Lucy's *joie de vivre*. He absolutely didn't want to mess that up for her with a one-nighter.

He studied the girl bending over the pool table. Her shorts' back seam separated her butt. As she studied her next shot, the shorts' hemline rode up to give everyone a peek at the tanned round cheeks above her thighs.

She made her shot, then straightened, and moved around the table for her next shot. Beneath her midriff top, her belly-button ring twinkled against her tanned, flat abdomen.

If anyone had been interested, behind her was one of the photos of the local shrimp boat that had beached on the island's northern shoreline during a windstorm a few years earlier. By the time Benedict's friend took the picture, the sands had covered it until only the masts stood above the crashing waves.

Like Benedict, the males in the bar weren't interested in the bar's decor. The view as the girl bent over the table was much more to their interests.

She wore no bra and her nipples showed dark peaks beneath the white, stretched material of her top. Her breasts swayed hypnotically while she assessed her shot. The cleft between them was as tanned as her arms. She either wore next to nothing on the beach or frequented the nude area further north away from the hotels and condos.

Technically, legally, there wasn't a nude beach. But county and state park officials had enough to do patrolling the tourist areas and trying to dam the tidal surge of illegal drugs beaching from the Gulf of Mexico. The least of their worries was people who were determined to get skin cancer on their asses. Besides, the only way to access it was with four-wheel drive vehicles. Some soul had white-washed a large cylinder that washed ashore years ago and wrote "Nude" in bright red six-foot high letters to warn the few unsuspecting families who might wander that far north. Fishermen getting away from the crowds to go surf fishing got an occasional eyeful, especially during Spring Break. However, most of the nudists kept a towel or beach robe nearby for coverage when vehicles approached.

"Going to fulfill the evening pleasures of the pool shark with your charms, Jones?" Miguel, his closer for the evening, slid behind the bar and began loading beer bottles into a bucket for one of the waiters.

"Considering her," Benedict washed glassware in the triple sink of detergent, antibacterial water, and clear rinse. "Should be a quiet night."

"Wednesdays usually are." Miguel dumped a second scoop of ice into the bucket of beer bottles. "And, yes, we'll page you if we have any problems, worry wart."

Benedict grinned at Miguel, the brother he never had, who loaded the blender with fresh strawberries, bananas, and rum for one of *The Sinking Ship's* specialty drinks.

"Yeah, well, when you inherit this place, let's see how casual you are about leaving in the evenings or taking a day off."

Miguel looked at Benedict somberly for a minute, his eyes darken with unshielded grief. He swallowed once, then sneered, "I hate like hell when you remind me I'm going to inherit this rat hole. I think I'll burn it to the ground and let somebody build a twenty story condo unit on the property."

"Yeah, right, sure you will. I'll haunt you forever." Benedict finished mixing a Cosmopolitan and plucked a scarlet hibiscus bloom from the bush beside the bar. After fixing drinks all evening, he knew what the pool shark had been ordering. He reminded himself to haul the hibiscus bush outside in the morning for it to get some sun.

Leaving the Ladies room, Lycida, whose acquaintances this time called her "Lucy," tramped down her lust yet again when she saw Benedict carrying a drink and a flower toward his latest objective. His brightly patterned Hawaiian print shirt was smooth across his flat abdomen and tucked into a pair of khaki pants that hugged his butt. His shaved head caught the light from the Tiffany-style shades on the lights above the tables. His face wore a predatory smile that told other men he had staked the female pool player as his. From watching Benedict in action over the months, Lucy knew his brown eyes held the light of the challenge and gleam of lust.

A couple of women whom Lycida knew to be former lovers sent him looks as if saying, "Choose me again." To them, Benedict gave a smile and a wink. They'd had their turn. Time to move on.

Other women shrugged shoulders, shifted bodies, licked lips, or sucked maraschino cherries in open invitation to choose them. Benedict spared them a glance and a smile. Next time, perhaps.

Lycida had never even received that much interest from him. Not that she invited his attention. Not that she wanted it. She shuddered at the idea of causing the death of such a vital man.

She purposely put on over eighty pounds to make herself unattractive in this society. She knew part of the reason she lusted after Benedict was because she was just so damn horny, especially for a young male body.

It had been a least a couple of centuries, maybe

three, since she had a young lover. It was just too hard living with the realization that Artemis meant her vow.

When she absolutely had to have a lover again, she looked for an old man whose interest in sex was more cerebral than physical. She had also been careful to pick men who made their wills beneficial to their rightful heirs. All she wanted out of the relationship was sex anyway. After living forever, she had all the money she needed.

But why she was putting herself through this every few nights was beyond her. For her own peace of mind, she didn't want to have sex with men like Benedict.

Once again, she reminded herself she really needed to stay out of *The Sinking Ship*. She ignored the framed photograph of The Titanic on the wall next to the hall leading to the bathrooms. She'd seen enough copies of that picture when the ship sank. She'd been "Lydia" then, living in New York City, and counted several of the victims and survivors among her friends.

Despite her firm admonitions to herself, she persisted in coming back to The Sinking Ship. Lusting after Benedict was an itch she wasn't able to scratch.

To hell with this. She needed to get out of here, go back to her condo, and use her toys. At least in this society, in this age, she no longer had to rely strictly on fingers or just the plain, solid reproductions of dicks. Lycida smiled at the thought of her collection of antique reproduction dicks, most of which she'd gotten for her personal use. She still had a particular fondness for the jade and ivory ones she's bought in the first centuries Japan and China opened up to foreigners.

She needed to say good-bye to her domino buddies. She ought to bring a mah-jongg set over and teach them how to play. The ivory from her first set had yellowed and the colors faded, but she held fond memories of playing with it. Idly, she flipped through her memory thinking which museum she might consider donating it to. That thought sent her to wondering if any museum was open-minded enough to display her sex toy collection, if she decided to donate it.

Concentrating, she suddenly bumped into something hard and yet resilient.

"Oh, shit," Benedict said simultaneously. Momentarily, he frowned at her. He still held the mostly empty glass of Cosmopolitan in one hand and the hibiscus in the other.

The hot bodied pool player glared around Benedict's body. The cranberry juice stained red across her blouse, down her midriff and her white shorts, and dripped down tanned thighs.

"What the fuck?" she shrieked. "You fat clumsy bitch. Why the fuck don't you watch where you're going?"

"I'm sorry. I wasn't paying attention. I was thinking of something else. Here," Lycida fumbled in her bag for one of her business cards. She held it out to the enraged blonde. "You can take this to any of the boutiques on the Island and they'll let you charge a new outfit to me. Let me write your name on the back and sign it so they'll know. What's your name?"

The blonde's face twisted with a sneer. "You fat cow..."

"My God," Benedict looked straight into the blonde's sneer, "your parents were so cruel to name you 'You Fat Cow?'"

He picked Lycida's card from her hand and tucked it into Lycida's t-shirt's neckline. Heat skittered across Lycida's skin at the brief touch of his hand against her neck.

"Lucy," he turned back to the blonde, "owes you nothing. I spilled the drink. You can send me the cleaning bill or replace them at my expense."

Benedict twisted the blonde around, checked out her butt, then pulled the back of her shirt away from her neck, and read the tag. "And now that I know the brands, don't try to rip me off and replace them with clothes from the Island boutiques."

Benedict handed the nearly empty glass to a passing waiter, then handed the hibiscus to Lycida. "Let's go, Lucy." He took Lycida's hand.

She felt the firm bones wrap themselves around her fingers and followed his gentle tug. She had no reason to go with him and every reason not to. Then she looked into his light brown eyes.

For the first time in years, she saw not the pity for the fat girl, not the pure lust she'd grown impervious to through the millenniums, but desire. The desire in Benedict's eyes and smile contained the sensuous look of wanting to explore the physical and the even more magnetic pull of wanting to learn the personality.

Lycida didn't know how many men she had had sex with over the millenniums. She'd become immune to lust and men who wanted no more than her body. She wasn't able to resist going outside with a man who wanted to know what made her tick.

Chapter Two

Outside the bar, Benedict stopped by the wall beside the parking lot.

"Do *not* let what that bitch said upset you."

Lycida leaned against the wall and looked up at his serious face. "It doesn't bother me."

At the skepticism that crossed his face, she continued, "Really. It doesn't. I've learned through the years that a lot of people think they can make themselves more important by criticizing other people. It just shows how small and pathetic they themselves are."

Benedict lifted a lock of her hair and rubbed it between two fingers. "You're very wise."

"No," Lycida shook her head, "just observant."

After all, she knew if she were wise, standing here watching this man was the last thing she should be doing, much less allowing him to play with her hair, and even worse, wishing and hoping he might kiss her. It had been so long since she'd kissed a young man. Was it so wrong of her to feel, for just a few minutes, the strength and texture of a strong young man's arms around her?

She knew nothing more than a kiss was going to happen. She was strong enough to resist more than just a kiss. She just needed a kiss.

Benedict stroked a knuckle down her cheek and leaned closer to her. "I've been watching you the past several months."

Lycida's breath caught. "Yeah, well. Um."

She had to think. Her mind was already short-circuiting. The warmth of his body radiated against hers. His clothes held the tang of cigarette smoke from the bar, but his breath was sweet.

"With my weight, it's kind of hard to miss me in a crowd." She needed to distract him, remind him she was *just* the fat girl who was everybody's friend. Then he'd go away and leave her. She needed to go back to her condo and get busy with her toys.

"No, it's not the weight and don't put yourself down," His voice was solemn. "I look for you every night. It makes me feel good to hear you laugh. I like your laugh."

The security light made his cheekbones stand out in sharp relief. Lycida tried to pull up a mental image of him when she first noticed him behind the bar to compare it to how he looked now. Had he lost weight?

No matter. Because now his lips were smiling and he was moving closer, slowly, as if asking silently for permission.

With a sigh of pleasure and a curse at herself for being so weak, Lycida accepted the pressure of his mouth on hers, then opened her lips at the tentative touch of his tongue.

The heat from his mouth went straight to her cunt. She ached with wet, hot longing. It took everything she had not to wrap her arms around him and pull his head closer.

She sucked in his tongue, eager to feel his texture, hungry to take advantage of as much of this experience as possible.

Oh, this was such a mistake. But, damn it, it had been so long and he tasted so good.

His tongue twisted around hers, then retreated slightly, only to push back in harder as though he were ravenous for her taste. He ran his tongue across the insides of her cheeks, against her gum line, as though memorizing the texture of the different parts of her mouth.

His hand twisted in her hair, separating strands, massaging her scalp, pulling her head closer to his. His other hand rubbed in the area where once her waist existed. He slid a hand up her shirt. Her skin tingled where he stroked as softly as if he were petting a newborn kitten.

Her nipples hardened against her bra, but she managed to keep herself from pushing her breasts against his chest to relieve their throbbing.

This time when his tongue retreated, she followed it into his mouth. It was her time to probe, to explore the dark reaches. She tasted his essence, inhaled his breath, exhaled her own to share with him.

Concentrating on his mouth, it took her half a moment to realize he'd lifted her thigh to step closer between her legs. His body pressed her firmly against the wall. He rubbed his rigid shaft against the apex of her legs. Even with two pair of pants separating them, Lycida's hypersensitive cunt appreciated the pressure. It flooded between her legs with moisture as wet as his tongue in her mouth.

She grasped his shoulders to hold herself upright. If she didn't hold onto him, she'd slide right off the wall. She'd missed this kind of deep throated kissing and heavy petting.

His hand left her head and slid between their bodies. He reached under her shirt and then pushed her bra down to clasp her breast. His fingers flicked across her nipple.

She gasped into his mouth. How long had it been since a man had stroked her nipple into an unbearable peak like that?

She twisted against his body, silently begging him for more. He balanced the weight of her breast in his palm and concentrated his fingers on tweaking and teasing her nipple. Feathery touches alternated with more aggressive light pinches and twists making her whimper into his mouth as they continued the mating rituals with their tongues.

His own groan of pleasure vibrated in her mouth and sent shimmers throughout her body.

She wiggled her hands under his arms to hold his shoulder blades, pulled him closer to her, and tightened her leg around her body. She rubbed her cunt against his shaft and wondered if she was going to come without him even touching her bare pussy.

She thought just his touch was going to be enough to make her happy, but she wanted more. She wanted his mouth on her nipples.

But this was not the time, not the place.

And she absolutely did not want to get naked with this man.

It wasn't the weight. Well, okay, part of it *was* the weight, but only a small part.

If she allowed him to suckle her nipples the way

she wanted, she didn't think she had the ability to stop from getting completely naked and taking him into her body.

If she did that, she automatically condemned him to death. Artemis' curse made sure of that.

She needed to stop this. She had to stop this. She had no right to continue this kissing, this petting.

But it felt so damn good. It had been so damn long.

Dimly, Lycida heard voices. She didn't want to listen to them. She wanted to just continue kissing this tasty man.

"Hurmph." Lycida recognized the voice of the blonde pool shark. "Look at that."

"Don't worry about it, baby," a man said. "He's just feeling the fat girl up. Guess he decided tonight's his night for a pity fuck."

Lycida abruptly pulled her leg from Benedict's grasp and her tongue from his mouth. Time to end this. And those two, slamming car doors and leaving, gave her the perfect excuse.

She pushed him away and adjusted her bra back into place.

Benedict tucked a hand in her hair again and angled her face up to his. "I thought comments from pathetic assholes didn't bother you."

Lycida jerked her face away from his hand. She dug for her car keys in her handbag still hanging from her shoulder. "They don't normally. But I've been watching you for months also. You've never picked up a woman who looks like me before. You always pick up the hot, thin, young girls. I don't know why you've chosen me tonight, but I'm not a one-night stand. And I'm definitely not a pity fuck."

"I never said you were. I said I liked it when you came into the bar. I like your laughter and the way you enjoy everything and everybody. When you bumped into me tonight, I realized I wanted to spend time with you, not drift from girl to girl."

"Yeah, right," Lycida forced herself to be sarcastic. "You mean from fuck to fuck, don't you?"

As if there wasn't a time in her life when she did that herself, until she realized exactly what Artemis meant by no man would ever enjoy other pleasures again. Never, ever try to get the best of the gods and goddesses. As people said in this society, 'It'll come back and bite you on the butt.' Not that Lycida hadn't occasionally enjoyed a good bite on the butt or biting on a butt. However, the price wasn't worth it any more. Oh, hell. She definitely had to get out of Benedict's life and never come back to *The Sinking Ship* again.

She continued her patented *Lucy's hurt feelings routine*. It wasn't hard to add a few tears to her eyes and the catch in her throat. She was so damn lonely, especially for a man to hold and enjoy her. "You've never been with any one of your women for more than a week before you move on. I'm not a one-night stand. I'm not even a week's playtime. I'm going home now."

And console myself with some of my toys, damn it. "Thanks for the kiss."

She pushed Benedict aside and he watched her walk to her car. Her spine was ramrod straight.

Stupid fool, he told himself. *You knew better to get involved with her. You shouldn't have kissed her. You knew you'd break her heart. Now you've ruined even the chance of having her for a friend.*

The thought of not being able to be around Lucy, to not get to know why she was so happy all the time, sent a pang through him almost as stunning as when he sat in the doctor's office with his sisters and had the medical reports spelled out in plain English. God-damn-it. He wanted to get to know Lucy. He wanted a friend, a female friend.

"Lucy, wait!" He got to her car while she waited at the parking lot exit for cars to clear for her to enter the street. She rolled down her window. Thank God, she wasn't crying.

"I'm sorry. Well, I'm not sorry for kissing you. God, you're a wonderful kisser. But I'm sorry you think I only want sex from you. Look, I came on too strong. I really do want to be friends with you. Can we start over?"

The way the streetlights faced, Benedict wasn't quite able to see her face. He found himself sweating even in the Island breeze off the Gulf of Mexico. He didn't know why it was so important to him to have Lucy in his life and he damn well didn't want to analyze it.

For the moment he just wanted to feel again. To be with a woman who wanted to be with him and didn't walk on eggshells, afraid to say the wrong thing, not wanting to talk about the elephant shitting in the middle of room. Someone to do things with and be with.

Someone who didn't know he was dying.

And he didn't just want the momentary hot explosion of sex. Because in the dark of the night, in the brightness of day, that wasn't enough. The girls he'd been picking up and using had been using him, too. Mutual satisfaction for a few moments wasn't enough any more.

"Lucy?" he asked again. "Can we start over? Take it more slowly. Get to know each other?"

"Um, okay," she said. She took a breath as though needing extra air to get the words out. "I guess so."

Relief flooded through him, totally disproportionate to the idea of losing a possible bed partner. Yeah, he really did want Lucy for a friend, although his dick still was rock hard and wanting relief. Too damn bad. He'd just take care of himself later. In the meantime....

"It's early yet. Want to go do something? Walk on the beach? Miniature golf? Go carts? A movie? Go bungee jumping?"

"Bungee jumping? Do you have a death wish?"

"Nope," Benedict laughed at her scandalized voice, "just trying to pack as much living into each day as possible."

"There's a lot to be said for savoring each moment."

"Yeah, well, I want a lot of moments," Benedict told her. "So? You want to do something?"

"Miniature golf?" The tentativeness in Lucy's voice reminded him of a little kid asking for something he was pretty sure his mom and dad weren't going to let him have.

"Let's go. Um, two vehicles? My truck's parked over there." He pointed at his four-wheel drive crew cab parked in his designated spot.

Lucy gave a sigh, almost as if she were regretting her decision to doing something with him. "Get in. I can bring you back for your truck afterwards."

Benedict normally spent the time playing miniature golf in public foreplay with the girl he was planning to take to bed later. He wrapped his arms around the girl helping her hold the putter, a great excuse for his arms to brush against her boobs. He managed to help her angle the shot just right while rubbing his dick against her butt. Then, there were always the happy squeals, hugs, and deep kisses when the ball finally went in the hole.

In the late spring night, Lucy, though, played as though getting the ball in the hole was the second most important thing in her life. She not only didn't need or want help on how to play, she was giving people instructions on angles to make bank shots and how to avoid the small hazards built into the course.

Unfortunately for his ego, Benedict realized he wasn't the most important for her this evening. All the people, especially the children, also playing miniature golf held her fascinated attention.

Whenever Benedict looked up from his shot, she was chatting with someone, laughing with someone else, juggling balls for a small child. Damn it, Benedict knew he'd invited her on this junket. Why did she act like she was with everybody except him? It was beginning to piss him off, especially since he still wanted her to *juggle* his balls.

He thought by being out in public with her, his dick would stop pounding for relief. But, no, not a chance.

"Hey, Benedict, watch this."

Benedict watched Lucy take her stance and hit the ball. He heard it clunk several times against the walls of the course for the hole, then the hollow thunk when it landed in the hole. He heard it all happen, but he was too busy watching Lucy's butt while she stroked the ball. When the ball landed in the hole, he was enjoying the view of her boobs bouncing under her tee shirt despite her bra when she jumped with happiness. He remembered how smooth her skin was under his hand, the hard kernel of her nipple under his fingers.

The rush of heat through him and surge of blood to his dick made him light-headed. He wanted to hold her boobs and hear her gasps while he sucked her nipples.

Damnation. There was one thing he was able to do though. And practically everybody on the miniature golf course was expecting it.

Benedict strolled to where Lucy had plucked the ball from the hole and was laughing.

"A hole in one! Congratulations, Lucy." Benedict put one arm around her and pulled her close to him. To hell with starting over and taking things slowly. He didn't have time for slow.

He angled her face upward and kissed her.

Once again his tongue plunged into the dark, welcoming wetness.

Chapter Three

Kissing Lucy held the same excitement of opening Christmas packages, the exhilaration of watching fireworks over the bay, the pleasure of having a cat purring on his chest. With all the joy Lucy celebrated life, she put into her kiss.

While she kissed him, time slowed. The pleasure Lucy spread around other people, the gusto she gave her strawberry margaritas, the zest she put into eating, she now focused strictly on him.

Her kiss gave him the illusion of being all-powerful, like everything in the world was his to just reach out and take. At this moment, he was going to live forever.

His senses sharpened. He smelled the fresh paint recently applied to the course walls and figurines in the miniature golf course. The arid scent of mosquito repellent combined with the leftover sweetness of coconut scented sunscreens used throughout the day still clinging to people's skin despite the moon rising. But mostly, he smelled the heady aroma of the aroused woman he held in his arm.

Her nipples poked hard through her bra. Her cheeks were smooth and silky between his palms. Her tongue twisted and teased around his, tasting of strawberries and desire. One of her hands gripped his waist.

While visions of her spread naked and wanting him danced behind his closed eyes, he felt rather than heard her faint moan of passion. He delved deeper into her mouth, drinking in her secrets with her flavor. Cars and trucks rumbled past. Parents called to children, friends talked with friends. Underneath all the noise of too many people and vehicles was the faint, constant swoosh, whish of the waves landing on the sand as it had since the Island formed.

Gradually, Benedict sensed Lucy withdrawing. As much as he wanted this to continue, this was a family friendly facility. The kids Lucy had been entertaining with her juggling didn't need to see his hands roaming all over her lush body, which was going to happen if this kiss kept going.

He let her go and looked around, surprised to realize only moments had passed and the family group behind them wasn't even ready yet to move to the hole where Lucy had just gotten her hole-in-one.

"Let's finish the game," Lucy said. Her eyes sparkled and her lips puffed out.

With an almost unbearable hard-on, Benedict didn't have much interest in continuing the golf game, but Lucy had already gone on the next hole.

"How about I just concede?" Benedict joined her at the hole and glanced at the number. With five more holes to go, he was afraid his own balls might explode before they finished the game

"Chicken. Afraid I'm going to beat you?"

"Would you use a velvet whip?" Benedict whispered in her ear.

To Benedict's surprise, Lucy laughed. "You so wish. Put your ball down and hit it."

"I think I'd like you to hit my balls with a velvet whip." Benedict leaned down to place his golf ball on the rubber mat used instead of a tee.

Lucy swatted his butt, then rubbed it. "You have no idea what you're asking for."

Benedict straightened and turned around to look into Lucy's eyes. "I think I do. Do you know what you're doing to me?"

Lucy's blue eyes, the same shade as the moonstones dangling from her ears, danced. "I suspect you're hard enough to use your shaft instead the golf putter."

"Damn right," Benedict growled. "Are you going to do anything about it?"

"Not tonight. Tonight I'm just going to be the tease. Besides, what happened to your 'let's take it slow and be friends' bit?"

Benedict tapped the golf ball sending it bouncing off the back wall of the course and nearly back to where he hit it in the first place. He divided his scowl between the ball and Lucy who smirked at him.

"It disappeared. I watch your butt when you bend over and your boobs bounce when you jump up and down."

"Oh," Lucy's eyes widened like an innocent child's. "You mean like this."

She jumped up and down, laughing at Benedict who managed not to grab a bouncing boob.

"You are a tease."

"Damn right. Had a lot of experience at it. Want me to show you how to play this hole?" She set her ball down and settled into her stance.

Once again Benedict watched her butt wiggle and thought he was going to die if he didn't get to put his hands on it. He wanted to hold onto her generous hips while he pounded into her body. He wanted her straddling him, his hands holding her tits, his fingers on her nipples, while she rode him.

Just as she started her swing to tap the ball, Benedict leaned in close and said, "I'd rather you let me play with your boobs."

"Not tonight," she said not in the least rattled by his interruption of her concentration. The ball she tapped ricocheted off his golf ball, bounced off a wall, and then a second, and slid into the hole. "I do believe that is another hole-in-one."

This time, she wrapped her arms around him and lifted her face to his.

Amazing, Benedict knew he was going to lose what was left of his mind. Three kisses now, two of them in very public places – okay, all three of them in public places – but this was the second one where nothing happened but lip-lock. Yet Benedict thought he was going to come in his pants.

After Lucy ended the kiss, her full lips lifted in a smile. "I think that needs to be my last hole-in-one."

"What's the matter, Lucy? You don't think you can finish the game with all holes-in-one?"

"Oh, I can do it, but the kissing needs to stop. I realize I instigated this last one, but it was a mistake."

"Not as far as I'm concerned." Benedict ran a finger along Lucy's lower lip. "Why? Getting too much for you?"

Lucy backed away from him. "It's getting too much for both of us. I'm not sleeping with you."

Benedict stepped closer to her again. "Sleeping is

the last thing I was to do with you."

A bit of the light dimmed in Lucy's light blue eyes. "Yeah, yeah. I'm just a sex object." Her deep, throaty laugh made heads lift with smiles across the small golf course.

"Me with my broad butt, fat thighs," She slapped both portions of her anatomy, then lifted her breasts. "and double-D boobs."

Lucy dropped her breasts and flapped her arms like a chicken. "And let's not forgot the flabby arm wings and stomach paunch that's a credit to a nine-months-pregnant-with-twins woman."

Benedict took Lucy's putter from her hand. "Let's go. Now."

He grabbed both golf balls and walked away. He didn't trust himself to speak or touch Lucy. Damn it all to hell. He just wanted a good time with a fun woman. He wanted to spend time with a woman who might become a friend. If it lead to fun in bed, too, so much the better.

But he *hated* the look in Lucy's eyes while she poked fun at her body. He hated society for causing her to think of herself as less than a woman because her body was nearly double the size of the magazine models. He didn't have time in his life to take on a *cause*, to try to build her self-esteem.

Why didn't she stay just the fun-loving, life-loving girl he wanted to hang around with?

Why did he have to look in her eyes and see the pain there? The sorrow? He knew pain and sorrow too well himself. He barely controlled his own. He didn't want to get involved with someone else's.

Lycida watched Benedict stalk to the distribution area and slam the clubs into the return barrel. He set the balls on the counter, then still rigid, anger practically radiating off him in waves, went to the main street of the Island. She didn't no why he was so mad. Happy fat girl with the in-your-face-I'll-put-myself-down-before-you-can routine was part of Lucy. Normally, the attitude made people laugh. As Lucy, she wanted people to laugh with her, not at her. It also reminded most men that they just wanted her for a buddy. She did admit pointing out her weight was adroit at keeping men at arm's length and away from tempting her, Lycida.

However, the standard I'm-fat-laugh-with-me made Benedict mad. Lycida tried to think, but didn't remember a time before when it made a man mad. A couple of women friends through the years made it clear they didn't like it. Around them, she dropped the routine. With them, she was able to relax her guard slightly and actually have friends instead of acquaintances. At least until they died of old age. Sometimes being immortal was the pits.

But a man who got mad at her for her self-derogatory act? Never, at least not until Benedict. Was it possible Benedict was like her few female friends? Her last true friend died twenty-five years ago. She was lonely without a friend. But if she let Benedict into her life as a friend, was she going to be able to avoid sex with him? Was it even possible to have a male friend without a sexual relationship? Lycida certainly never experienced one in her long life. Several lovers turned into friends before their deaths, but never a friend into a lover. Of course, she was very careful not to have male friends, just female. And she was *so not* into the lesbian scene.

Benedict's anger about her fat-girl act seemed to be an indication he truly did want her to be a friend, not just a pity fuck. But if she wanted to take the chance that he did want to be a friend, she needed to talk to him and not shut him off.

Benedict stood under the streetlight on the Island's main drag. The halogen light gleamed off his shaved head and made his skin look sallow and yellow. Lucy saw the Island's shuttle bus down the road and hurried to him before he boarded it to go back to the bar and his car.

"Hey," Lycida tapped Benedict's arm. Might as well play the role of wide-eyed innocence. Lycida hoped he was upset over the way she demeaned herself. Lucy was *young* enough not to understand. "Why are you so mad?"

Benedict pushed his hands into his khaki pants' pockets. He glared up the road as though he was pulling the open-air mock trolley faster to him by using telekinesis.

"Benedict?"

"Look, Lucy, this isn't going to work." He directed his glare to her.

In his eyes, Lycida saw annoyance, affection, misery, compassion. She didn't see irritation or pity. She knew damn well what those emotions looked life. Generally, they were the ones she cultivated because men whose eyes held those two did not appeal to her.

But affection and compassion. Oh, goddesses.

She told herself once again she absolutely had to get away from this man. Far, far away and fast. Because those two emotions were too close to love.

In Lycida's past, an occasional sexual partner fell in love with her. While she often experienced sadness when a lover died, she had a much harder time facing the next days when a lover who actually loved her died.

She probably needed to find another old man who wanted someone to warm his bed and remind his body of younger days during the last days of his life. It was easier for her to accept their deaths even when they fell in love with her. She knew she made them happy at the end of a long life.

Lycida firmly reminded herself that if she accepted the friendship Benedict appeared to want to give her, then she had better kept it to *filios*, the love between friends. *Eros*, sexual love, held no place in a relationship with someone as young as Benedict.

Her resolve in place, she tapped her foot. "What's not going to work out?"

"This relationship."

"What relationship? Fourteen holes of miniature golf does not a relationship make."

Benedict's eyes locked with hers. "And three kisses that are enough to kill a man."

Lycida mentally rolled her eyes and thought, *You have no idea.*

"Lucy," Benedict rubbed her forearm.

Heat radiated from his hand through her body to her cunt. Lycida reinforced her resolve, especially since he kept his eyes on her face and not roaming across her tits. Hard enough to resist a man who was horny for her, but damn near impossible to resist one who was interested in her.

"You are one of the sexiest women I've ever met. And it kills me to hear you put yourself down. But," he put a finger on her lips to stop her from speaking. "Do you realized how much you insult me when you make comments about how ugly you are?"

"I never said I was ugly. Just pointing out how fat I am." Lycida kept her tone reasonable, curious to where this conversation was going.

"In that sarcastic, mocking voice that tells everybody you hate your body."

"Ah," Lucy twisted her mouth as though in comprehension, "and this insults you, how?"

The shuttle slowed down, preparing to stop for Benedict. He waved it away. After it rumbled past, he turned back to Lucy.

"It's an insult because I kept telling you how sexy you are. When you imply you're not, you're basically calling me a liar."

An odd expression slid across Lucy's face, then her face lit with a smile. "Oh. That hadn't occurred to me. I'll try keep that in mind."

Benedict had to touch her again. He ran his fingers through her hair enjoying the way it slid through his fingers. He touched her cheek, then rested his hand on the side of her neck. "Have you ever seen a *Peter Paul Ruebens'* painting? A real one, not a print."

"Yes."

"They glow. The skin is so beautiful. When you

smile like that, when you laugh, that's what you remind me of. A *Ruebens'* painting."

"Thank you," Lucy said softly.

"Can we spend the day tomorrow and I show you what a gorgeous body you have?"

"We're not having sex."

"Of course not." *Damn it all to hell. His cock throbbed.* "Do you have a bikini?"

Lucy looked at him like he lost his mind. "Of course not."

"Fine, then wear shorts." Benedict looked carefully at her. He'd check a couple of the beach wear shops and find her a bikini, after he got over his morning-after meds crud. He needed to get home and take his meds. "I have to check on the bar at noon. I'll pick you up after lunch, okay?"

Lucy frowned at him. "This isn't because you've got a savior complex, is it? I really don't think my self-esteem is so low that it needs a pity date."

"Hell, no. I don't have time in my life to play amateur psychologist. I just want to spend the day with you and your gorgeous body."

Lucy still looked a bit dubious, but nodded. "Okay."

Benedict slid his hand down her arm and took her hand while they walked back to her car.

"There'll be no sex," Lucy warned again. "Promise."

"Right. No sex. Promise." It might kill him to keep that promise, but he made it. But, tomorrow he planned to see and feel as much of her body as he was able to manage without having sex.

She'd wear shorts and they'd go parasailing. Then to talk her into a bikini and go to the water park. After that, they'd have a picnic supper on the beach. The nude beach.

Chapter Four

Lycida's hands shook while she held the straps of the harness out of the way so the college-age boy who was hooking and buckling the harass.

"You okay?" The boy asked after everything was snapped and clinched. "You can let go of the straps now."

"Okay." Lycida heard the quaver in her voice. "Are you sure this is strong enough to hold both of us?"

"Sure will. The two of you together don't even come close to the weight limit. Are you afraid of heights?"

"No," Lycida told him.

Not as long as I have something solid beneath my feet. Lycida thought longingly of her condo balcony, wishing she was there and not getting ready to be launched into the air to dangle from a giant parachute.

She kept thinking of Icarus' plunge into the sea when the wax on his wings melted. She remembered the early years of motion picture's newsreels of the first experimental airplanes collapsing. The icy white of Challenger's explosion against the bright, clear blue sky still hung in her mind's eye.

Benedict massaged the back of her neck. The heat from his hand, the texture of his skin, the strength of his fingers ceased some of her tension.

"Are you okay with this?"

"Um, maybe."

"They're not going to let you fall. They do this a couple of dozen times a day."

"What if the harness breaks?"

"It won't. Hey," Benedict called to one of the crew, "what's the weight limit on these harnesses? And how often to you inspect them?"

"We inspect them daily and they'll hold three hundred and sixty pounds."

"See?" Benedict hugged her. "No problems. It'll be good. You'll see."

Lycida let herself relax against his body. Standing next to him in the sunshine she realized last night's suspicion was true. He *had* lost weight since she first saw him last March. From the smooth, delineated muscles of a surfer, he had shrunk more into the thinner, wiry build of a marathon runner. She knew he bicycled. Idly, she wondered if he were in training for a triathlon with the combined swimming, bicycling, and running. As he had since she first saw him months earlier, he kept his head shaved. Now she saw very little body hair gleaming in the sunlight.

She mentally shrugged. Athletics were so damn obsessive. Even back in the first days of the Olympics, she knew athletics who kept their body shaved to help keep down wind resistance.

The crew was unbuckling the pair who they'd just pulled in from their float across the bay. The couple chattered excitedly, but Lycida didn't listen.

She watched the parachute billow off the back of the boat. Its primary colors shone vividly against the slate blue bay water.

"Come on." Benedict tugged her hand. Numbly,

she followed him to the back of the boat and sat
where the crewmembers indicated.

Deftly, they double-checked the cinched and
tightened straps around her and Benedict, then
hooked up the parachute to them.

"Hey," one of the crew caught her eye, "you
know, we won't send you up too far right at the
beginning. If it bothers you, we can haul you right
back in. If you need something to hang onto, use these
straps here." He grabbed the straps in front of her.

"You don't need the straps, Lucy. You can hang
onto me," Benedict generously offered and covered
her fist clenched around the strap with his hand.

Damnation. Flying in airplanes never bothered
her. She loved sitting on her balcony and looking over
the Gulf of Mexico. She even liked roller coasters.

But this felt so fragile. The wide nylon parachute
billowed behind them. They were held onto it by no
more than a bunch of wide webbed straps. When they
got in the air, they were going to be totally dependent
on these straps and that nylon.

Once again she remembered the screams of
Daedalus and Icarus while Icarus plunged into the sea
below them. Even if she fell into the bay, she was
immortal and death didn't happen to the immortals.
But damn it, she didn't want Benedict to die.

Benedict ran a hand across her cheek. "This is
going to be fun."

Lycida pried one hand off the strap and held
Benedict's hand. Grimly, she reminded herself this
was a nylon parachute held by strong straps,
emphasizing the *strong* to herself. This wasn't made of

wax and feathers and had no chance of melting in the sun. She wasn't escaping The Labyrinth of King Minos of Crete.

She was going to ride up in the air with this man who made her blood boil. Her big concern needed to only be she had no chance of joining the mile-high club with him. In the first place, the parachute didn't go up that high. In the second place, as much as she wanted him, she wasn't going to condemn him to death for having sex with her.

"I'm okay." Lycida swallowed. "Let's go."

"Pick up your feet then. Ready? Launch." With that, the crew released their hold on the straps and the winch holding the cable to the parachute.

Almost before Lycida had time to blink, they slid across the smooth back of the boat and were in the air. She glanced down at the boat suddenly ten feet below them.

"Okay?" the crew chief yelled.

"Okay," Lycida yelled back.

The crew released more of the cable and the chief revved the boat's engine. Within moments, the faces watching them were tiny blobs.

"Look down there," Benedict said.

Lycida followed the direction of his finger. A pod of five dolphins streaked and breached through the water.

"Wave at the people on the bridge." Benedict waved with his free hand, the other still holding Lycida's hand.

The metal die-cast vehicles toy stores carried for children to play with loomed in size comparison to the ones on the bridge. Lycida didn't even bother to look for the occupants' faces. She just waved also.

"There's my bar. Look how small your condo is. Look at the Gulf."

The boat pulling them turned in a circle.

Benedict continued a running commentary. "Lighthouse looks like a toy. And over there, across the ship channel, is Boca Chica, the last of the mainland of Texas south coast. Have you been over there yet?'

"No, not yet." Lycida relaxed enough to realize the harness that felt so awkward when fastened around her thighs and across her back now fitted as comfortably as an old porch swing. She watched a dozen brown pelicans fly in a V underneath them. How lovely that a bird on the borderline of extinction no longer held a place on endangered species list.

"I'll take you. It's great for shell hunting."

"That's nice."

"It's still pretty much a wild beach like South Padre near the Port Mansfield ship channel. We can stand at the mouth of the Rio Grande. My truck has four-wheel drive. We can drive to Brownsville, then out to Boca Chica from there."

"Benedict."

"I thought though, after we finish this, we can go to the water park for awhile. Then we can take a drive north up the beach and have a picnic supper."

"Benedict," Lucy shouted, "will you be quiet just a few minutes?"

"Huh?"

"Let's just sit here and enjoy this peacefulness for

this moment. Look at the sunlight dancing across the bay, the clouds' shadows sliding across it, changing its colors. Listen to the quiet. Relax."

As many times as Benedict had been parasailing, never had he had a woman he was with tell him to be quiet. They always wanted to chatter about the view, about the landscape in miniature. Way up here, they didn't even hear the motors of the vehicles on the bridge and the boats below them, much less the calls of the seagulls and pelicans flying beneath them.

Quiet wasn't something Benedict liked. It gave him time to think. Right now, he didn't want to think. He had too much he didn't want to think about. He wanted distractions.

But then Lucy was quite a distraction herself. He draped his arm across her shoulders and Lucy wrapped her arm across his back. Her skin was soft and smooth, her shoulder under his hand reminded him of how cuddly her body was. Pity they were tied in these harnesses and he wasn't able to really cuddle her. But he'd fix that later. One step at a time.

To his pleasure, she leaned sideways and rested her head on his shoulder. Her hair, tied back in a ponytail against her neck, smelled of oranges. If she had on a sunscreen, she hadn't used one of those with the too sweet scent of fake coconut that so many of the sun lotions had.

The silence settled down into his ears with only the slightest wisp of wind whistle.

He grew aware of the sound of his breathing and matched it to Lucy's. His heart kept pumping. Today, this moment, he was still alive and had a warm armful of happy girl.

He tilted her head upward. Her eyes crinkled when she smiled at him. He leaned around the harness straps and gave her plenty of time to draw back.

Lucy opened her mouth to his kiss. Her tongue slid around his welcoming him into her mouth, inviting her into her soul.

His vow to just be friends with her and not to push her into a fast fuck started to crumple with the taste of her mouth. Every atom in his body wanted to feel bit of her skin.

She sucked his tongue deep into her mouth and swirled her tongue around it. His imagination went straight to his cock.

He saw himself stretched out on the bed while Lucy put her head between his legs and sucked his cock the way she now savored his tongue. In his imagination, he saw how she might kneel on the bed and let her tits rub against his belly while she deep-throated him.

In his mind's eye, he saw her honey colored skin next to his. His palms ached to feel the shape of her ass. His fingers twitched to stroke her cunt and feel how wet she was.

Lucy continued to eat his tongue the way he wanted her to eat his dick. If he was able to ever persuade her to have sex with him, he promised himself the first thing he wanted to do was to taste and eat her pussy the way he now tasted her mouth.

Resolutely he kept his hands on her shoulders. His cock already strained against his shorts. If his hands got to roaming her body, he might embarrass himself when they landed back at the boat. He didn't think he had time to jack off while they were up here. The crew was probably ready to begin hauling them in soon.

Hell and damnation, why had he gone and bought her that skimpy bikini? He was going to explode at the water park when she wore it. The water park, with all the kids around, was absolutely no place for him to be able to have a jack-off in the Men's Room.

Firmly, he reminded himself he wanted Lucy as his friend. He was going to resist this temptation. Then, when they got far enough to have sex, it was going to be all that much better.

He just hoped it was a "when," not an "if."

As Lucy ended the kiss, Benedict realized Lucy was rapidly spoiling him for other women. He wanted "when" to be soon.

"Oh." Lucy's eyes grew large when she realized how far down the boat crew had pulled them.

"Do you want to drop into the water before they pull us in or stay dry?"

"It's so hot, we'll probably dry off before we get back to the dock. Let's drop all the way in."

"The deepest we'll go is waist-deep." *Which should be enough to cool his dick and get some shrinkage before they landed back on the boat.*

As if she read his mind, Lucy glanced at his crotch then grinned. "That's probably a good idea. It'll cool us off for awhile."

Hours later, Benedict still needed cooling off. He

was definitely glad of the cold water in the water park's artificial river. He hung onto a large plastic floater and let the jet propelled current push him around, keeping his waist below water level, once again hoping for shrinkage.

Lucy balanced in an inner tube while she floated. Her face lifted to the sun as though she were a flower drinking in its rays.

To his surprise, she hadn't balked in the least at the bikini he bought her. She stepped out of the Ladies changing room with the expertise of a professional stripper flaunting her body for the crowd.

When Benedict's mind came back into focus, he glanced around at the people milling about. Sure, there were a few sneers, mainly from some teenage girls, while she walked toward him, her body jiggling and bouncing with each step, but there were also a number of appreciative looks from other men. A couple of women looked appreciative, not to mention downright envious. Benedict figured they were sorry they hadn't opted for a bikini.

They'd done some of the water slides and water equivalent to roller coasters, but they'd spent most of the time just floating along the artificial river. Inconsequential conversations mixed easily with deeply philosophical ones.

Like during the parasailing, throughout the afternoon, Lucy stopped him in mid-sentence to direct him to concentrate and focus on different things.

Through her enjoyment, he saw the different

colors in flowers he never noticed before. Before Lucy, he hadn't noticed the shapes of clouds blowing across the sky since he was a child. Ice cream tasted better than it had in years. Lucy's joy in life even made the normally crabby kids tolerable.

Now, floating in the inner tube, Lucy's body once again was sending him into testosterone overload. Her boobs filled and overflowed the bikini's top, her nipples crinkled into tight buds from the water's chill or maybe she was as turned on as he was.

Her belly rounded with softness that made him itch to stroke it. Earlier, he watched her smooth sunscreen across her breasts, belly, and down her arms and legs. His tongue stuck to the roof of his mouth at the sight of her touching herself.

He jumped at the chance when she asked him to put sunscreen on her back for her. He managed, just barely, to keep his hands from rubbing lotion under the bikini bottom. He wasn't able to see her ass at the moment, but she climbed the stairways to the tops of the slides and water roller coaster rides in front of him. Several times they stood so he was able to put his arms around her and pull her close to him so he was able to feel her ass against his cock.

"Um, Lucy?"

She smiled over at him.

"Are you ready to go? The picnic supper I ordered will probably be ready to be picked up now."

"Sure. I'm getting hungry. How far up the Island were you thinking about going?"

Benedict looked into Lucy's shining eyes and

knew he wasn't going to be able to lie to her. "I was thinking about the nude beach."

Lucy flipped herself upright and pulled off the inner tube. She made her way to the ladder out of the artificial river.

Benedict followed her slowly. Kids, teenagers, and adults floated around him laughing and yakking.

Benedict knew he'd blown it with her. He'd apologize for suggesting the nude beach. They'd just have their picnic on the public area.

Lucy turned around at the top of the ladder. Water sheeted down her body and made it glow in the sun.

"Well," she said with a smile, "are you getting out of the water or not? It's a long drive to the nude beach."

Chapter Five

For the most part, Benedict kept his truck on the damp, smooth sand of the tide line, but occasionally debris or driftwood logs forced him to churn through the dry, loose sand. He tried to keep his mind off the near future with Lucy not even wearing the scanty bikini, but that was like telling himself not to breath.

Lucy and her abundant body sat within an arm's length of him, safely fastened in the passenger side seat belt. He wished he was able to touch her, but he needed both hands on the steering wheel to get through the sand.

At the moment, she wore the bikini top with a long scarf thing tied around her hips like a skirt. He almost regretted letting the salesgirl talk him into buying it when he bought the bikini. It covered her thighs and down to her ankles. Then, when he hit a bump, it slipped open like a mini strip show to reveal her golden thighs before Lucy readjusted it.

With the need to watch the debris and twist the steering wheel through the soft sand, he just got quick glimpses of Lucy. Whenever he did glance at her, her attention was riveted on the waves crashing on the sandbars, on the seagulls standing in formation which they broke only long enough for Benedict to drive past. She waved at the fishermen and families enjoying the surf and solitude away from the county park manicured beach.

"Stop at the shrimp boat, please." Lucy hauled a large squashy tote bag from the backseat of the club cab. She rummaged in it and triumphantly hauled out a camera. "I want to take some more photos of it. I'm working on it up in strained glass."

"I didn't know you did stained glass."

"There's a lot you don't know about me."

Benedict didn't understand the dry note in Lucy's voice, but easily replied, "That's one of the reasons I suggested we spend the day together. So we can get to know more about each other."

"I thought you said you wanted to spend the day with me so you could show me what a gorgeous body I have."

"That, too." *Oh, yeah,* his groin agreed when he looked over at her boobs barely contained in the bikini top.

He'd had a hard-on most of the day, but managed to mostly conceal it or shrink it in cold water. Oh, hell. He might as well admit it to Lucy. It was going to be visible soon anyway.

"Once we reach the nude beach, you'll see exactly how much I appreciate your gorgeous body."

He spotted the shrimp boat, wrecked and pushed onto the tide line during a winter storm, now almost covered by sand. The masts stood above the waves, nearly the only part still visible. He parked the truck and then joined Lucy at the wave edge.

She studied the battered shrimp boat as though it was the finest piece of sculpture she ever saw.

"It's just a wrecked boat."

"No," Lucy said firmly. "Look at it. Watch the way the waves hit the masts. Watch how the spray flies off the rigging and scatters in the sunlight."

Benedict watched the surf come in and hit the boat. The spray didn't look special to him. It was just water bouncing off the wires angling down from the masts.

The waves foamed with a crashing slosh. Seagulls quarreled and called. Time stretched while they stood quietly watching the sea and sand slowly bury the boat deeper with each wave.

Lucy lifted her camera and began taking photos.

"I saw the photos of this boat at *The Sinking Ship*. Did you name the bar after it?"

"No, I named the bar months before this happened. A friend took and framed the picture. He thought I needed some local color in with all the pictures of famous boats that have sunk." He watched the wind plaster Lucy's skirt against her butt. He hoped when he got her to the nude beach he was going to be allowed to cover her ass with sunscreen. Despite it being late afternoon, it was still hot and the sun was pretty intense.

His cock twitched at the thought of Lucy's bare ass in his hands. It throbbed harder at the realization that he needed her to rub sunscreen on his own butt.

While he spent the day touching Lucy as much as he was able to get away with in public, she only occasionally touched him. He definitely needed her help putting on sunscreen, all over his body.

"Why did you name the bar *The Sinking Ship*?"

Like a lovesick hound dog sniffing after a female in heat, Benedict followed Lucy around the water's edge while she took photos from different angles. He watched her handle the camera, adjusting focus and the zoom attachments like a pro. He wondered if he might ever feel her fingers dance along his dick as decisively as they twiddled the length of the camera lens.

No, first he wanted her for a friend, he ordered his dick. His cock pulsed telling him he was such a liar. Resolutely, he reminded himself he had a brain, not just a cock. He also promised her he wasn't going to push her for sex today. If he wanted Lucy for a friend, he needed to ignore his dick and reengage his tongue before he started drooling. What had she asked? Oh, yeah.

"Just thought it sounded good. At lot of people come into a bar thinking their lives are out of control and they're standing on the deck of a sinking ship." *Like me,* Benedict glumly thought. "In the bar, they relax, enjoy the other people, forget their troubles for awhile."

"I go to visit with people." Lucy stowed her camera back into her bag. They went to the truck.

"You always look like you're having fun. People like to be around you."

In the truck, Lucy refastened her seatbelt. "I like people. No one is the same and very few people are totally unlikable."

"You always look like you're having fun."

"I try to enjoy each moment. Every moment is different. Every thing is different. It makes life more enjoyable when each moment is savored for its uniqueness."

"Don't you ever get down?"

"Of course, but I don't let myself dwell on it."

Like he tried not to dwell on the cancer growing throughout his body despite all the treatments. For a few brief months, everyone celebrated the remission. But now....

"How do you cope with the blues?" *Shit*, even he heard the desperation in his voice and Lucy was more perceptive than most people.

Without looking at her, he knew by the smalls sounds Lucy had twisted in the seat to look at him.

"What's wrong?"

"Nothing." Benedict focused on getting through the sand. "Don't worry about it."

"Why don't you stop at that big stand of dunes?"

"Is this a ploy to delay me from seeing you naked?"

Lucy's laughter curled around him as comfortable as an old pair of workout pants and tee shirt.

"No. I want to take some photos of the dune plants and the way the sand flows for one of my projects."

"Is this more of the stained glass? Are you a hobbyist? Or trying to make a living at it? Hell, I don't even know what you do for a living. When I first saw you, I thought you were a perpetual college student playing on Daddy's money."

"I'm older than I look," Lucy said with another laugh. "But, yes, I do have trust accounts and don't have to work. However, my stained glass artwork is already bringing in a good income. I've had several excellent gallery displays. I make it to please me, but I'm happy others like it so much."

"I'd like to see it," Benedict pulled to stop at the

base of the dunes.

They got out of the car. To his pleasure and agony, Lucy left her skirt in the truck. He let her lead the way so he was able to watch her butt as she climbed. They worked their way up the slippery slope, being careful not to grab the grasses and rip them from their delicate hold.

Midway to the top, Lucy stopped and sat in the sand.

"You okay?" he sat down beside her, grateful to have a chance to catch his own breath.

"Fine, just a breather. I'll never make it as a mountain climber again."

Benedict put his head between his knees and breathed deeply. "I guess this means the trip to Mount Everest is out."

"Been there, done that," Lucy said with an airy wave of her hand. "Cold. Prefer heat myself."

She unhitched her camera from its protective case and used it to take some careful photos of the twisting morning glory vines. She replaced the camera and stood. "To the top now."

Once again they carefully climbed in order to not disturb the dune's fragile vegetation.

"This wouldn't be such a bad trek," Lucy gasped when they reached the top, "if there was something to hold onto and the sand wasn't so hot."

"And this is late May," Benedict said with a gasp. "Wait until August." "My feet and legs feel burned already. Impossible to do this without long pants in August." Lucy brushed sand from her knees and calves. "Probably end up with major burns.

"And heatstroke. Of course, pants would guarantee heatstroke."

"No shit."

They sat in a hollow near the top of the dune and watched the waves continue to roll in. While it cooled his hot, sticky skin, the breeze brought the smell of decaying kelp on the tide line along with the familiar scent of salt water. Sea grasses rustled in the light wind.

Gradually, Benedict became aware some of his tension eased and part of his constant depression lifted.

"When I'm blue," Lucy's quiet voice simply added to his easy, peaceful feeling, "I think about moments like this. The sound of the waves. The pattern of the dune grass leaves on the sand when the wind blows it. The shape of the sand itself."

Benedict never before noticed the thin lines drawn by the tips and edges of the grass bending across the sand. He realized the wind had blown the sand not held in place by the plants into a wave like pattern with a knife-edge ridge at the very top of the dune beside them.

"I focus on happy memories. Like the taste of my favorite foods and drinks."

"Strawberry margaritas," he said. "What about the people in your life?"

"Them, too. But also strangers. Like the toddler we saw at the water park who had on the Tinker Bell bathing suit and looked like a little fairy herself. She'll be one of my happy memories."

"Like Peter Pan, you think happy thoughts?"

"Yes, because every day can have a bit of pleasure in it. Even sad moments."

Benedict's memory sent him the feel of his sisters' hands clasping his when the doctors confirmed the remission had ended. He had to be strong for them throughout their teens, raising them after their parents' deaths. Now, without their continual strength and support, he would have swallowed his bottle of Valium and all the pain pills at one time months ago. He owed it to them to live out the rest of his days, no matter how much pain and crap he was going to have to go through.

Lucy continued talking, "But mainly I concentrate on the happy days. Like today has been."

She smiled again at Benedict. The last of his depression scattered the way the water droplets shattered against the masts of the wrecked shrimp boat.

Lycida saw the haunted look leave Benedict's face. His light brown eyes held hers. She knew he was going to kiss her. Kissing him was not something that was good for her peace of mind. Oh, goddesses, she wanted him to kiss her again.

His mouth settled on hers with the gentleness of the brush of butterfly wings, just the lightest of pressure that silently promised more if asked.

She asked. She slid the tip of her tongue along the seam of his lips, then welcomed the warm wetness of his mouth. Their tongues tangled and embraced.

Her clit ached for the heavy pressure of his penis deep inside, retreating and thrusting as his tongue did now. Her nipples grew tighter. Her breasts swelled.

She needed his hands on her, holding her breasts, thumbing her nipples. She was dizzy with heated desire.

Benedict was being the damn gentleman and keeping to his promise about not pushing her for sex. Her body was screaming for his touch. She wasn't going to be able to enjoy his dick, but she might get a bit of release. She knew was making a big mistake, but she did it anyway.

She reached between their bodies and released the bikini's fastening between her breasts. Her breasts hung heavy and free of their constraint. Being no fool, Benedict filled his hands with them.

She eased back into the hot, stinging sand to lie down. Benedict followed her down, still kissing her, his hand kneading her breasts.

He pulled back from her mouth and gazed at her. She lifted her arms above her head offering her beasts to him. She'd seen that look of absorbed adoration on people's faces when they looked at *Michelangelo's Pietá,* when they looked at the *Mona Lisa,* at weddings when the bride and groom looked at each other.

She memorized the incredible sight of his face. No man had ever looked at her with that much joy before. She felt honored and blessed.

Benedict stroked her body starting at the top of her bikini panty. His fingers skimmed across her skin sending shivers throughout her. Her cunt flooded with moisture.

His hands were on her breasts. He cupped them and cradled them with sublime gentleness. Then he released them. Before she moved, his index fingers lightly circled the outside edges of her areoles. They tightened impossibly hard as he slowly moved up to her nipples finally stroking them and lifting them into peaks.

He looked into her face as though asking permission, then slowly, so slowly Lycida thought she was going to scream, took a nipple into his mouth. First he simply held it in his mouth while his hand kept circling the other nipple. Then his tongue began to flick across it.

Lycida rubbed her aching pussy against his thigh when he began to suckle her nipple. She needed to stop this. She was the ultimate tease, she criticized herself, especially when he changed sides and suckled the other nipple leaving the first wet one open to the sea breeze.

His hand dipped below the elastic of the bikini panty and slid into the slick wetness of her cunt. Deftly he slid his fingers between her folds all the while sucking on first one nipple, then the other.

Her body started to come apart. Shudders of fire rippled through her. She wanted to open her legs to give him full access. She wanted to come.

This wasn't fair to Benedict. She wasn't going to give him back what he was giving her. She had to stop this. She couldn't let herself take this pleasure when she wasn't going to give it back.

With every part of her body screaming, her body spiraling to hot orgasm, she wrenched herself from him.

"Stop. No more," she ordered.

Chapter Six

"Lucy."

"No." She ignored the raw hunger in Benedict's voice. She fumbled at the bikini top. She needed to pull it together and get away from him. She needed to pull herself together.

Damn, damn, damn it all to hell. Damn her for letting this get out of hand. Damn her for letting him get his hands on her. Damn her for having sex with Damian in the first place knowing Artemis had expressly forbidden it.

Damn this fastener on this damn bikini. She blinked back tears of rage and tried to focus on the damn clip.

Benedict's hands came over her shaking hands and hooked the bikini together.

Lycida hastily blinked away more tears.

Men cursed and raged at her for taking them to the brink, then backing away. Men walked away from her at that point.

Men didn't touch her hair or apologize in a gentle voice, "I'm sorry. It's too open here. Everybody driving past is able to see what we almost did."

Lucy stood and dusted off sand. "I want to go home now."

She picked up her camera case and started down the dune face. Her legs shook. Her breasts ached. Her cunt still wept with twinges of heat, wanting, screaming for the touch of a hand, the pressure and stretch of a penis filling her.

She heard the shush of sand behind her while Benedict followed.

When she got to the truck, she pulled the shorts and baggy tee shirt she worn parasailing out of the backseat of the club cab. She kicked off her flip-flops and put on the loose clothes to cover the bikini. She dusted off her feet and put the flimsy flip-flops back on. When she got in the front seat, she wrapped the sarong around her shoulders like a shawl.

Benedict got behind the steering wheel. He had put on a tee shirt himself. He started the engine and turned to her. "I guess this means the nude beach is out, huh."

Lycida saw no reason to respond. She watched the waves. She always loved the sea.

The waves rose and banged on the shoreline. Other days, only ripples slid across the water. She'd seen blue ice glaciers and swum at the Great Barrier Reef. The deep blue of what was now called the Mediterranean still remained her favorite shade of blue.

Wherever she lived, she tried to live on the ocean side. In her lifetime, she'd been on ships where for days nothing was visible but the ocean. From her balcony, she watched the sunrise across the water, tinting the sky from navy to bright yellow.

On the nights of the full moon, she stood by the water's edge. Artemis' chariot shone silver-white on the water. Its reflection stretched across the water as though it were a pathway to tempt and tease Lycida with what she never was to have again.

Although for years she tried to blame Damian for enticing her into welcoming him into her body, she knew she had only herself to blame for Artemis' anger. She was the one who had taken the vow to be Artemis' handmaiden. If she had gone to Artemis for permission, Artemis would have released her from service.

But, no, she was selfish. She wanted both: the power and prestige of serving a goddess and the earthiness of sex.

She was not going to be selfish with Benedict. She experienced many orgasms with men through the years, men whom she never repaid for the pleasure they gave her. Like women through the millennia, some men also were available for a price. Men who did her biding, gave her orgasms, but whom she gave nothing in return.

She wasn't going to treat Benedict like that. He deserved better. He needed a nice woman who loved him and made him happy. He was not a human sex toy for her use and pleasure.

Lost in her brooding, it caught her by surprise to realize Benedict had already pulled up to her condo building. After they used her security card to open the gate, he drove to the visitors' area and parked.

"Am I going to get to see you again?"

"No," Lucy said firmly.

"What happened?" Benedict asked, trying to keep a rein on his temper. Raising his two younger sisters taught him that yelling just led to tears and tight lips. "You're not a virgin."

For the first time since he met her, Lucy's laugh

held a bitter note. She undid her seatbelt and opened the door. "No. Not for years."

A horrible thought flashed through his mind. He grabbed her hand before she managed to get out of the truck. "Oh, God, Lucy. You were raped, weren't you?"

"No! Oh, Benedict." Her eyes were soft and gentle. She leaned over and stroked his cheek. "No, I've never been raped. I just can't make love to you. There's things about me you don't know. Things I can't tell you. Don't ask me to."

She placed her fingers on his mouth. "Before you ask. No, I don't have AIDS either. It's nothing medical and nothing you can help with. It's my burden, part of my life. Have a good life, Benedict."

Still looking at him with a sweetness he never saw before, Lucy swung her legs out the door. She stepped down and screamed.

Benedict shot out of the truck and to the passenger side where Lucy had sat on the truck's door jam. Blood poured from the arch of her foot where a jagged wedge of brown glass had gone straight through her plastic flip-flops and into her foot.

Benedict kicked the rest of the broken beer bottle to the curb edge. He held her ankle firmly and jerked the glass from her sandal and foot. He grabbed a bottle of water from the cooler holding the uneaten picnic supper and poured it over Lucy's foot.

"Let me get a towel and wrap a pressure bandage. The clinic's closed by now, but I'll take you to the fire department. The paramedics can put a better bandage on it so I can drive you to the emergency room."

"Benedict." Lucy had her hand pressed against the deep cut. "It's okay. Don't worry about it."

"Lucy, look at this glass." He held it up in the light of the dying sunset. "There's blood at least two inches down it. You might have torn ligaments in there. You definitely need stitches and a tetanus shot."

"No, I don't. See? It's already stopped bleeding. I'm fine. I'm up-to-date on my tetanus shot anyway."

Benedict stared from the broken glass in his hand to Lucy's foot. She poured more water over it and even the last bit of oozing washed away.

"Lucy, what is going on here?"

"Um, I'm a fast healer. It just bled a lot. It wasn't as deep as you thought."

"Don't bullshit me, Lucy. I pulled out the damn glass. I know how deep it was. What's happening to your foot?" Even as he spoke he saw by the truck cab's light that the jagged line where the glass had gone in was now fading.

Lucy bit her lower lip.

"Lucy."

"Hell," Lucy said with a sigh. "I really like living here. I hate like hell to have to move again."

"Why do you have to move? What the fuck is going on?"

"I'm going to tell you something I've never told anyone. But I think I kind of owe you an explanation. You can't tell anyone, not that they'll believe you anyway. I'll be gone by morning. You won't see me again. I have a lot of practice at disappearing."

"Lucy." The woman was making him crazy. Even his sisters at their most unstable, hormonal rampages in their teens didn't make him this nuts.

She looked at him solemnly. "I am immortal. The cut healed fast because I can't die. I've lived since before the Greeks began exploring philosophy."

"Oh, right, sure."

Lucy laughed, the deep throaty laugh that always made his dick hard.

"I knew you wouldn't believe me." She took the broken glass from him and, before he was able to stop her, ripped opened her wrist. She gave a hiss of pain, then set the glass on the truck cab floor. "Watch and don't touch it."

Benedict stood beside the truck and watched the tear stop bleeding and heal in a matter of minutes. His stomach churned. *Why her? Why did she get to live forever? He was dying. Why did she lie forever and he have to die before he saw his sisters marry, have children. Before he married and had children.*

"I was a handmaiden to the goddess Artemis."

"Why are you living here? Now?" *Why wasn't he going to live longer?*

Lucy's face twisted with grief. "The key word is *maiden*. Suffice it to say that when I got curious about sex and no longer qualified as maiden, Artemis threw me off Mount Olympus. But not to be mortal, to wander the earth forever to have sex whenever I wanted to."

"And the problem with that is?" Benedict didn't give a shit why Lucy was sad. "Sounds to me like everybody's dream. As much sex as you want and living forever. Your life so sucks. Excuse me for not being sympathetic."

"There's a catch. There's always a catch when the gods and goddesses give you a gift. Any man who has sex with me, whose penis entered my vagina, dies. Like a black widow spider, having sex with me kills men."

Lucy studied his face. "I knew you wouldn't believe me. I didn't believe Artemis' curse at first either. Between wars and diseases, it took me awhile to realize what was happening. Every man who ever has sex with me dies. They don't have a heart attack and die during intercourse. Wait, one did, but he was eighty-nine and had a dicey heart anyway. But, they've all died through the years. The longest a man lived after having sex with me was a year."

"But you still go on living." Benedict didn't care about living forever. He just wanted to live longer, like to be eighty-nine and die in the middle of a great fuck.

"Yeah. I do." Lucy's body drooped when she got out of the truck and picked up her flip-flop from where he tossed it when he took the glass from her foot. She put it on and gathered her tote bag and camera case. "Have a good life, Benedict."

She pressed her lips to his, but Benedict refused to kiss her. She had life ahead of her. He didn't. He watched her walk to the condo entrance, but she didn't turn around.

Back in his truck, he drove aimlessly up the main drag. Neon lights shone from restaurants and bars.

He passed his own and automatically noted the locals' vehicles filling all the parking slots. Miniature golf was in full swing. He kept driving north and turned off the pavement to the beach. The masts of the wrecked shrimp boat gleamed in his headlights.

Once again he parked at the bank of dunes. He pulled on a pair of blue jeans he had in the backseat of the club cab and picked up a denim jacket against the night wind.

He sat in the shelter of the dunes, in the hollow where Lucy offered her breasts for him to enjoy. He thought of the look on her face when she lifted her arms and her breasts spilled out from the bikini top. In the sunlight, her breasts were golden, the areoles like dark pink roses, the nipples sweet buds made for his mouth. Briefly, he tasted paradise and touched the slickness of her cum.

The moon rose lighting a shining pathway across the water.

He was alive at this moment. The waves and he shared the moonlight. The waves rolled onto the shore the way they had since before he existed and would after he was gone. This moment with the dunes, the surf, the moon, the smell of kelp and seawater, the gritty sand under his feet and hands, this moment mattered. Not tomorrow, not yesterday. Only this moment.

Each moment needed to be treasured for its own special goodness. A wise woman told him that.

Benedict knew what he had to do. He rose from the sand and stretched, amazed anew at how his body was assembled. He was unique, just like everyone else.

He drove back to town, stopping along the way to watch the spray bounce off the wreck's rigging. Each drop was different, catching the moonlight differently, falling back into the waves at different angles. When he got to the pavement at the county park area, he called Lucy's cell phone.

"Lucy? Can I come up and talk to you? There's something about me I need to tell you."

"I'm sorry. We have nothing to discuss. I've got a plane to catch in the morning. Have a good life."

"Lucy, that's the thing. I don't have much life left. What I've got left will be better if I can make some happy moments with you. I have cancer. I'm dying."

Lucy was so quiet Benedict started to panic that they'd been disconnected. Then her voice came back on the line. "Call me when you get to the security gate and I'll buzz you in."

Lucy solemnly greeted him at the door of her condo and led him to the secluded balcony. Although they had a view of the Gulf, the balcony situated so no one in other condos, walking along the beach, or at the hotels was able to see them.

Benedict explained how he raised his sisters after their parents died, his brief law career, then the diagnosis, treatment, temporary remission, and now re-emergence of the cancer. When she suggested experimental treatments, he told her the names of his doctors and the hospitals he'd been at and made her realize everything had been tried.

"Lucy, will you marry me?"

Stunned amazement washed across her face. "But why?"

Benedict walked around the table and knelt at her side. "Because from you I've learned to enjoy life. And I'll enjoy it even more with you with me. It's not like you're going to kill me. Hell, my body's already dying. But I realize now that this moment, each moment is special. I love you. I want to spend my moments with you. Will you marry me? Please?"

Lycida wrapped her arms around him. This was important to him. Despite the other men who asked her to marry them, she never said the vows. They wanted her to be their exclusive property.

But Benedict was different. He looked into her eyes and saw her, what was important to her, the joy of living each day.

"Yes. I'll marry you."

They tossed cushions from the chairs onto the floor and there on the balcony, in the moonlight, Benedict lifted the silk caftan from her body, then stripped off his own clothes.

He turned her slowly around and studied every inch of her skin, first with his eyes, then his fingers. He eased her onto the pillows, licked, and tasted from her toes to the tips of her ears. When he suckled her breasts, Lycida thought her body was going to explode in flames. Then he turned her over and licked down her back to swirl his tongue around her rump. Her body jerked and shuddered under his hands and tongue eager for him to touch her cunt. Her moisture drenched her thighs.

She started to lift herself to her knees, but he

said, "Wait."

He rolled her to her back, then moved her around until her body was in line with the full moon.

Benedict spread her knees wide apart and smiled at what he saw. He moved to her side, then drew a finger through her wet folds. Her cum flowed thicker, hotter.

"This woman whose legs are opened before you, Artemis, is the woman of my heart." Benedict dipped his fingers deeper into her and held them up. In the moonlight, they glistened with her cum. "Your curse on her joy will not harm me."

Benedict moved between her knees, then lifted her butt. He put his mouth on her cunt, his tongue probed deeply, his mouth sucking ands savoring. Lycida grasped the cushions under her, wildfire whipped through her.

He lifted his face to the moonlight. His lips and chin gleamed with her moisture. "Artemis, I vow to you. This woman I will treasure, enjoy, and love all the days of my life."

Lycida wiggled herself out of Benedict's hands. She knelt in front of him. She filled her hands with his burgeoning penis. She took his penis into her mouth and sucked. He groaned and jerked. She swallowed the first bit of his cum, then looked to the moon.

"Artemis, just as he has taken the woman's moisture of my body into his being, I have now swallowed his man fluid. Artemis, this man is the man of my heart. I will treasure, enjoy, and love this man for all the moments we have together. The moments with him will remain with me until Eternity ends."

In the moonlight, Benedict entered her body. Lycida's heart opened to receive him as easily as her body accepted his. Joined together, they climbed the spiral of heat and passion until their very beings became one and danced, for the moment, along the silver pathway to the moon. At that moment, they knew love lasted eternity.

*****

To all world news wire services: Astronomers announced today photos from the Hubble Telescope confirmed the new star in the constellation Orion is actually a nova more than a million light years away. In accordance with tradition, the astronomer who first discovered the nova has named it. His choice is 'Benedict' in honor of Pope Benedict the Sixteenth. Benedict is most easily viewed on the nights of the new moon.

The waves continued to foam around the wrecked shrimp boat, the spray flying through the rigging. Lycida stood at the shoreline watching the stars, gazing at Orion as he and his dog chased the stag through the star spangled sky.

"Greetings."

Artemis' voice didn't startle her. She'd been expecting Artemis ever since she first heard of the new star in Orion's constellation.

"Thank you for giving Benedict a place in the constellations."

"You are welcomed. It honored me to be presented with your vows to each other. A great love such as he had for you should be honored the way Orion's love for me has been honored all this time. However, after you exchanged vows with Benedict in the mortal ceremony with his mortal family and friends watching, you had no need to tell him of my offer to extend his life if you became mortal. That was my gift to you. He had no need to know."

Even without looking at her, Lycida knew the great goddess was frowning. When Artemis made the offer, she tried to extract Lycida's vow not to tell Benedict. Lycida refused. She'd betrayed her vows to Artemis too many years ago. She had no intention of betraying her vows to Benedict. She took her eyes off Benedict's star for a moment and stood straighter to look into Artemis' eyes.

"Yes, I did have to tell him," she said, proud of herself for sounding decisive not defiant. "He knew there was no mortal cure for his disease. If he suddenly was healed, he would know that as an immortal I, a former handmaiden of the Artemis who is sister to Apollo the god of healing, must have had something to do with his cure. I gave Benedict my vows of honor and trust. Trust includes not lying to him. To not tell him of your offer was a lie by omission. I tried to convince him I was happy to become mortal. Being immortal among mortals has its drawbacks. I've lived so long, to actually see an end was a refreshing thought. But he chose not to let me."

"Lycida, my love," Benedict's voice still remained strong in her ears. "I don't want you to give up your immortality for me any more than I would want one of my sisters to sacrifice her life for me. It gives me peace to know you'll live forever, that my sisters will have children whom they'll tell about me. As long as you live, as long as the stories my sisters tell their children and grandchild remain, *memories of me forever live. Forever's a long time."*

"Benedict loved you greatly to not want you to give up immortality in exchange to extend his own life," Artemis said solemnly.

"Yes, but we had nearly a year together." Lycida looked up to Benedict's star again. It blurred monetarily and she blinked away her tears yet again. "And even though he's dead, I'll remain forever and cherish his memory as he asked me to."

A second woman walked out from the waves, her long hair streamed down to her knees.

Lycida smiled at her. "This is not a nude beach, Aphrodite. Perhaps you might conjure a robe."

Aphrodite snapped her fingers. Not only did a white terry cloth robe wrap around her body, but her hair dried.

"Do you wish to return to Mount Olympus?" Artemis asked Lycida.

Lycida peered at her in the dark. "I don't think virginity is retroactive."

"Not as her handmaiden," Aphrodite said with a laugh. "As one of mine."

"One of yours?"

"Yes," Artemis said. "It has taken you many centuries, but your love for Benedict and his love for you has finally taught you the importance of sex."

"Not just for the body pleasure," Lycida said slowly, "but for the joining of the inner being."

"Which is only accomplished through love," Aphrodite concluded. "Now you understand love. Perhaps you wish to be in my service? To help others learn the value of love? Someone is waiting for you."

Aphrodite waved her pale, ivory arm. The starlight showed brighter.

For the first time since she was banished, Lycida saw a glimpse of Mount Olympus. Amongst her friends, other handmaidens of Artemis and those who served other gods and goddesses stood the image of Benedict.

Made of glowing stars, he smiled down at her. His hand reached down to her, to lift her up to join him.

Every fiber in Lycida's being longed to go to him, this mortal man who showed her the value of love.

Lycida knew though that part of love is trust. Trust includes keeping promises. She had promises to keep. Her heart bled with pain, but she forced the words out. She had to keep her promises to him.

"Benedict asked me to keep watch on his sisters until they marry and are happy. I need to keep my promise to him."

Aphrodite and Artemis both breathed quick sighs.

"You truly have learned the importance of love," Artemis said. "The sacrifice you make to remain separated from Benedict until you have completed the task he has asked of you is a much greater sacrifice than giving up immortality for short lives for both of you."

"This solid love you demonstrate," Aphrodite said, "completes the process."

She waved her arm again.

Benedict's body solidified on Mount Olympus. No longer was he the glowing star being. Now his body was firm and healthy, as real as Aphrodite and Artemis standing beside her, as real as Lycida herself.

He smiled at her and nodded in agreement with her decision.

"When you have completed this task for Benedict and you are ready to join him, you will both serve me as examples of eternal love."

"Yes. Thank you." Lycida smiled back at Benedict knowing eventually she would be with him forever.

"You know how to contact us," Artemis said. "when you are ready."

The two goddesses walked into the starlight, leaving Lycida alone with her memories of moments with Benedict and her dreams of the eternity with him.

To learn more about Betty Hanawa visit

http://www.bettyhanawa.com

Look for her EPPIE & CAPA nominated

Falling Star Wish
On sale now.

And in January 2007, her award winning ebook

ONCE UPON A FAMILY

Comes to print.

For the best in both otherworld and real world
contemporary romance, come over to the wild side:
Triskelion Publishing
www.triskelionpublishing.net
All about women. All about extraordinary.

HEX & THE SINGLE (WEIRD) WERE-MONSTER
or

How Janice Got That Way

TERESE RAMIN

For Gail
Whose patience is Legion
and
For Kristi
Who never gives up

Notes:

[1] Refers to the poem, **"The Legend of Braugh Naughton" by Jennifer St. Giles**, at the beginning of *Bewitched, Bothered & Bevampyred*, *Season 1* (*Proceeds benefit the Red Cross disaster relief fund.*)

TO BEGIN WITH...

In which things that shouldn't happen to anybody, happen.

Once upon a time in a land called Up North there lived a bunch of natives called the *Pesquiwatamis*.

The *Pesquiwatamis* were descended from an exquisite blend of peoples. Among them were Mongols; some democratic Iroquois and Algonquins; a number of Ojibwa peoples; a few Micmacs and Mohawks; and various other native tribes. There were also quite a number of exiled Frenchman, (also known as French-Canadian trappers before they came down to da U.P., aka the Upper Peninsula and became Yoopers and Pesquiwatamis). To top *that* off, there was also a sizeable bunch of lumberjacks of indiscriminate origin and the odd Jesuit or fourteen. Eventually, (though not right away), some Finns, Swedes, a few lonely Norwegian bachelors and a number of copper miners joined the clan. (This is why the best pasties in the world still come from da U.P.)

Also mixed up among this exquisite blend of peoples was the occasional black bear or badger, a wolverine and perhaps a coyote, a hawk, a raven or an eagle and (of course) a wolf–among other mystical, but earthly, creatures....

Beyond that, there were, of course, Wendigos.

Due to the abundance of heritage and ancestry, there was an equal overabundance of philosophy, mythology and taboos to reconcile within each subsequent generation.

In plain English, that means the gods squabbled among themselves over which of them received top billing over everyone else, who governed what seasons, which of them held sway over what feasts, and what goddess got to be queen of the winter carnival. (This was important because Up North had a lot of Winter, so the title actually meant something and got used A Lot–unlike the title of say, Cherry Queen or Peach Queen or, worse yet, Wild Asparagus Queen. That one was particularly short-lived because if the asparagus was left to grow just one day too long, and you were given the stalk end to eat... Yech! It was woody, nasty and inedible.)

But the greatest battles took place over the simplest and most basic subjects of all: sowing and reaping; plowing, planting and harvesting; fallow and fertile fields–of all sorts...

And sex and sexibility.

Coyotes and like creatures were indiscriminately for it. Lonely Norwegian bachelors and (some) Jesuits (generally) against. Wolves and a few of the tribes and intermixed clans were for mating for life. The French-Canadian trappers (well the French) and a number of the lumberjacks were for having sex-with-someone available, period. This often meant having a wife of any sort was a good idea, so they sent away for one, kidnapped one, or bartered with a native tribe or a trader for one.

Wendigos, on the other hand, simply increased their numbers by biting, clawing, scratching and infecting whomever they wanted, so sex for them was sort of a side issue.

In short, where there wasn't any sex, and where

people were scarce, sex boiled down to a matter of procreation and species survival coupled with taboo and recreation.

Frankly, the gods not only got tired, but just plain bored out of their freaking minds of hearing about it all the time.

Now, many people believe desperation is the mother of invention. By the same token, boredom is the mother of all mischief. But boredom coupled with intelligence, a challenge and a dose of power is the mother of the worst (or best, depending upon your point of view) kind of mayhem: the creative kind.

And so it happened that the most intelligent and creative of the many deities grew bored and decided to fuck with their believers and non-believers alike by teaching them that The Almighty has a sense of humor even where sex, souls and shapeshifting are concerned.

To this end they decreed that the chief/queen/tribal leader/matriarch of the Pesquiwatamis should not be fully menopaused by her late seventies (they were an extremely hearty people, the Pesquiwatamis) and they put a flirty little bug in the breechcloth of her consort of nearly sixty years that some serious frisky might be in order. By the end of six weeks worth of "serious frisky", the matriarch and her eighty-year-old consort felt like kids in their teens again—

Until the matriarch started suffering flu-like symptoms every afternoon right about lunchtime, then thinking she was dying of some dread disease.

A consult with her life-long shaman suggested otherwise. The extremely elderly woman, who'd presided at not only the matriarch's birth and subsequent childhood illnesses, but the birth and illnesses of each of her children, (sons all, and therefore not eligible to run the tribe as males other than the consort–and even he was prone to the occasional wander–tended to sow seeds and roam willy-nilly without looking back) cackled at her in most un-shaman-like fashion. Then the shaman let the matriarch in on what the gods had done, and when she could expect the "blessed event" to arrive less than six months hence.

Gobsmacked and intimidated to be put in charge of such a "miracle" at her age, the flabbergasted matriarch recrossed the tribal compound to lay the news–and half the blame...er, *awesome responsibility*–on her consort...

Who immediately vowed to join the Jesuits at the earliest opportunity–right after he stopped gleefully boasting that he still had the stones to "pop one into the old lady" no matter how ancient they both were.

Meaning not only his testicles, but his late-seventies, un-menopaused tribal chief old lady.

Since pride has a habit of going before a fall, this was no doubt the reason the gods saw to it that he laughed himself right over the side of the tallest mountain (people from Out West where they have real mountains would probably call it an exceptionally high hill) in the U.P. less than a week later while embellishing his "fertile *cajones*" tale at his (ahem!) "old lady's" expense.

In due course the tribal matriarch–who interestingly enough began to feel younger, (and a helluva lot more sexy!) the more her pregnancy hormones kicked in, and despite her swelling feet, varicose veins, aching back, and a belly that made her feel the size of a bloated whale–dropped her child. The baby was a strapping, healthy, black-haired, black-eyed girl with prodigious lungs, an unnatural hand-grip and an almost frightening ability to look into a person's eyes and see straight into his soul from the moment the after-birth and mucous were wiped off of her. Even the gods were amazed–and half-afraid–to see what they'd wrought in the name of a good joke.

Still, they'd wrought it and they couldn't back up now; that would show cowardice. The very last thing the gods could do was show fear in front of a people who might already be braver than they were. Instead on the babe's public naming day, they sent down three of their most powerful gods with special "soul gifts" with which to imbue her.

When the shaman shook her turtle rattle over the infant and invoked the tribal spirit of the great she-wolf, then followed by summoning the spirits of the she-bear and the lioness, the first god entered the child and lit the flame of her mind, throat and belly, saying, "I give you the soul of a powerful warrior. None will overcome you unless you wish it. You will be truth, chastity and purity always, a great guardian, the most courageous of the brave even in the face of loneliness."

Then the god breathed eternal light through the flames so they would never die and retreated into the shadows at the edge of the circle where the mortals couldn't see.

The second god gave the first a look of huge disgust. "Truth, *chastity*, purity and courage in the face of loneliness? Why would you do that to anyone? Especially forever?"

The first god thumbed its nose at the second god. "Immortality is its own burden, why clutter it up? Do better."

"Easily," the second god snarled, thumping the side of a hand into the crook of the other elbow and causing that fist to jump skyward in an exceedingly rude gesture. "I am from an underground place that will eventually be called Seattle. I will make her the greatest legend their night creatures will ever know."

Then the second god settled into the infant's heart and lungs. With thumb and forefinger, it flicked the tiniest grain of pearl-sand into her loins (where it would take years–or possibly even centuries) to grow and ripen. Satisfied that the child would become a woman who could (eventually) feel *desire* instead of merely winding up the chaste, asexual warrior princess the other god seemed determined to make her, the second god then placed the embryo of a Second Soul inside a hot emerald-amethyst-topaz flame deep within the emotional center of her heart.

"There." Satisfied, the god ignited the fire of forever within the hidden soul, cursed it with a bond of True Love and Oneness and Faithful Soul Mate Through The Sands Of Time Even If It Belongs To A Vampyre–and withdrew, dusting its godly hands together in triumph. "Hey-nonnie-nonnie and a nyah-nyah-nyah," the second god told the first, swaggering. "Too bad on you. The kid's gonna get to have sex *and* protect a vampyre's soul from evil."

"Yeah, *eventually*," the first god scoffed, "if anyone around here ever figures out what a *'vampýre'* is when they don't even *believe* in 'em" –and the second rounded and cuffed its rival soundly upside the head.

And the squabble was on, loud, fierce and long.

Round and round the forest they battled, bitching and moaning, biting and scratching, bickering and calling each other names while each attempted to break the other's noggin.

Since they were gods, this was, of course, impossible. But gods will be gods, and roughhousing–also known as thunder and lightning among the common folk–tended to break up the monotony of immortality.

This time, however, these two particular gods fought so long that they whirled a huge crater–and then carved a deep path up it–into what used to be an ordinary riverbed. They churned the waters so hard that the river took on permanent rough-water-rapids and began to spill hard over the rocks and into the crater, creating the most brilliant and intense waterfall ever seen anywhere. Then they spun and squabbled their way *counter*clockwise upriver from this awesome waterfall and corkscrew-hewed out–and up–the steps of an even grander and more dangerous set of falls.

The third god–really The Goddess, for it was She, Mother and Mistress of all Nature Herself who last waited to gift the newborn–ruefully watched the two lesser gods bicker over *who* and *what* the tiny princess should/would be. Privately she thought them Total Fuck-Ups and Personal Glory Seekers, sticking not one but two conflicting souls into an innocent infant who had enough growing up pressures to look forward to (for the love of Mike, her mother was almost eighty-freaking-years-old; talk about your generation gaps!), without tying the little darling up with souls that came with psycho-neurotic-bloody-strings attached.

Shoving her undulating mantle of ferns-leaves-moss-flower petals-and-sifting-natural-elements away from her face, she regarded the unnamed babe with thoughtful circumspection. She couldn't undo what lesser gods did, but she *could* do her best to gum up their works.

A slight moue of perfect understanding forming her mouth, she slipped over to where the tiny princess's cradle-board hung suspended near the naming-fire. The little one blinked her perfect, almond-round black eyes at the Mother and Mistress of All Nature, and waved a chubby infant hand uncertainly in the air. Mother Nature bent forward so wildly quixotic tresses the mixed-earth shades of tree bark, clay, sand and healthy soil swung close to the little fist.

When the tribal princess grabbed hold of a few tickling curls, tugged and started to laugh, Mother Nature chucked her under the chin and smiled. The babe gurgled, bubbled and cooed brightly, kicked inside her cradle-board–and then socked the Mistress of All Nature in the eye.

Startled but delighted, Goddess chuckled. "You *are* precious," she said.

Accepting the attention as her due, the baby merely burbled merrily back at Mother Nature and yanked harder on her about-to-be godmother's hair. "Right," Goddess agreed, smiling. "Get on with it."

So saying she leaned in closer than close and breathed her own essence and soul into the fearless princess.

"I give you the gift of freedom to choose your own path, your own person," Mother Nature whispered fiercely, "and the strength of will to hold it, the right to know what's best for you and what is not–and the ability to be responsible for your own actions." Her voice gathered strength, and the trees bowed down and cowered before her. "You will be a bitch among bitches, a beast among beasts, woman among women and, should you require it, the greatest demon avenger man has ever feared." She raised a hand and the earth's fauna appeared: salmon leaped from the stream, deer, wolverine, badgers, wolves, and all of the other animated pieces of creation slunk to the edge of the clearing at her bidding to hear what she had to say. "You are *my* godchild, my own Precious One. You carry my spirit within you. No man, creature or god will own you as long as the wind blows and the earth lives and I am mistress of this world."

Then Mother Nature kissed Precious on both eyes so the child would see clearly no matter who or what she looked at. She kissed her on both ears so her goddaughter would ever remain unburdened by the uncertainty of wondering whether words she heard were false or true. Last, she kissed the tiny, wild rosebud mouth, promising the princess that only pearls of truth would ever pass her lips.

Then she tickled the princess's tummy, dropped

a quick parting kiss on the babe's brow (right over her third eye), and walked away, snapping her fingers as she went.

On the snap, a brilliant sun-colored full moon burst through the storm caused by the battling gods and a unique double rainbow waltzed right out of the waterfalls' mist to splash across the little one's face. The tiny princess chortled gleefully, pulled her feet out of her cradle-board and set about dabbling her minute toes and fingers in the river of color.

Then right there, before everyone's eyes, she shapeshifted into a wolf for the first time, dropped to the ground on all fours and trotted fearlessly over to her mother without a thought to the sparking bonfire nearby.

Since most Weres didn't come into their wolf natures until *at least* reaching the age of reason (seven for girls, thirty-five for guys–though frankly, both genders usually hit their shapeshifting abilities about the time they hit puberty and lost all reason *and* sense), it was a precocious event for a one-month-old, even without the fire fearlessness.

Awed, the tribe crowded around the littlest werewolf. She growled and trembled and showed her fangs, backing up butt-first against her mother's legs. But even bewildered as she was, she didn't back down from anyone, not for an instant. She stood her ground and snarled–and some Pesquiwatamis thought they saw the infant lupine grow bigger and more dangerous-looking while they stood there. Muttering under their breaths about "evil maejicks afoot," they backed away hastily, giving the tribe's newest she-wolf room.

Predictably, her mother ignored what she didn't want to hear.

"See her already practicing to lead us in battle against our enemies?" Crowing with pride, her mother picked her up and held her aloft, declaring, "We will call her Precious Child, hope for our tribe and our future!"

And so they named her–until she got a bit older and discovered that her *precious*ness was really just an Independent Streak that was, oh, a heckuva lot more trouble than anyone (including the gods and Mother Nature) ever dreamed. Then they renamed her Causes Trouble...

...Because she sure as hell did.

SEX ON THE BITCH

Wherein Causes Trouble turns eighteen and fully lives up to her name.

Causes Trouble stared blankly at her elderly mother. "You want me to change into a werewolf, turn around, lift my tail and let one of those dumb hounds climb on and do what up my what-what with my whoo-haa?"

"*Mate!*" her ninety-late-ish year old mother crabbed waspishly for the one hundred and fifty-fourth time. "Dance dirty under the flowering moon. Snog. Get your groove on. Do the deed. Get pregnant and start your own household. It's high time you moved out of mine."

"Get pregnant?" Causes Trouble shuddered. "By one of…" She grimaced and gestured in the direction of a bunch of lounging male tribal members– bodaciously attractive, hunkly gorgeous specimens all because werewolves, well, tended to be. They were all *eying* her. And *drooling*. "…*them*?"

"Yes," her mother said. "Choose one. Heck, choose them all. I'm not fussy, no need for you to be. Every one of them is prime mating material, and you should be in season. Why aren't you?"

"Because I'm a shapeshifter, not a Were-slut?" Causes Trouble (sometimes known to her mother as a Fuss-budget of the Worst Kind, and at others known simply as Picky-Picky-Picky) snapped irritably.

The Matriarch of All She Surveyed (AKA Tribal Chief, AKA Alpha Bitch, AKA Mother-May-I) stared goggle-eyed at her daughter. Causes Trouble stuck her nose in the air and glared rebelliously (and a trifle belligerently) back. The M.O.A.S.S.'s mouth opened and closed fish-like in disbelief. She displayed a perfect set of teeth and gums when she did this, I might add. This was remarkable not only for a woman-wolf of her exceedingly advanced years, but particularly for a woman-wolf in her late nineties who'd spent the last eighteen of those "exceedingly advanced years" raising Causes Trouble, AKA Mother Nature's goddaughter and FKA (formerly known as) Precious Child.

Squared off against her recalcitrant would-be successor, Causes Trouble's mother gathered her ire and desire for grandchildren about her and remembered every bit of who and what she was, and what that allowed her to do. Catching up her somewhat taller daughter by the scruff of the neck and the seat of her (doeskin) pants (I'm pretty sure there was a painful bit of hair trapped at both ends, too), she launched her at the flap of their summer lodge. "Get out there and get humped, *now*! And don't come back without a litter, that's an order."

"But mo-o-o-oooo-*oommm*!" Causes Trouble howled as she flew through the air.

The howl cut short when she splashed face-first into the whirlpool below (the recently named[1]) Braugh Naughton Falls. Sputtering, coughing and furious, she surfaced, swam to the edge of the pool and climbed out onto the mossy rocks.

"'s'not fair!" Fuming, she picked up a flat piece of shale the size of a six-foot-four-inch (in human form) male werewolf's chest and skipped it across the pool. It hopped out the other side and skidded neatly into place below the last several hundred chest-size pieces of shale she'd played skip-stones with, forming another step up the precarious slope beside the falls. "Nobody forced *her* to go out and have a litter when *she* was eighteen. Noooo." Morosely she picked at a crevice between two rocks with a steadily thickening and elongating nail. "*She* waited 'til she was older than *old* then she only had *me*! But what does she want? Me, buggered up the hoo-haa until I'm in heat, preggers and abandoned by ten or fifteen of those studly yahoossss –"

"Wah-hoo-hoo-hoo-*hooooooo!*"

"*Gauuugh!*"

Hit from behind by Studly Yahoo number too many to remember, Causes Trouble slipped off the rocks and belly-splatted smack back into the pool. She surfaced spluttering.

"*Bastard!*"

The bastard grinned. "Man, that was fun! Do it again? This time you bounce me."

"I'll bounce you all right." Puffing wet hair-strings out of her face, Causes Trouble (who didn't know she was about to earn the name she'd live with for the rest of her life–*Janice*) straightened and squared off opposite her opponent in the diamond-dropletted pool. It was amazing how many prisms the sun could find in a few water sparkles. "Right off the end of my foot and into the tops of those trees."

Studly Stupid had the gall to look delighted. "Oooo, feisty. The chief said you wouldn't be *too* easy. That's good. Males like a chase before a good tuck 'n cover." Head cocked, he canted his chin and nose in her direction and sniffed. Circled carefully closer while Causes Trouble moved with him and sniff-*sniffed* again. "Tell you the truth, though...you could be a little less gen'rous with the grousin' you're doin' 'bout the whole traditional male-female-wam-bam-scramming thing and a lot more gen-r-*nice*—"

(Hoots and barks of adolescent-giggly male laughter erupted from the nearby tree line.)

"—'bout turnin' your tail around and gettin' your c'mon musk up so we c'n get on with it. Lotta fellas up there waitin' a turn if I can't do anything with ya. Chief said she'd...*ooof!*"

Teeth bared in a man-eating snarl, and halfway through wolf-transformation without benefit of the moon or anything resembling twilight, Causes Trouble crouched over the startled would-be Stud, who now lay belly up and terrified, contemplating the large, extremely white teeth at his throat.

"Leave. My. Mother. *Out*. Of. My. Sex. Life. Or. You. Won't. Have. One. Ever. Again."

"N-no problem," her thwarted suitor agreed readily. When she eased off slightly, he crab-scuttled backwards until he was out from under her. Then he splashed hastily out of the pool and beat feet into the trees where his buddies...weren't waiting for him. "You know you don't just Cause Trouble," he shouted from the relative safety of a few yards between them, "You're a freaking societal menace. In fact, more'n that, you just ain't nice!"

"*Just Ain't Nice! J'ain't Nice! J'ain'nice, J'ain'nice...*"

The jeer echoed among the trees, reverberated off

the rocks and pounded into Causes Trouble's half-transformed being until she doubled up her human fists and shoved them into her wolf ears, threw back her head and howled. "I *am* nice! I *don't* cause trouble. What's wrong with knowing who and what I don't want? I'm *gen*tle, I'm good, I'm *nice, I'm nice, I'm niiiiiiiicccce…*"

But of course it was the contracted form of "You Just Ain't Nice" –*Janice*–that took.

A BITCH WITH A GLITCH

In which a lovely afternoon of lost virginity and beach sex goes wrong. Very, very wrong.

"O, O, OOOOOOOOO!" Janice (formerly Causes Trouble) warbled ecstatically.

Naked and alone, but for the young, newly arrived (exiled) three-foot Wyvern conspiratorially (and grumpily) standing guard at a peep-hole deep inside its cave, she bathed in the faster and extremely aptly named Screw-in-a-Cork Falls that lay well above Braugh Naughton Lake. A (very) late bloomer, she'd only lately discovered (some…twenty-five or fifty years after her mother first sent her out to "get humped") that if she poised her nether regions *just so* beneath the pulsing, twisting fall of water, it tickled her crotch in a most amazing way.

At first, she'd been startled and embarrassed by the tingly-pleasurable-liquid sensation forming low in her tummy and pooling between her legs. Surely, That Sort Of Thing (meaning not only the tickly-giddy sensation, but also its unwarranted and involuntary long-drawn-out-oh'ing of *ecstasy*) wasn't supposed to happen, which meant that surely it must be *wrong*. I mean, no one had ever mentioned *That Sort Of Thing* to her before so…was she the only one who'd ever experienced it? Perhaps the only werewolf? Or more to the point, the only *female* werewolf?

And what was *it*, anyway?

And why did she feel it around, well…er…*there*, where a male was supposed to come up behind her and stick his…ahem…then bump and grind and grunt and bite and howl until…

Oh…! It was too embarrassing to even *think* about it!

Not to mention, how could that possibly be *fun* (AKA *pleasurable*) for anyone, males and females alike? Getting the job done, sure, Janice could (unfortunately) picture that, but not…not…*this*.

Then the sensation twisted higher and tighter inside her, suffused not only her nethers but her lower spine, jacked heat into her breasts and tweaked her nipples into hard dots, and caused her throat muscles to shorten and convulse.

"Aahh," she whimpered, somewhere between terror, curiosity and ecstasy, "*Aaahh…*"

Guided by impulses beyond her control, she slid a hand between her legs and touched the apparent center of her culminating fear and torment, the source of her body's gathering lightning. Pleasure seared through her, plundered overwrought nerve-endings, caused Janice to utter a shocked, high-pitched squeak, "*Uuh?*"

Poised on the crest of a wave right out of a five-hundred-year storm, she paused, uncertain of whether (and how) to ride it, and survive. Then the corkscrewing waterfall pulsed hard against her waffling fingers. On the whirlpool's command, Janice found three of them thrust deep inside her. Her mouth opened, head jerked back in surprise.

And then the pleasurable little "*O'ing*" she'd experienced when the falls pulsed *just so* around her nethers turned from a panicked little questioning "*O?*" to a rising howl to a prolonged scream of

ecstatic   and   disbelieving
"*ooooOOOOOOOOOOOOOOO!!*" of bliss as she
bucked her hips involuntarily against her hand…

And discovered for the very first time ever what
it was to feel not only good, but sublimely, limply,
relaxedly happy and yummily fine and dandy.

L'GRAND(EST) 'O' & L'PETIT (meaning "really huge") 'OOPS!'

Wherein Janice is condemned to spend an eternity in Brokenoggin Falls as everything that means "flatfooted-cop-etc." but not sex-kitten.

Once Janice discovered her body's affinity for sudden, intense, prolonged, transcendentally earth-shattering *bliss*, she became a far more frequent visitor to the violently screwy Corkscrew Falls.

She became so enamored of the bliss of screaming "O-O-*OOOOO!*" in fact, that she wanted to do it everyday, more than once, morning-afternoon-and-night, and no matter which form she was in, human or wolf.

Now, everyone knows wolves don't have "Os". They're beasts, and it's not part of their natures. So Janice figuring out the "O" as a wolf...hmmm... That was even more disturbing to her than when she'd figured it out as a human. No one talked about *"It"*, which meant *"It"* couldn't exist. So not only had she discovered something sublimely, delightfully, *cravenly* satisfying, she must also have stumbled upon something forbidden.

She felt wonderful and guilty at once.

It was quite a predicament for an acknowledged monster to muddle out. But since "talking about your feelings" wasn't yet encouraged, she kept the wonderful-terrible discovery to herself and fed her addiction at the wilder falls (and anywhere else experimentation seemed practicable and discovery unlikely)—

And felt guilty about it afterwards.

It was an unholy cycle, but every time Janice determined to break it, something rubbed her "down there" and...

Sigh.

The "O" was a difficult task-monster, and since she'd been the one to turn the creature loose...

She really couldn't do anything less than keep it in check by responding to it—

—Over and over and over again.

*****

Alack, there came a moment when playing diddle-me-fingers all by her lonesome (even with the help of the waterfall) started to get...

...Boring.

Oh, the shrieking *"O"* itself as well as all the shuddery physical sensations that accompanied it were still pleasant enough, but it came to the point where Janice knew *exactly* what would happen when, not to mention *how*, along with what buttons attached to which screams and...

Her interest–and even her guilt–in the coming attractions eventually began to wane.

She started to get distracted during the course of events.

This is probably why, while in the midst of a rather frustrating attempt to find satisfaction diddling about beneath the fine rush of the falls one warm Indian summer afternoon in mid-autumn, Janice (who'd undergone a partial wolf-change in an effort to rekindle her relationship with herself–don't ask) suddenly pricked her furry gray-black ears in fascination. Somewhere in Pesquiwatami territory, someone was singing. Since Pesquiwatamis tended to howl rather than sing, it had to be a stranger.

Slicked up and ready as she was for other things to take place inside her body, Janice nevertheless stopped what she was doing with the large-ish, long-ish, smooth-polished bulbous-shaped piece of agate in her fist and twitched her ears toward the song.

> *I'm a lumberjack*
> *and that's not bullocks*
> *I work all day*
> *then I sleep with trollops*

Sung in a fine, jovial baritone in a language that made no sense to her, the ditty tickled Janice's beast-sensitive ears. It also stirred something funny and fluttery in the region of her lonely heart and just south of it, in the sex-ready muscles of her tummy.

Prompted by an instinct well beyond her ken, she replaced the nearly fist-sized end of the agate at the mouth of her nether-lips and pushed it upward at the same time the baritone sang,

> *I dine on joe and mutton*
> *and I've got a huge cock*
> *'neath my buttons!*

"Oh goddess!" she groaned immediately, keenly gratified by the instant sear of satisfaction that flared out of her lower spine and tightly upwards when she arched into it.

Deliberately she clenched and unclenched her muscles around the agate bulb in time to the song, holding onto both the sensation and the rock tormentor inside her while forcing her hand to remain still. Simultaneously the sound of an axe pitting wood pounded time with the song, kept rhythm with her blood–with the increasingly wild, primitively harsh, involuntarily heavy pulse of her muscles around the stone inside her…beating…beating…*beating*…

Until Janice couldn't stand it anymore.

Surging out from underneath the waterfall, she stood shaking and shivering in the center of the pool, entire being shimmering in the spray of the falls and glorious orange-gold autumn light, a finger-snap away from the grandest climax in the history of the known universe.

And her still her body waited, anticipating something greater–and indeed larger than the fist-sized stone–surging, plunging, *plowing deep furrows* inside her—

And refused release, declined to *come*.

Needs urgent, Janice snarled even as her face changed shape, elongated into enough of a muzzle so she could throw back her head and *howl*.

Then still on human legs and hands, she plunged to the river's edge, scrambled up the mossy, rocky bank. From there – ears pricked, nose high, bulbous agate clenched muscle-tight and tormenting inside her–she dashed off to get what her body (in complete and total confusion) insisted it craved at the hands (and *body?* What was that about?) of "The Voice."

*****

Janice skidded to a stop roughly seven miles downriver from Braugh Naughton Falls.

The song emanated from a male.

She knew it had to be *male* because although it didn't smell like any kind of male creature she'd ever before come in contact with, it definitely didn't smell female. Ergo—

The autumn breeze shifted more firmly in her direction, bringing with it a wash of odors so powerful that her virgin senses cried out and literally flung her into the scent.

In full wolf form, she leapt, covering the ground between her and her…intended…on wings of magic.

Until she noted the fact that he was…

A very strawberry-blond, bushy-faced, one-eyebrowed *human* and she'd never before met a human.

Then she panicked in mid-fall/drop when she tried to change back into "Just Janice" and crashed down atop him whilst he was in mid-axe-swing…

All a-jumble of naked arms, body and legs, and hot, sweat-glistening, molten, bosom-bobbing, wanting, long-haired, female, agate-clenching, juice-slick sex.

"*Aaaaauuugghh!*" he screamed, trying to make sure his axe didn't cut off anything–or more particularly anything vital–when they fell. "Fuck the *hell* out of me!"

"Yes, please," Janice said eagerly, though she didn't comprehend a word of his strange language. The sentiment seemed perfectly clear to her–especially when his axe handle came in contact with her cunt and joggled the agate bulb still lodged tightly within her nethers, causing it to bump some squooshy little button inside her that she'd never before found. Her belly muscles wavered and clutched. She bucked and whimpered. Then a sudden sensation of liquefying flowed through her, and her powerfully scented cream bathed the use-smoothed wood.

The fallen lumberjack's (for clearly, though Janice was too sheltered to know it, that's what he was) battered-looking nose twitched. The well-chewed pipe clamped between his strong, (off-)white teeth fell by the wayside when his eyes glazed over and his jaw went slack. The previously sung about *"huge cock behind my buttons"* expanded to meet advertised proportions and then some–out-girthing, in fact, the palm-size girth of his axe handle.

Strained to maximum bulge, *all* of the (probably about ready to come un-sewed anyway) copper buttons on the fly of his (overworked, bibbed) overalls burst off. The threadbare red flannels underneath didn't bother with their buttons; they simply shredded around the buttonholes. The massively engorged, angrily aggressive, purple-red cock no longer fully constrained behind polite fiber trappings busted free–to jab roughly at Janice's brushy black shorthairs and hunt instant imprisonment within them.

Flabbergasted but enthralled, Janice stared wide-eyed and slack-jawed at the immense, bobbing, tumescent *thing*. Her (long, curling, slavering, hot, pink, wolf) tongue fell out of her mouth in excited anticipation, dropping (with her chin and her jaw) toward the tip of the lumberjack's (impossibly, impressively) expanding shaft and strangling (inside cotton duck fabric that refused to give despite the pressure) balls. The lumberjack's already popping eyes got wider and more frantic-looking; discombobulated along with the rest of him, his single (bushy, reddish-blond) eyebrow scrambled closer to his (bushy, reddish-blond, watch cap covered) hairline. His lips (buried deep within his extremely bushy, reddish-blond-and-calico beard) elongated in a snarl of extreme (if painful) lust while his nostrils flared wide and he snorted his full of sex-laden female fully primed. It was sort of like (how TV and movies depict) getting a straight hit of one hundred percent Colombian home-grown appears: so stunning the brain freezes and the senses go into overload, and the digits that continue to function do so of their own accord.

In other words, he'd been overpoweringly, unadulteratedly, not-comin'-down-without-a-sledge-hammer-to-the-brain drugged.

And it only got worse when he yanked his axe handle out of Janice's crotch to throw it aside and a drop of her (rich, spicy-sweet) spilled cream flew up and landed just inside his lower lip.

For the barest, *parchest*, drag of an instant, time froze while the single-eyebrowed tree-feller's eyelids washed down over his (somewhat pupil-exaggerated but still mostly crystal clear) blue eyes. His tongue slid experimentally forward, dabbed at the cunning little drab of moisture, slipped back into his mouth and rolled the flavor around and around for a moment. Came back for more.

Savored.

Then his eyelids flipped up, and the crystal blue irises were all black pupils; inhuman yowls and growls rumbled through his chest. He tore at the cloth restraining his testicles while his cock pressed straighter to reach Janice's (appreciative) lolling tongue. The turtleneck of foreskin protecting the most delicate area of his frenulum rolled down as his glans poked free.

A bead of some pearlescent, milky substance bubbled and eddied from the meatus, shiny, lickable. It bobbed there just below her tongue in succulent invitation, literally *begging* for attention and Janice found it absitively, pantingly, *insanely*, gimme-gimme-*GIMME!*—

—Tortuously tantalizing. She wanted it–*all* of it. Now.

Almost hypnotized by the groping, glistening glans mere millimeters below, Janice dipped her head to send her unusually long, prehensile tongue curling around the rod protruding from the full sacs at its base. The heavy penis flexed within the pink confines of her tongue; the involuntary movement roused Janice's predator. Excitement for the chase flared inside her. Her tongue tightened, massaged the sensitive sheath of foreskin up and down the shaft, lubricating it before drawing it toward the dark wet well of her mouth. The lumberjack made a choked sound of pleading anticipation. She bit down and sucked him in…

The fist-sized agate dildo inside her vulva trembled and quaked, so wildly did her inner muscles pump around it seeking a satisfaction its smooth, un-living surface could not provide. The ridged sheath surrounding the huge, hot shaft in her mouth seemed to speak directly to her loins, call to them–to *it*.

Releasing the lumberjack's shaft from her mouth and throwing back her head on a yowl that was neither quite human or wolf, Janice grasped his cock in one hand and plucked the agate from her betwixt her nether lips with the other. Then holding her labia open, she fitted cock to cunt and impaled herself on him.

Surprise was followed closely by a, *"Oh, goddess, yes!"* of intense relief.

And then Janice rode her conquest hard, harder, hardest, until they were both wringing with sweat, both grabbing whatever they could find for purchase, both shouting without knowing it—

"Jaaaaaa-nnnnice!"

Hollered at the top of her mother's considerable (if ancient, and now centenarian plus) lungs, the bellow carried all the way from Brokenoggin / Braugh Naughton Falls and landed in Janice's (well-tuned) ears as though the Tribal Matriarch stood *Right There* next to them, *Watching*. Instantly (even though no other werewolf worth his or her salt cared who saw them humping because what the hell, it was just procreating) guilt reared its head. In mid *"OOOOOOOOOOOO-O!"* Janice's ecstasy shrieked to an abrupt, *"Eeeeek! Quick, my mother!"* and she tried to leap off the ride of her life without losing it, and while also trying to hide what she'd been doing at the same time.

Being a Man In The Throes Of Dispersing His Seed (meaning he was pumping it as hard and fast as he could bang his buttocks off the ground and into Janice because his weapon was still firing and man, he'd never had it like this before!), the tree-feller grabbed for her thighs to pin her in place. Understandable though the move was, it was also a decided tactical error on his part. Feeling trapped, Janice panicked.

From there it happened quickly. Even as her mother's canoe appeared upriver and the Pesquiwatami chieftess hollered, *"Yoohoo, Janice, I've found a mate for yooooouuuuuu…"* Janice panic-shifted from one creature to another: human-wolf to wolf-wolf to wolf-something…

Really weird no one had ever seen before.

Her entire furry wolf body hugified beyond belief, stretching and straining and…her hind legs turned into something that resembled Wyrm haunches and…some kind of fuzzy scales formed over her back and along her sides and her ears turned into a sort of horned-over ridge along either side of her wolfish-looking head and—

Pulled out of his (bodaciously magnificent) *cum*-induced stupor by the (enormously) increased weight of the creature atop him, the lumberjack opened his eyes.

And screamed. And screamed and *screamed*.

At the same time the Tribal Queen (AKA Mom or She Who Must Be Avoided) parked her canoe high up the riverbank near the freshly logged area wherein Janice had recently foisted her virginity off on the (now) screaming logger and stomped toward it leading the werewolf she'd chosen to boink and impregnate her daughter.

Scared to bits by the screaming and guilty as hell over being found naked and beastly, Janice did what any normal monster would do under the circumstances–the only thing her terrified, monster-y brain could think of to shut up her lover so her mother wouldn't find him.

She reached down, picked him up, put him in

her mouth and ate him.

The *"oops"*-factor ~~didn't sink in until~~ after she'd chomped down and swallowed him. Then she was horrified. Eyes wide, she put a tiny, still-human hand to her over-large, elongated, wolf-dragon snouty-mouth. Her cheeks pooched dangerously and her face turned a hideous and unhealthy shade of bilious yellow-green–with whiskers.

Bushy, reddish-blonde, single-eyebrow-whiskers, that dangled from her lower left molar, to be exact.

"Janice!" her mother, the (not so) regal Pesquiwatami Queen (who couldn't seem to help but speak loudly in italics even when Janice was *right there* in front of her) shouted up at her aghast, coming to an abrupt halt below her daughter's gagging and *"gurgging"* maw. "What the hell's gotten into you now? I brought you a lovely young wolf—" she shook the (quailing) male Were at Janice as though he were nothing more than a pinecone "—to turn up your posterior for and *this* is how you repay me?"

Miserably, Weird Were-Monster Janice gazed down at the scene before her. Something had happened to her brain during all the shapeshifting and she…well, she couldn't seem to understand what her mother was saying. She was pretty sure she didn't want to hear it, whatever *it* was, but even so, what with the brain her mind presently occupied…she didn't comprehend a word.

And that was not to mention the state of her belly. Apparently lumberjack lunches did not agree with it. She put one (relatively) dainty paw in the vicinity of her tummy and tried to soothe it by rubbing. The other she placed (delicately) to her mouth.

"Janice, are you listening to me?" the queen-chief-tribal leader bawled.

The lumberjack kicked the inside of Janice's stomach once then started jumping up and down in an effort to get out. Janice lifted the paw off her belly and brought it up to help cover her mouth, trying to keep everything (including her sanity) in.

Suddenly she belched.

The bushy, reddish-blond single-eyebrow dislodged from her left molar and drifted down on the noxious waft of gaseous fumes to land on her mother's upper lip and pause there–a splendid strawberry handlebar on a crinkled-up prune face. And for a sparse hint of an instant, Weird Were-Monster Janice got a big kick out of the sight.

But only for the sparsest shadow of an instant.

Then her lunch backed up and stuck two fingers the wrong way into her craw. Janice had just enough time to croak, "O—" before the fingers (frankly, they were really more like just bones now) tickled their way fully out of her throat, pried open her jaws, leaped to the ground and scuttled away fast.

Shocked, sickened, disgusted and appalled–no, not by the sight of bones, but by the sight of Janice trying to hide the fact that she'd eaten them–the male werewolf made an effort to escape this (albeit most honored) round of planned parenthood. Simultaneously, the chief made an effort to stop him. Concurrently, Janice's gag reflex (temporarily overridden while the finger bones made their getaway) took over and the logger's skeleton…made a hurried departure...from her queasy stomach.

It landed on the (attempting to flee) male werewolf and the (strident, bossy) Tribal Matriarch and caused Janice no end of grief for the next two hundred plus years during which she never again got to experience anything like the *"OOOOOOOOOOOO-O!"* and instead learned an awful lot about the agony of the "Oh shit!"

An Excerpt from

My Fair Apprentice
By
Rose Lyley

Available now from
Triskelion Publishing

CHAPTER ONE

Bored, bored, bored. Great Stars, he was bored out of his mind! With a disgusted sigh, Alasdair MacCorran leaned back into the darkened corner of the coffee shop booth and watched the snow outside drifting lazily toward the ground, where people in far too much hurry to do absolutely nothing important would trample it. He knew how that felt. Not the trampling part– no one in their right mind would even attempt to run over a MacCorran– but the having nothing important to do. He'd become jaded to it all.

His eyes traveled the interior of the coffee shop, and he suppressed another sigh. *Hole in the Wall*, whimsically named by its original owner for the since-patched holes in the brick exterior, was a small, secluded hangout for Seattle's more offbeat crowd. The last place anyone would ever expect to find Alasdair MacCorran, Master *Draoidh* of the *Sgàil Ealdhainean* and descendant of the *Cheud Draoidh* of the *Sgàil Taighean*. Not that he gave a damn, he decided with a disdainful snort, for the world he'd left behind. Come to think of it, he didn't care about anything in three dimensions, anymore, not even his magic. That thought had troubled him for a while. Magic had always thrilled him, the rush of power in his veins too seductive to resist. So, why did it suddenly bore him? What was missing? Why did he keep feeling like something important was lacking?

"Mac? Hela's teats, man, snap out of it!"

Roused from his musings, Mac quirked a dark brow at his companion. They were probably as different as any two friends could be, he and Geoff. Mac bore all the hereditary traits of his Celtic ancestors – he had their wiry, athletic build, skin of a smooth olive tone, hair darker than midnight, and eyes that were a pure, deep bronze. Geoff Grayson – Geoffrey Grayson IV, Master *Skald* of the *Thorolfkin*, to be proper – was Norse from the roots of his moon-blond hair to the toes of his fur-lined biker boots, a giant who appeared at once intimidating and approachable. Mac was the dark side of their duo, and always had been, ever since they'd suffered through Madame Luminare's Elementary Magic at the age of six. Geoff was the very definition of laid-back observer, half-lost in his stories. Now, though, he sounded more like the *Thorolfkind* – the dark wolf – he really was. He was miffed about something.

"What was that?" Mac enquired blandly, leaning back in the booth and twisting a strand of shadow around his finger, pulling it around to mask his face.

Geoff shoved a large hand through his long, blond hair in a frustrated gesture, his sharp, canine teeth flashing in the light as he grated out, "I swear by all the Gods, Mac, you're getting senile, living out there in the woods! I asked if you're ready for *Luna Ascesa*, yet."

Ready? Mac bit out a sharp laugh. *Luna Ascesa*, or Rising Moon, was the biggest gala and trade conference in the magic world, and each master of a field had to choose one apprentice under them to represent their Craft with a display of skills. As Master of the *Sgàil Ealdhainean* – the realm of shadow magics– Mac should have a dozen or more apprentices to choose from. Only, he'd grown bored with apprentices, and teaching, years ago. He'd dismissed his last pupil after *Luna Ascesa* last year. Hellfire, he was bored with magic!

"I'm not going."

Geoff, in the process of taking a drink of his coffee, nearly spit the contents of his mug across the booth. Choking, he finally spluttered, "What do you mean, you're not going? You don't have a *choice*, Mac! None of us do."

Mac shrugged indifferently. "I've been banned, by now."

Geoff sat back, frowning. "How's that?"

Gods and demons, shape-shifters could be thick, at times! Mac rolled his eyes expressively. "Because I broke taboo."

Understanding dawned in Geoff's keen azure eyes. "Ah. The infamous female apprentice." He leaned forward, resting his arms on the table as his eyes sparkled with interest. "I've been wondering about that one, myself. You knew it was taboo for a man to teach a woman – we have different arts and different training techniques where the arts overlap – so why'd you thumb your nose at tradition? You're not a rebel, Mac."

Mac sighed, leaning further into the shadows, wishing he could just make himself disappear into them. He could, of course, but it wouldn't get him out of this. Geoff already knew that juvenile trick. Finally, he faced his friend. "You're telling me you haven't found it odd that, since I took on this apprentice, you've never seen her?"

Geoff's frown deepened. "There is that. Who is

she?"

Mac bit out a sharp laugh. "I have no idea."

"*Excuse* me?" Geoff blinked, hard. "You've been living with and mentoring this woman for almost a year, and—"

"Geoff," Mac leaned forward suddenly, and saw surprise flicker through his friend's eyes. Shadow magic tended to have that effect, even on magic users. "That's the whole damned point! There *is* no woman."

There was silence from the other side of the table for a full minute before Geoff loosed a low, disbelieving groan and slumped back in his seat. "I'm not hearing this! Mac, please tell me you didn't deliberately falsify yourself to the *Illuminata*."

Mac nodded glumly, sinking back into the shadows again. "It gets worse."

"I don't want to know how, buddy."

"Tough," Mac returned in dark humor. "You asked. I'm sick of magic, Geoff. There's no thrill, no challenge, anymore. I can create or conjure anything I want with a wave of my hand." He demonstrated, sugar and cream poured out of thin air into his coffee.

"Uh, Mac," Geoff said hesitantly. "You drink your coffee black, man."

Mac waved his hand and the coffee returned to the dark, inky brew it'd been before. "That's not the point."

"Okay, so you've hit a slump," the blond giant said with a shrug. "We all do at some point. What's that got to do with lying to the *Illuminata*? Man, they can take away *everything* for that!"

Mac snorted disdainfully, spreading his hands

wide in indifference. "They can have it all, if they want it. I don't care anymore."

"That's it," Geoff muttered with shake of his blond head. "You've officially run mad from all that communing with nature. Mac, you know as well as I do what happens if they find out you lied. You'll lose it all. Not just the money, or the license to practice magic in this dimension, man, but *everything*! They'll give you the Mark of the Damned, man. You'll be stripped of your magic, and you'll disgrace the MacCorrans forever. What about your parents? What about Ysabet, Mac?"

Mac straightened, his bronze eyes blazing. "Leave Ys out of this."

Geoff snorted derisively. "I didn't bring her into it, *you* did, you dumb bastard. The *Illuminata* find out you lied about an apprentice, and Ysabet won't have a snowball's chance in Hell of ever getting into a Bardic school, no matter *who* sponsors her."

Mac groaned, slumping back into the comforting embrace of the shadows. Geoff was right! He'd been a self-centered ass to submit that false résumé. Ysabet was barely sixteen – their parents' late-life surprise and joy – and the only thing that still shed any light in Mac's dark existence. He couldn't let his sister pay for his stupidity!

"What am I going to do? *Luna Ascesa* is only a little over a month away, Geoff."

Geoff shrugged nonchalantly. "Hey, it's your mess, Mac. But I'd suggest you find someone, and quick. You've got a lot of work to do in a month."

Mac snorted. "You know the *Sgàil Ealdhainean* are way too complicated for just anyone to learn."

"But I'll bet you can do it.   If there's anyone pigheaded enough to turn a nobody into a *Sgàil Ealdhainean Bhuitseach*, it's you."

Mac rolled his eyes. "Fat lot of help you are."

"Fine."   Geoff leaned forward, suddenly all hunter. "How about a little wager, MacCorran? You get off your ass and use all that charm and magic you ooze all over the place to turn the next woman who passes this table into everything you put in that résumé, and I'll personally browbeat Kyna Ravensfall into slating your sister for the next entry sitting at Dalamor."

Mac's brows shot up as his eyes widened. Ysabet would give her right eye to get into Dalamor Bardic Academy. It was the most prestigious Bardic school in three dimensions, and entry sittings were impossible to get without the approval of the highly critical Headmistress. Ysabet would be ecstatic, and really, how hard could it be to train a woman in the *Sgàil Ealdhainean*? *Hole in the Wall* was a meeting place for Seattle's Pagan types. Surely, he could train one of this dimension's *Draoi*, or even a Wiccan, with a minimal amount of fuss. It was an easy win. A slow, confident smirk sliding over his face, Mac met his friend's challenging gaze.

"You're on, Grayson."

Geoff looked up, and grinned wolfishly. "Good. Don't look now, my friend, but your subject's headed our way."

Mac blinked and looked around, but there was no one there. No one except a harried-looking and unkempt waitress, her dark hair working loose from her braid in flyaway strands of curly frizz.

"Where? I don't see anyone."

Geoff tipped his head back and laughed as the waitress passed their table, scowling. "You now have an official apprentice, Mac. You just saw her."

Mac's eyes landed on the waitress, and horror settled. "Not her."

"Remember the bet, Mac. The next woman to pass our table." Geoff gave the waitress an once-over, his eyes twinkling. "Well, she's female, and she walked right past us. Looks like she's your girl, buddy."

His eyes fixed on the woman's stormy scowl and flyaway hair, Mac bit back a disbelieving groan. He'd heard of turning sow's ears into silk purses before but this was ridiculous. He was going to lose this bet, big time.

CHAPTER TWO

That did it, it was official. The Universe at large was out to get her. Meg Tempest slapped her damp cleaning rag down on the sticky surface of the window table where someone's kid had smeared honey handprints. This was supposed to be her day off. And not just any day off, this was supposed to be the day her life changed, and she got out of the massive disaster it had been for twenty-eight years. She'd had it all set up, at last. She was supposed to audition with the Seattle Philharmonic Orchestra, for the chance to sit as their new pianist, in exactly three minutes. Yet, here she was, cleaning up someone else's messes and missing her dream, all because whatever god there was up there was one sick practical joker.

"Murphy's Law," she muttered to herself, shaking her head at the phrase her mother had used one too many times in her life, to explain all the mishaps she suffered. "I'll show you Murphy's Law. If I ever find Murphy, he's a dead man!"

A throat cleared, somewhere near her, startling Meg. She turned from her furious scrubbing, and felt the air stop in her lungs. God. She hoped this was Murphy, because she could handle a little drawn-out revenge. Beside her stood the most gorgeous specimen of male beauty she'd ever laid eyes on.

He was probably six-foot-two or three, towering over her five-foot-six and a half inches and making her feel positively diminutive. His olive complexion was deeper than her skin tone with eyes that gleamed like pennies in the dim lighting of the coffee house. Molasses-brown hair curled against his collar, looking so thick and silky her fingers itched to run through it.

She licked her lips, and saw something dark and dangerous flash in his eyes, before wry humor curled on his lips. Her heart pounded so loudly she was sure he could hear it, and her skin tingled with the touch of his eyes as they skimmed over her. Did he find her reaction funny? Defensive fury roused in her, and she lifted her chin belligerently and said, "Seen enough? Maybe you can tell me what you want, now?"

An ebony brow quirked, but Meg refused to back down from the humor that flashed there. He'd be laughing out of the other end once she got through with him, boy-toy material or not.

He must have read her intention in her face, because he suddenly chuckled, and the deep, mysterious sound quaked along her tautly strung nerve endings, sending heat lightning ricocheting through Meg. She shivered at the wave of heat, and barely controlled a small moan. She wasn't going to let a stranger see that he affected her at all.

Especially not this one.

He had dangerous written all over him. From his severely handsome, exotic features to his tight black jeans and gray silk shirt, he was the stuff dark fantasies were made of. In fact, he'd probably feature in one or two of hers, in coming months. Yet, there was something else about him – a shadowy self-confidence, a powerful presence – that made her insides melt at the thought of what kind of lover he'd make. Fantasy material, for sure.

"When you're finished…"

His husky brogue rolled over her, taking Meg's breath away. It took her a moment to register what he'd actually said. When she did, she blinked hard.

"Finished what?"

He chuckled again, his eyes sparkling with mirth. "Stripping me with your eyes."

Of all the arrogant, conceited… "I was not."

He leaned closer, until she felt surrounded by him, his scent all around her, as dark and mysterious as a shadow, and so utterly perfect her heart nearly stopped.

"No sense lying to me, lass. Your eyes give you away." He reached out and tilted her chin up until she was forced to meet his bronze gaze. A spark kindled there, and he seemed almost surprised. "Such lovely eyes they are. Like sweet, dark honey…"

Meg swallowed hard, and yanked her face from his light grasp. She felt too raw, too exposed, under that piercing gaze of his. She could feel her hackles rising, and welcomed the return of her control.

"What do you want?" She snapped as she went back to her task.

"Your name."

"Can't have it," she replied flippantly. "I already own it, and it's not for sale."

His hand moved to her hair, and she felt the light tug as he wrapped one dark, unruly strand around his index finger. "Sarcasm, my pet, doesn't become you."

"At the moment, it's the only thing standing

between you and a mouth full of broken teeth, so don't knock it, buster." Meg scrubbed harder. His *pet*? How obnoxious could a man possibly get? This one might be sexy as hell, but it was no wonder the man was still single. A glance at his left hand confirmed that. He'd drive any woman crazy inside of a day, with that attitude. "And I'm not your *anything*."

A brief smile flickered at his lips as she shot him a glare. "Have it your way, *leannan*. I'll learn your name soon enough."

Her eyes narrowed at the smug confidence in his smirk. He was arrogant, and yet, there was a steely determination to his eyes that told her he spoke only the truth. She sighed resignedly. *Might as well get it over with, now.* She slapped the rag down on the table and turned to face him, planting her fists on her hips as she glared up at him. "Meg, okay? My name's Meg. Now, leave me alone, or tell me what you want. I'm busy."

He reached to remove one fist from her hip never knowing how close he was to a quick, painful death, and raised it to his lips in a smooth European fashion she imagined melted other women. Not her. Well, okay, maybe her knees trembled a little as his warm, firm lips brushed her skin, but that was because she hadn't had any in so long she was probably an honorary virgin, again. It had nothing to do with *him*.

Swallowing hard at the sudden image of how she could end her dry spell with this man, she snatched her hand away. The images were just too tempting, and she couldn't afford the distraction. "Who are you?"

"Alasdair MacCorran, Laird of Lachulan Castle, among other things." He quirked a smile full of wry, self-mocking humor, and Meg nearly groaned in disbelief. Oh, great. Another escapee from the loony bin, trying to get her attention. How did she always end up with these morons?

"I see."

A small frown furrowed his brow, just above those sensual eyes, as he studied her. Then, his brow smoothed, and he smiled. "I doubt you do. However, I do have a proposition for you."

Those words stabbed Meg with surprise, before angry heat fanned her face. Did she *look* that easy?

"Okay, that's my cue. This conversation is over, Mr. MacCorran, or whoever the hell you really are." She snatched up her rag and turned away, before she hauled off and socked a customer. Phil the Pill wouldn't like that.

"Wait!" His hand closed around her arm, causing Meg to spin around in automatic defense. "Just listen—"

"No." She shook off his grip on her arm, her eyes stormy. She'd had enough. This had been the day from hell already, and she'd had to sacrifice her dreams, once again. She wasn't about to listen to any crackpot. "You listen to me. I'm sick and tired of being pestered by men like you, who think the only way to get to know a woman is to flatter her with a bunch of syrupy endearments and crawl inside her panties. Newsflash, buster: I don't want you, I don't plan on sleeping with you, *or* with your friend over there, and I certainly don't need your kind of trouble in my life. So just take your noble ass back over to your booth and—"

"Miss Tempest!" A nasal, grating voice screeched from behind her making Meg wince. Great. Phil the Pill, owner of *Hole in the Wall*, finally puts in an appearance and, of course, it would be just in time to hear her tell a rude customer off. "What do you think you're doing?"

"Nothing," she muttered, glaring up into Alasdair MacCorran's wry grin.

"Well, you can take your nothing right out that door and down the street to the unemployment office," Phil huffed, puffing up like an overstuffed penguin. "You're fired."

Mac watched the look of stunned disbelief that crossed Meg Tempest's intriguing honey-brown eyes, and wondered whether she was more surprised she'd been fired so easily and publicly, or that she'd let her temper get the best of her like she had. Then, as fury whipped to life in her eyes again, Mac decided it must be the former. He sighed in resignation, wondering if his friend had set him up once again. There was no way he could teach this woman the complexities of the *Sgàil Ealdhainean* in a month, he'd be lucky if he could teach her to control that storm brewing in her eyes.

Without a word, Meg whipped off the apron around her waist and threw it straight into the face of the pompous little ass who'd fired her, and then, shooting Mac a glare that told him she reserved the top slot of her shit list for him alone, stormed toward the front door. But, rather than the fury he supposed he should rightly be terrified of, it was the flicker of raw vulnerability that had crossed her eyes that intrigued Mac. And, just as he saw her figure disappearing down the snowy Seattle street, there was a hiss and a pop, and the entire interior of the coffee shop plunged into darkness.

An excerpt from

Dancin in the Moonlight
By
Beverly Rae

Available now from
Triskelion Publishing

Chapter One

"Five."

"No way. He's not even a four."

"Okay. So how about that guy?"

Two of her friends questioned Carly at the same time. "Which one?"

Carly rolled her eyes at the other women and shook her head. "The lean, mean-looking one by the bar. The one staring at Tala."

Tala darted her eyes toward the bar, found the object of their discussion, and whipped her gaze back to her Cosmopolitan. "Figures."

"Just because he looks mean, doesn't mean he is mean, Tala. Besides," Sara licked sugar off the rim of her glass, "I like 'em a bit rough around the edges."

"Sara, don't razz Tala. She's just being cautious." Carly managed to appear delicate while nibbling on a piece of sushi. "You know what she's been through."

Oh, crap. Pity from her friends was worse than suffering through an abusive relationship with Mark Winston. Well, almost. "You know, ladies, I booted Mark to the curb over four months ago. Can we give the pity party a rest now?"

She glanced around the table at her three closest friends. Carly, the oldest one of their thirty-something group, leaned against the back of her stool and regarded Tala with cool eyes almost the same gray-blue as her own. Sara caught the unspoken communication between the two women and tucked her head, giving her silent agreement to keep the conversation light. Yet Melinda, normally the quietest one of them all, decided to add her two cents.

"I mean, damn, how long can you last, girl? Four months and counting without any sex. How the hell do you keep from going insane?"

"She spends a lot of money on batteries."

Tala started to laugh at Carly's impromptu response. "Hey, I can have a different fantasy every night. One night I can savage Brad and the next night I'm licking up and down Clooney's body." Figures the quiet one in the group was the most sexually active. "Actually, Mel, four months isn't very long. I mean, for most of us."

Mel adopted a perfect coquettish smile and nodded. "I guess. But if you ask me, I'd rather die than go four long, lonely months without male companionship. Much less without the Big O. Still—"

"Still, no man is better than an asshole, right?" Tala flicked back a loose strand of hair. "Okay, here's the deal. I broke up with Mark because he hit me. So maybe I'm not ready to leap into the pond again. It's a sad fact, but all the guys I meet aren't worth the time of day anyway."

Carly opened her mouth to speak, "Honey, we've all been there. Not the violent part, but the lack of quality fish in this pond.

"That's what I'm talking about." Tala jumped in and headed her off. "Besides, I'm good to go, at least until my vibrator dies." She winked at Carly when her friend snorted at her joke.

Tala gulped in a breath of much needed relief, released the air, and relaxed. Now maybe their *Girls' Night Out* tradition would get back to normal. This was the first time she'd gone out with the ladies since she left Mark, and she didn't want anything spoiling the night. "But hey, don't mind me. If you want to search for your perfect man," she added finger quotes to the description, "then, by all means, don't let my self-imposed celibacy stop you."

"Uh-oh, Tala. Don't look now, but Man-At-The-Bar is headed your way." Carly's warning barely made it out of her mouth before the "lean, mean-looking" man appeared at Tala's side.

The stench of alcohol and smoke smothered the atmosphere around Tala and she had to shift her head to the side to gasp in semi-clean air. His hand slid behind her, stopping to rest on the top of her stool. "Hey, beautiful one.

Tala, right? Name's Fred. How about you excuse yourself from these other gorgeous ladies and join me for a nice private drink?"

Oh, shit. A fan. He must have recognized her from the zoo's public service and promotional spots, *Tala's Animal Facts.* Just what she needed. Not. She tilted her head up and batted her eyes at him. "Wow, Fred, I haven't had such an enticing invitation in a really, long time. How can I refuse?"

His stained, toothy leer didn't do anything for his bloodshot eyes. "You can't." He snaked his hand around her arm and tugged, "Come on, babe, let's go back to my place and you can show me what you've learned from all those wild animals. In fact, I bet you're the wild animal. You know. In bed. With Fred?"

Tala slipped her thumb under his fingers and ran her fingers over the top of his hand. Putting on her best airhead voice, she tossed her hair away from her shoulders in a perfect imitation of the stereotypical blonde bimbo. "Oh. My. God. You're a poet and don't even know it."

Fred blinked, her barb slipping straight over his head. "Huh?"

"Poet? Know it? Get it?" When he clearly didn't get it, she shook her head, trying not to let her jaw drop to the ground. Was this guy genetically stupid? Or was he drunk stupid? "Never mind. Don't strain your brain."

His face lit up as her joke finally hit home. "Oh, I get it now. Bed and Fred. Strain and brain." His loud horselaugh echoed through the room, stopping conversations and swiveling heads in their direction.

"Let me give you a little tip, Fred. Unless you want a broken hand, back off. Now."

Sara giggled and nodded. "She's been taking karate."

Carly chuckled, "Isn't it *tae kwon do*?"

Fred got a little green around the gills, "Aw, but she wouldn't hurt me." Yet, he carefully withdrew his hand before adding, "Would you, babe?"

Damn, how she hated anyone calling her "babe." But before she could open her mouth, Carly twisted on her stool, knocking over her drink. The cool liquid splashed onto Fred's bright orange shirt and green pants, a dark stain spreading over his crotch.

"Oh, I'm so, so sorry!" Carly feigned a contrite expression while winking at Tala.

Fred's curse only added to the ladies' enjoyment, although they all tried to go along with Carly's ruse. With a groan of disgust, Fred flicked drops of drink off his hands. "You bitches are crazy." Adding a few more choice expletives, he slinked back to his hole at the bar.

Giggles erupted from all four ladies as Tala high-fived Carly. "Thanks, girlfriend. Fred doesn't realize he got off easy."

Carly grabbed the rag from the waitress who'd arrived to clean up the spill. "I'll take care of this." She nodded toward Tala. "You can get the drink my friend here is buying me."

Tala sipped a little of her Cosmopolitan and echoed Carly's nod. "You bet. You deserve it."

Sara pointed an accusing finger at Tala. "You need to let yourself go. Free your inner goddess. Run naked through the woods. Do something and get over it."

Tala tried to control her infamous temper, but some sneaked out anyway. "Well, you know what you can do, don't you, Sara?"

"No. What?"

"Bite me."

"Ooh, Tala. I didn't know you got into women."

Leave it to Sara to turn a jab into a joke. Of course, that was part of the reason she loved these women so much. Sure, they were tough, yet they were loving, too. After all, they'd had to be strong to rise to the top of their professions, but they cared about her. Accepting Sara's lead, she quipped, "I don't usually swing that way, but for you, Beautiful, I might." Sara batted her eyes, ran her tongue over her lips, and wiggled her fingers in a come-and-get-me gesture. Tala faked a lecherous smirk at Sara just as a couple of good-looking men passed by them, shooting them a disgusted look. The two friends reached out for the men, pretending to pull them to the table.

"Hey, don't go. We're only kidding!"

Tala crossed her heart. "Yeah, really. We love men."

Carly slapped her hand down on the table. "Will you two cut it out? Do you want gossip getting around the bar that we're lesbians? Which would be okay if it were true, but when you're trolling for men that's the last message you want to send."

Mel sipped her wine cooler and agreed. "Right. Besides, let's not lose focus. Keep your eyes peeled for the perfect man." She copied Tala's earlier use of finger quotes. "This is the hottest club in town."

Tala's sarcastic laugh turned heads in her direction again. Lowering her voice, she explained. "There's no such thing as the perfect man. It's an oxymoron, not to mention an impossibility. Especially for women our age. And especially for successful women like us."

"Maybe we *should* become lesbians. I wonder if the whole sex thing and finding the perfect partner would be easier if we eliminated men altogether." Tala, Mel, and Carly raised their eyebrows at each other. When Sara caught their reaction, she held up her hands and backpedaled. "Hey, I'm only wondering. I love men, too, you know."

Mollified, Mel picked up where they'd left off. "I agree with Tala. I don't think a perfect man exists. To be perfect, a guy would have to be half man, half god. Like Hercules, or Zeus, or whichever mythical hunk you can think of." Mel sighed. "You know, someone with major brawn."

"Yeah, but he'd have to have brain power, too. I don't want a pretty boy toy. If I wanted a handsome dead-head, I could take home half the men in this bar."

Carly's assessment rang true to Tala. "As long as the head that's dead is on the shoulders instead of in his pants, then at least he'd provide some fun for a little while. But she's right. The perfect man has to possess all the right traits. Looks, intelligence and a—"

"A wild side." Mel ripped tears into the edge of a napkin. "Your definition of the perfect man would include animalistic qualities. Probably need a hairy chest, too."

"Ewww, I like mine smooth."

Tala blushed, hating the heat spreading across her cheeks. Yet she couldn't help telling them more. "Well, if you want to know the truth, I think the perfect man would be like a wolf."

Sara sputtered into her drink. "A wolf?"

"Told you, she wants a man with a hairy chest. Never mind Tala. She's always had a thing for wolves. I think she wants to make it with an animal. Personally, I think she's worked at the zoo a little too long for her own good."

Tala's hair stood up on her neck and she fought the urge to change the subject. "You know what I mean, Mel. I want a man to be *like* a wolf. Beautiful, with muscles and endurance. And loyal to his woman."

"His woman? You make 'woman' sound like female. Or bitch." Sara tilted her head back and gave a teeny howl.

"Yeah. I've heard wolves mate for life." Carly sipped her Chocotini and waved at Tala to go on.

Tala let her mind envision the ideal mate. "Hey, go with it for a sec. I mean who wouldn't want a guy like this? Wolves are tough when times call for tough, but they're also loving and playful, too. And they're rarely cruel."

"You'd have to make monthly appointments for him."

"For his shots?"

"Nah, the groomer."

Tala smacked Carly in the arm. "I'd take him where I get my bikini wax done, thank you very much."

"Forget the grooming. Think about the dough she'd have to shell out for training. I mean he's got to be housebroken. Not to mention taught to sit up and beg. Or should I say, lie down and beg."

Immersed in her thoughts, Sara was the only one not laughing. "Immortal." Sara played with the swizzle stick, tapping it on the table in rhythm to the music blaring through the speakers on the dance floor.

"Immortal?" Tala was aware that sometimes Sara came up with some good ideas. Tala squinted at her in the dim light of the bar and waited.

"Yeah, immortal. Forever young and virile. Forever hunky. Forever mine."

"Yuck. If he were immortal, then you'd grow old while he stayed yummy. I'm not sure even an immortal man would stay with some dried up old prune." Leave it to Carly to pop up with the negative in the situation.

"What if loving him made you immortal, too?" Sara winked, enjoying her dream.

"Okay, I guess we're going deep into this fantasy, aren't we?" Carly raised her glass to Sara. "But I do like the way you think."

The ladies stopped for a moment, letting the thought sink in.

Immortal, huh? The word "immortal" jogged Tala's memory of her cousin's recent visit. Would her friends think she'd gone nuts if she brought up the idea? She checked their faces and decided to risk it. Besides, she could always blame it on the booze later.

"Funny we're on this subject." She hesitated, and then took the plunge. "Because my cousin brought up the same subject not long ago. In fact, she and her friends had a similar discussion."

She searched her memory, dredging up all the details she could remember. "They're like us. Thirty-something, successful, and manless. So they brought up the plan of summoning an immortal man."

Mel leaned forward. "You mean like Hercules? Or Adonis? Or Zeus?"

"Okay, we get it. You want a Greek god." Carly downed the rest of her drink and motioned for the waitress. "Or are those guys Roman?"

"Who cares? I don't care if they built Rome or Athens. I just want *them* built." Mel followed Sara in ordering another drink.

"Maybe mine would be part elf. Like the cute one in the movie we saw last week." Sara grinned and ran her tongue over her lips. "No wait. I've changed my mind. Maybe I'd prefer—"

Carly's sarcastic tone interrupted Sara's musings and brought them back to reality. "And did they have any luck finding their immortal men?"

Sometimes Carly could be a real killjoy. Tala scowled at her, unhappy with her negativity. Which made the truth even better. "Come to think of it, I think they did. Well, at least they found love. I can't say about the immortal part. But here's the really weird part. They did some kind of ceremony to call the men to them."

Carly Killjoy smacked down the others' exuberant reactions. "Now we're getting silly. A ceremony to attract an immortal lover? Get real, Tala."

A stab of embarrassment for letting her whimsy run wild zipped through Tala. Until Sara spoke up, keeping the dream alive. "Let's do it."

Carly sputtered into her drink. Dabbing her chin dry, she threw an exasperated look at the others. "Do what?"

All eyes squared on Sara.

"Let's summon our immortal men."

"Are you kidding?"

"Carly, shut up. Sara, are you serious?" The excitement in Mel's voice mimicked the shiver running through Tala.

"Yeah, I am. I mean, what's the harm in trying? Besides, it'll be fun."

The conversation stalled as the waitress returned with fresh drinks. Once she'd left, Sara took up where she'd left off. "What exactly did they do, Tala?"

Are they seriously considering summoning their perfect men? She tried to recall how they'd ended up on this topic, but the alcohol fogging her brain kept her memory on a leave of absence. Just how desperate could they get? Tala bit her lip and shook her head. "I'm not sure."

Sara clapped her hands. "Hey, I have an idea. Since Tala's perfect man is a wolf," she paused at Tala's warning glare, "uh, wolf-like, then how about we do something under a full moon?"

Mel gasped and slapped her hand over her mouth. Lowering her hand slowly, she whispered, "I think the moon's full tonight." She checked her watch, and met their eyes with wonder in her own. "In fact, the moon should be high in the sky by now."

Without finishing their drinks, the ladies pushed away from the table, grabbed their purses, and headed outside.

*****

"This is so ridiculous. I hope nobody sees us."

Carly stood with her arms crossed, tapping her foot, and glaring at the other women standing in the middle of the bar's parking lot. "Are you all actually going to do this?" Nonetheless, she clasped Tala's hand in her own and reached for Sara's hand.

Ignoring Carly's outstretched hand, Sara giggled, spun around, and let the cool breeze of the summer night ruffle her hair. "Come on, Carly. Let yourself have some fun. And who knows? Maybe we'll get lucky and it'll work."

"Yeah." Mel grabbed Sara's arm to keep her from toppling over. Acting like giggling teenage girls, they hugged, squealed, and hopped up and down.

"Look, Tala." Mel pointed toward the heavens. "I was right. A full moon. Talk about your premium conditions. Perfect for calling up your wolfie, don't you think?"

Tala grinned at them and tapped Carly on the shoulder. "Lighten up and stop worrying. If anyone sees us, we can always claim we were drunk out of our minds. Besides, who's going to care?"

Carly shrugged and linked hands with Mel to begin their circle. After Mel pulled Sara to her side, Tala grabbed Sara's other hand. Once in place, all eyes fell on Tala.

"Okay, Tala. So how do we do this?" Sara squeezed Tala's hand and scanned the faces around her. "Do we make a silent wish like when you blow out candles on a birthday cake? Or chant something about immortal men?"

Tala paused, trying to recall her cousin's description of the process. But, when she couldn't remember any details, she flung caution to the wind and guessed. "Uh, how about we, one by one, speak our wish out loud? How else are we supposed to know what everyone wants? And I'm dying to hear everyone's wish. Especially Carly's."

Sara shook her head as intense determination creased her forehead. "We need to do something more dramatic along with just wishing." She scanned her friends' faces, searching for suggestions. "Like maybe a dance after we're through describing them."

"Sure. Why not? If we're going to do this nutty thing, then let's go all out." Carly fixed her steely-eyed glower on Tala, making her squirm, but she held her ground. "Any volunteers to go first?"

Mel nodded toward the horizon. "Better hurry. We want to catch the moon at its highest peak. So I'll go first." Staring into the night sky, Mel took a huge breath and described her perfect man. "My Immortal One—"

"Now there's a title to live up to."

"Shush." Tala nudged Carly into silence. "Go on, Mel."

Mel's description went on for several minutes with exact details given to every aspect of her man. From eye color to length of his shaft, Mel left nothing to the imagination. From his spiky white hair to his exact height, she described her perfect man, making it easy for the other ladies to visualize him.

"Wow." Sara's whisper spoke for the group as they all nodded in awe. "Something tells me you've given this some real thought."

"I hope you get him, Mel. He sounds incredible."

Heads turned at Carly's warm declaration and she scowled at them. "What? Just because I think this is stupid doesn't mean I don't want the best for my friends. Sheesh." She tossed back her hair in defiance. "So here's my immortal hunk. He'd be tanned, dark, rippling with muscles, impeccably dressed and…"

Tala stared at the moon above her, allowing her mind to drift away from the sound of Carly's voice. Wouldn't it be great if she really could summon her dream man? If she could beckon her very own half-wolf, half-man stud? A punch in the arm broke her out of her reverie.

Catching Sara watching her quizzically, she wiggled her hand for encouragement. "Okay, Sara. You go next."

Taking a deep breath, Sara spread her lips wider, unable to hide her excitement. "Well, let's see. My Immortal One would be a man like no other."

As Sara continued to describe her version of the faultless male, Tala's mind drifted off again, letting the image form in her mind's eye. Within seconds, the form appeared, drawing her deeper into her trance.

His long, toned body, sleek and glistening in the moonlight, slowly rose from a crouched position. Muscles rippled across his chest, highlighting the broad expanse while large, brown nipples accented his hardened pecs. A sprinkling of silky black hair running from his six-pack abs led to the full, curly patch below and Tala wetted her mouth at the sight of his richly endowed self. Yet more magnificent than his body, his face drew Tala's attention away from his torso. Straight, black hair teased the tips of his shoulders and flowed around his angular face, while his strong, square jaw beckoned for a woman's touch.

And then she saw his eyes.

Amber eyes. Golden, compelling, magnetic eyes drew her to him. He commanded her to be his while he promised to be hers. Eyes she recognized from pleasurable nights of lustful dreams.

Her respiration quickened with the ache, the need clutching at her heart. Could he exist? Even as she wondered, he bent, inching back into a crouch. His image morphed, blurring the lines of his physique while outlining another. She blinked, trying to see him better but, instead, she lost the vision for a moment. She whimpered while a small, tortured sound escaped her lips.

Blinking again, Tala saw the new image. The amber eyes were the same. Golden, compelling, magnetic eyes. She blinked again and stared into the mesmerizing eyes of a black wolf.

"Tala?"

"Hel-lo? Tala? Are you okay?"

She jerked to awareness to find the others gawking at her. All three of her friends had their cell phones pointed at her, snapping pictures. Then she noticed why. She was down on the pavement, on all fours, gravel digging into her knees and palms. She must've fallen over from too much alcohol. "What's going on?"

Sara reached over and helped her to her feet. "Well, for one thing, you're sweating like a pig. Gross!" Releasing Tala's hand, she wiped her palm on her jeans. "Having hot flashes already?"

Tala shook her head to both answer the question and to clear the remnants of the dream lingering inside. "Excuse me?" She lifted her hand, noted the clamminess and copied Sara's gesture. "I, uh, guess I'm a little hot. Probably from too much alcohol."

"Yeah. Sure." Mel's tone left no doubt of her disbelief.

She glanced around her, clarity forming again. She tried to make a joke. "What's the big deal? I zoned out for a minute and fell over. No biggie."

The ladies dropped their hands, but remained focused on Tala. Unnerved by the intense scrutiny, she tried to pick up where she thought they'd left off. "So Sara's finished, right?"

When no one nodded, she swallowed and continued anyway. "Carly, I think it's your turn. It's Carly's turn, right?" Uneasiness crawled down her spine at their lack of response. "Cut the crap, would you? Or are you trying to scare me?"

Carly patted Tala's arm, bringing her into a hug in the process. "I already took my turn, remember? You haven't been ill lately, have you, Tala? I mean, with a fever or anything?"

Tala broke free and stepped away from the group. "Will you stop? You're acting like I've done something crazy. Haven't you ever gotten a little tipsy before? Damn it all to hell and back, knock it off."

The three women glanced at each other and back to Tala. Mel dropped her head while chewing on her bottom lip, but Sara and Carly returned Tala's glare. Carly flipped open her cell phone.

"What is the matter with you guys?" Tala's nerves strung tighter and she tried hard not to fidget. Was this a joke? Or did she have a problem? She gritted her teeth and asked the question she didn't want to ask but had to. "You're acting like I've gone over the edge. What the hell did I do to make you act this odd?"

Several tense moments passed until Carly broke the silence. "We're not the ones acting strangely, Tala. You are."

"Yeah? So what strange thing did I do, huh? And didn't all of you do something just as weird?"

Turning the cell phone to face Tala, she revealed the snapshot. "Just look at the picture."

Again her friends exchanged telling looks. Taking a deep breath, Carly gave her an unexpected answer. "You howled."

Tala's mouth dropped. "I did what? You're kidding."

From the expressions on their faces, joking was the last thing on their minds. In fact, Mel still couldn't meet Tala's eyes.

"You lifted your head, stared at the full moon, and howled."

"I did not." No way could she believe such an outlandish accusation. She'd daydreamed, sure. But howled?

Carly lifted an eyebrow at her. "Take a look at the picture, honey. Head laid back, baying at the moon in full color."

Tala shook her head, but held out hope for a better explanation. "No, but—"

Carly dipped her chin and raised both eyebrows. "I swear, girl. I am not lying to you. You stood there and let loose with an actual throw-your-head-back, no-holds-barred, canine-loving howl. Hell, I thought we'd have a wolf pack on us before the sound died out."

Sara nodded. "It's true, Tala. You bayed at the moon."

"I did?" Had she really howled? If she had, she needed to come up with a good explanation and quick. "Hey, I was just kidding around." She forced out a laugh. "And you all fell for it."

"Looked real enough to me."

"Yeah. Too real."

Needing a major diversion, Tala hopped a few feet away, gyrating to an unheard rhythm. "Come on, ladies, let's dance." When the others eventually joined her, she grabbed Carly by the hand, pulling her into a spin. "Dance. Now."

Whooping and shouting, the other ladies stretched out their arms and began twirling in circles. Sara bumped into Mel, sending the two crashing to the ground in a fit of hilarity while Tala and Carly skipped around them.

Exhausted, Tala and Carly pulled the two women to their feet and hugged each other. "Well, if nothing else, □ancing' in the moonlight was fun."

Sara's silly smile reinforced Tala's statement. "Yeah, it was."

Mel stumbled to a stop and blew out a long breath. "I don't know about you girls, but I've had enough excitement for one day. But I gotta say I thoroughly enjoyed everyone's performance. Whew! I'm danced out."

Carly caught Tala's eye and rolled her eyes. "Especially Tala's. She proved she deserves her wolf man."

Sara leaned against Tala and nudged her in the arm. "Yeah, who knew you could howl?"

More books in

THE STILL SEXY LADIES GUIDE TO DATING IMMORTALS

FALLING STAR WISH
BY
BETTY HANAWA

STRUCK BY LIGHTNING
BY
LIZZIE T LEAF

Can't wait for your favorite books to come out in print?

We have a huge selection of ebooks just waiting for you at www.triskelionpublishing.net

To learn more about
Janice and Brokenoggin Falls read

Bewitched, Bothered & BeVampyred

Available through a bookstore near you or from
Amazon.com.

*Proceeds from BB&B benefit the International Red Cross disaster
relief fund.*

And watch for
BEWITCHED, BOTHERED & BEVAMPYRED season 2

Coming in October 2006 from Triskelion Publishing and
starring

MaryJanice Davidson, Susan Grant, Gena Showalter, Alesia
Holliday, Sophia Nash, Kathryn Caskie, Terese Ramin,
Lynn Warren, Linda Wisdom, Yasmine Galenorn, Michelle
Rowen, Judi McCoy, Julie Kistler, Betty Hanawa, K. J.
Barrett, Marianne Mancusi, Robin T. Popp, Kelle Z. Riley,
Barbara Ferrer & more!

Author royalties from season 2 will benefit
Breast Cancer Research.

Triskelion Publishing
<u>www.triskelionpublishing.net</u>

All about women. All about extraordinary.

Ms. Pendragon

Coming this fall from
Triskelion Publishing

If you ever wished Guenevere would've had second thoughts when it came to King Arthur, you're going to want to pick up this spellbinding urban fantasy by Michele Lang.